Call
of the
Wattlebird

Victoria Carnell

Willowbank Series
Book 1

Copyright
Call of the Wattlebird
Book 1 of the Willowbank Series
© Victoria L. Carnell 2017
2nd edition © 2019
www.victoriacarnell.com
Published by Lilly Pilly Publishing

Lilly Pilly
PUBLISHING

Cover Design by Lilly Pilly Publishing
Interior Layout by Lilly Pilly Publishing
Cover image of wattlebirds © Alan Fletcher (Birds in Tasmania http://tassiebirds.blogspot.com.au/). Used with permission
Cover image: Girl in the Garden *Edward Killingworth Johnson* (1825-1896) Public Domain

National Library of Australian Cataloguing-in-Publication entry

Creator: Carnell, Victoria
Title: Call of the Wattlebird/ Victoria L. Carnell

Print Book ISBN: 978-0-6481853-3-8
eBook ISBN: 978-0-6481853-2-1

Call of the Wattlebird is a work of fiction. Where, names, characters, establishments and incidents, are used they are used fictitiously. All other elements are a product of the writer's imagination.

Dedicated to my wonderful adult children who are my greatest cheerleaders. Their encouragement has kept me dedicated to the task of writing. Over many years, with their dad and I, they've traversed dark valleys and climbed joyful mountain peaks, but always with the knowledge, *they are loved.*

Chapter One

Catherine Nicolson gripped the handle of the landau with both hands, her knuckles white with strain, and her mouth as dry as a bag of chaff. At any other time, she would relish the exhilarating dash between the towering poplars, but as she looked across to her mother, she knew, that rollick was unsuitable. Mother's face, as pale as the morning fog, stared back. Her arms twitched with the strain of cradling her new babe, trying to protect him from jolting his head against the side of the swaying vehicle. The horse-drawn carriage careered all the way down the gravel driveway, slewed around the corner and jerked to a stop at the far end of the courtyard.

'Ooh, Mother, I thought we'd end up in the ditch.'

A sigh escaped—Mother sucked-in an accentuated breath and drew the baby close. 'There's no doubt, Aunt Elizabeth's substitute driver is in desperate need of lessons,' she said.

'It had been better if we'd accepted Mister Fraser's offer of a ride, even if it meant we left earlier,' Catherine said.

'Aunt Elizabeth would never have approved.'

'Aunt is stuffy.' Catherine waggled her finger back and forth imitating her aunt.

Catherine, hands still damp from the reckless ordeal, gathered her skirts in preparation to disembark, but her mother did not move.

Instead, she scanned the expansive grounds developed under the watchful eye of Father's first wife. What thoughts stirred and held her mother's interest?

Only yesterday, her mother had spoken with Elizabeth, "Willowbank parklands lent a sense of opulence to our Georgian mansion, but of late, I've neglected the garden." Elizabeth had scoffed, "Really, Arianna, why you, a genteel woman, insist on tending the garden yourself with so many children to care for, I'll never know. My brother, Francis, surely doesn't approve."

Catherine loved Willowbank, Francis Nicolson's estate, perched on a small knoll overlooking the expansive plains of the Tasmanian Midlands. In the early eighteen-hundreds, her grandfather, Nicolson, a gentlemen settler in the colony, received the land via a grant. Her father, like all sons of the landed gentry, wore his distinction proudly as he inherited his lot and increased his wealth.

'I must cut the wisteria back otherwise poor nymph might choke.' Catherine grinned at her mother's comment in keeping with her jovial temperament. Her humour remained intact, despite the frightful spin they had just experienced.

The vine entangled the small statue, covering all but one white hand that stretched skyward, the scene reminiscent of the one in Grandma's picture book illustrating Eden after the fall, and bearing the caption, "Where art thou, Adam?"

'She's like a guardian angel watching over us, Mother.'

'Or maybe a mischievous fairy ready to spring the lock on a treasure trove.'

Catherine bit her cheek. Her lips moved, but no sound escaped. Had Mother discovered her notebook located in the pump-house down by the river? The lockable, leather-bound book was one of two her father had received from the local wool-merchants. She had begged him for the spare.

She glanced in the direction of the weeping willows along the river's course and past the cherubic Sentinel guarding the entrance of the path to the pump-house. Hardly visible, the shingle roof of the small purpose-built hut symbolised deception—hers. Her frequent digression to the shed in recent days, to add to her secret jottings, against the express command of her father. However, she was not the only one who trekked the path. One of Willowbank's female servants often passed by the hedge leading to the track, her elusive visits a mystery Catherine was yet to unearth.

Swivelling to fetch her bonnet from the carriage floor, Catherine exhaled, satisfied her mother had not noticed the fleeting look, but she would need to take care. No one must find her chronicle.

'Lucille, they're back.' Adele's voice floated from an upstairs window.

Catherine watched the front entrance for her older sisters, thankful the call redirected her mother's attention. Her sisters bounded down the steps with Evelyn, Willowbank's Scottish governess, in pursuit.

'We want to see our new brother.'

'All right, just a brief peek,' Mother said.

She lifted the coverlet, and Lucille grasped the baby's tiny fingers.

'He's teeny, just like a doll,' Adele said.

Evelyn pulled Lucille's sleeve. 'Come, now, back to your books.'

Father rounded the corner of the house, glancing from the coach driver to the mare's sweaty flank and frowned. The handler retrieved a cloth from his belt and proceeded to wipe the hide.

'Father.'

'Hello, big girl, I missed you. It was good of you to accompany Mother.' Catherine's father tousled her hair, his usual way of showing affection, and she hugged him.

'Even as a twelve-year-old, I can rely on her, though I'd say, she must be pleased to be out from under Elizabeth's rule.'

'Surely am glad to be home, for all I heard was, "Catherine, do this, do that". You'd think I was a scullery maid the way she bossed me around, and she already has a lady of her own, and a cook too.'

'Bossed you, eh?' Father's eyes twinkled his countenance forming a smirk.

Catherine nodded but for once did not retaliate.

'It is wonderful to have you home, my dear. I have missed your cheerful self.'

The new mother turned her face toward her husband and pursed her lips. His eyes crinkled, and he brushed his lips across her cheek.

She ran her finger along his day-old whiskers, tinged with grey.

'Here, let me hold our new son, I want to get acquainted,' he said, lifting his son from her outstretched arms, the baby tiny in his big arms as he flexed his muscles.

He studied the child's face, 'Such dark eyes, but in my reckoning, they'll be just like Catherine's.'

Catherine laughed, delighted her father deemed her new brother's features like her own, undoubtedly inherited from Grandma Nicolson.

'Elizabeth's sentiments entirely, and indeed she said, he has the same button nose.'

Catherine screwed her face and groaned. Aunt Elizabeth was far too blunt and did not regard the feelings of others. Her father chuckled, leant and kissed his wife, demonstrating his approval of the new addition to their family, his affection returned with a smile.

'I'll ask Sarah to bring the remainder of the luggage and attend to your needs.'

Lifting Baby Simon over her shoulder, the new mother retired upstairs. Catherine carried her bag and traipsed behind her mother, dropped her satchel on the floor inside her bedroom door—her intention to dash to her parent's room and play with her new brother, Simon.

A flash of light bounced from her bedroom windowsill, and she leaned against the pane catching a glimpse of the covert servant—the old woman. The figure passed nymph, darted through the foliage and hurried down the path, startling a flock of birds. They swooped into their nest at the top of the giant eucalypt towering above the pump-house. Perhaps Mother's remark about treasures referred to matters other than Catherine's memoirs. She would ponder this twist while remaining cautious. She must avoid detection.

♫♪ ♫♪

The tiny babe was all but covered by the stuffed bedcover. Catherine smoothed the lumps so she could see him, mesmerised by his little chest rising and falling. She already loved her littlest brother.

Mother examined her plump figure in the dressing-table mirror, wiggled and grimaced. 'I'll need to go easy on the puddings now.'

'That's unlikely, Mama. Smell those luscious flavours wafting up the stairwell. I reckon Sarah, with the help of her ma, has cooked up a treat to welcome us home.'

'Indeed, I can. My, those girls do such a wonderful job and are a deal more affable than Elizabeth's help.'

Mother removed her bonnet and let her auburn bun unravel, rubbed her back, kicked off her shoes and stretched out on the bed.

Simon whimpered. Catherine picked him up, pulled him close and touched his cheek with her own. She warmed at the softness of his face and the distinct smell of his skin, re-wrapped him snugly and placed him in the cot.

'I want to marry when I'm grown and have babies too.'

'Catherine, I pray you will. If you follow your heart, dear girl, just as I have done, at the right time love finds you.'

Catherine slipped around the large four-poster bed and flopped into her mother's armchair.

'Run along now, Sarah is coming shortly.'

Catherine sighed but meandered toward the door, tidying the cushions, straightening the counterpane and fluffing up the pillows on her way.

♫♪ ♫♪

It was Betsy, Sarah's mother, Catherine passed on the landing, the woman's face hidden behind a large vase of roses. Her tell-tale boots peeked below her black skirt. A pardoned convict, Betsy was a simple woman with little formal education. Catherine did not see her about the house often because the old woman avoided association, evidently due to her embarrassment about her scarred face. The servant was never without her cumbersome bonnet, but even the covering could not hide the jagged line running from her mouth and passing under her chin. When Catherine enquired of Betsy's injury, Mother told her an estate owner treated the servant abominably in her previous service. Mother cosseted Betsy, allowed her to pursue her favourite project, and the reason Willowbank's vegetable garden was among the best in the district.

♫♪ ♫♪

'Oh, Betsy, the roses are lovely.'

'Mister Fraser dropped them in, ma'am, when he visited today.'

Catherine's mother's voice softened, barely audible. 'I was blessed he introduced me to Willowbank.'

Catherine spun at the top of the stairs to listen, the wave of guilt, less intense than the desire to eavesdrop. Her father's words of a fortnight ago ringing in her head, "The child is more inquisitive than is good for her."

'Mister Fraser said to tell you the deep blush ones are for a lovely lady and the pale ones for her bonny boy.'

'Has he already left for home then?'

'Yes, spent a few moments with Mister Nicolson but said his young lad has a bad case of measles, and he needed to get back to cheer his wife.'

'That's too bad.'

'Yes, though, 'tis as well. We're not in want of sickness,' Betsy said.

'Home, ah! I don't like being away from Mister Nicolson. Francis adores me and regards me, landlady of the estate, though, Betsy, I will always think of myself as an ordinary woman.'

Catherine frowned. She mulled regarding her mother's relationship to Willowbank's servant, Governess Evelyn, describing their accord as familial.

A footfall sounded behind Catherine. She swung around. Sarah, clutching a small trunk, stepped onto the landing.

'Oh, Sarah, you crept up behind me.'

'No, miss, I did not creep, but you is looking mighty like a rabbit caught in a snare.'

'Here, give me that, I'll take it in.'

Catherine yanked the luggage from Sarah's hand, barged into her mother's bedchamber, dropped the trunk beside the robe and hovered. Betsy busied herself with the unpacking while her mistress leant back and rested her shoulders.

Smiling at the newborn in the cot beside her and lightly touching the baby's blanket, Mother said, 'He's so serene and peaceful now, but

I think he's going to be a lively one and quite demanding already.'

Betsy nodded, but only asked, 'Do you need anything, ma'am?'

'A glass of milk and a biscuit please, Betsy. Just leave them on the duchess. I'm sure I'll be well asleep on your return.'

The seasoned servant brushed by Catherine without turning her head.

'Catherine, look at him.'

Catherine chuckled, the invitation to stay with her baby brother assured. A tiny arm stretched over the top of the blanket and fingers curled about the satin edging.

Mother's tired eyes shifted to the family portrait on the far wall. 'My little one is certainly tarred with the Nicolson brush,' she said.

Catherine followed her mother's gaze but was surprised at the fleeting frown etching her brow. Perhaps she also disliked the picture. Catherine loathed the photograph because her likeness reflected her angry mood on the day of the sitting. The operator had taken an inordinate amount of time ensuring everyone faced the contraption, but the moment he was ready to snap, brother Stuart twisted Catherine's hair about his finger and yanked. She had thumped him and demanded another sitting, but the rigmarole involved in repeating the exercise was too much for her mother to endure. At least, now Simon had arrived, Mother would order a new portrait.

'It is hard to believe Adele was just a year old when I came here eighteen years ago.'

Catherine focused on Adele's face. The petite brunette with deep brown eyes was the prettiest of her sisters. Catherine liked her because she was quiet-natured and kind. If she could emulate anyone, it would be Adele.

'Adele's mother, my poor mistress … it was awful when we lost the dear. Her wet hair matted and stuck to her forehead, her lips cracked, though damped with a cool cloth, gasping for her final breath. Also, the poor baby born the day before lived no more than a few hours.'

Catherine glanced at the photograph once more. She could see no sign of distress on her father's face.

'I was a housemaid at the time, one of the ordinary folk.'

Catherine shook her head. 'No, Mother, you're a lady, and to be sure, never a servant in the manner of Betsy and Sarah.'

Her mother's eyes wandered toward the roses. She drew the bed-jacket about her and re-tied the straps. Catherine moved the vase to the dresser, the fragrance of the blooms filling the room.

'Mister Fraser is very considerate, daughter, and I thank our Heavenly Father for his every kindness.'

Mister Fraser, a special friend of the Nicolson family, often stopped by for a visit. He had brought her mother to Willowbank before her marriage, but Catherine did not know why. For the first time she understood, her mother was the first Missus Nicolson's lady in waiting, which explained why she appeared beholden to the kindly gentleman.

Her mother's cheeks quivered, and she brushed a wave from her brow. 'I was amused, having overheard your father discussing our marriage with Grandma Nicolson. He revealed his heart when he said, "I'm very pleased to have acquired a lively young companion for Adele and myself."'

The recollection caused her mirth. Her nostrils twitched, and she drew a deep breath. Catherine giggled and pulled the covers across her mother's lap.

'Catherine, as each of you arrived, your father expanded his heart, and now, he has another to pet.'

Catherine loved her father, a devout Christian believer, patient and impartial in his dealings with his family and servants alike. Francis Nicolson was a firm but fair boss, and according to Evelyn, he agreed with the colony principle, that to educate the servants and teach them Christian virtues would produce upright citizens.

In the early days, being a member of the estate, her mother and the other workers attended worship with the Nicolson family in the Willowbank chapel where the minister from Evandale visited for the preaching service. The reverend, a Church of England cleric, rode his horse to the property monthly. At one such service, her mother knelt at the penitent form along with Edward, the Nicolson's head groom, husband to Betsy, and repented of her sins, determined to live to honour God.

Her mother chuckled. 'Your father has a big heart.'

Betsy returned with a tea tray. 'Not asleep yet?'

'No, I've been thinking about how happy I am here, our household as contented as Ginger the barn cat's pampered kittens.'

'Truly, we all are, Missus, Mister Nicolson is so kind to us.'

'Sit with me, Betsy, we'll have tea together.'

'I'd like that A … Missus Nicolson.'

'Catherine, please fetch another cup and saucer.'

Was Catherine's imagination deceiving her? The tone between the women certainly struck an air of familiarity. She scampered down the stairs, in no doubt, her mother wished to speak with Betsy in private. The dismissal made her resolute—she would discover their common accord.

Chapter Two

Catherine sought an opportunity to visit the pump-house to add to her jottings. She ought to record the titbits she had learned about her mother at Aunt Elizabeth's. However, in the weeks since she returned to Willowbank, the requirement to take care of the younger children, Celeste, Stuart, and Louisa, in the front garden, while Mother attended to Baby Simon, stole her free time. Before the family rose from the table, Mother asked Catherine to take the children out to play in the warm midday sun. She rolled her eyes, resentful at the frequency of being the babysitter, especially given the lack of cooperation from Stuart. There must be a way to evade the task or convince him to follow orders.

Stuart stood at a distance, staring at her, his arms crossed, her brother as stubborn as she—like a couple of starlings scrapping over a worm. However, while they were alike in temperament, they were opposites as far as appearance: Catherine chubby, Stuart pole thin, her hair honey blonde, and his ginger like Mother's, surely the reason for his spoiling.

Instead of joining in the games Catherine suggested, Stuart found a hollow reed and began to puff seeds in his sisters' direction.

'Stuart, that stung.' Celeste rubbed the mark on her arm.

'Stop.' Catherine shooed Stuart away, but he grabbed and

punched her.

'Don't tell me what to do, sis. I'll do what I want,' he said.

Catherine flopped onto the garden seat and called Louisa and Celeste to her. She would make daisy chains with the girls and ignore Stuart.

♫♪ ♫♪

On hearing her name, Catherine stopped short and listened.

Mother, clearly agitated, said, 'He said, she slapped him hard, and, Francis, I did see finger marks on his arm.'

'A normal reaction I would think, my dear.'

'I simply asked her to mind the younger children for a while. She's a strong-willed child. You must chastise her.'

Catherine clenched her jaw. Stuart had run to his mother to tittle-tattle and had lied. She could scream. Why did Mother always take his side?

'I agree, Catherine is a determined lass, and for worthy pursuits not to be thwarted,' her father said.

'She's so impatient with Stuart. He's merely an exuberant boy. She has overstepped the mark this time.'

Catherine looked at the bruise Stuart left on her arm. She would show her father but not now.

'I'll have a word,' he said.

'I'd appreciate that, Francis. She adores you, but she's insolent toward me.'

'You must take the matter in hand, Arianna. Perhaps ask Lucille to share the responsibility for the younger ones.'

'I will, but Lucille doesn't manage as well as Catherine.'

Catherine stomped up the stairs and poked her tongue at her angry reflection in the mirror. 'It's just not fair.' She flung herself onto the bed and thumped her pillow. 'Mother picks on me, and the others get off scot-free.'

She stared at the ceiling, mouth puckered. Mother's soft touch was irritating. At least her father's ways were even-handed. She was glad the day Evelyn commented on her reliability and her calmness during a crisis, the reason for her mother's trust, but now, stymied because Mother excused Adele and Lucille from their responsibility. The elder sisters received copious invitations to visit with friends on neighbouring properties. Adele's young man, Robert, also spent considerable time courting her in the Willowbank parlour with the door closed.

To make things more disagreeable, Catherine was sick of rooming with Lucille, because while Catherine's corner was neat, Lucille's resembled a hen house raided by a fox. Catherine had giggled when she expressed her opinion to Lucille. There must be a way to get her sister to do her share of the work.

Hearing a shuffle, Catherine caught sight of Lucille sprawled on the floor, colouring-in near the window. She picked up a cushion and hurled it.

'Hey, that hurt. What have I done now?'

'Can't you tidy up before you laze about?'

'If I did everything you wanted when you wanted, I'd never have any fun.'

'Silly, I get my stuff done fast, so I can go outside and play.'

'I've watched you, coming up from the path.'

Catherine flinched. The girl's east-wing bedroom window was the only one facing the trees lining the riverbank, and it was very likely her sister had seen her.

'Somewhat indelicate isn't it, a girl spending time alone near the river. Father has warned us about the dangers down there. What could be so inviting?'

'More than you could ever dream, Lucille.'

'Little sister, your tongue is as sharp as flint.'

'Sorry, Lucille, I'm cross because of that brat, Stuart. He got me into trouble.'

Lucille would keep Catherine's secret since she had not blabbed regarding Lucille's latest indiscretion. In the past month, her sister read by candlelight until the early hours of the morning in defiance of their mother. Though Catherine was unlike her mother or older sisters to look at, the one thing she possessed in common was clandestine causes. Nevertheless, she would be more careful, not to provoke Lucille to blather.

Catherine rolled to the other side of the bed. Her head ached, her bossy behaviour causing her misery. She could not understand why her mother expected so much of her. Was it to keep her away from the pump-house? Pulling the covers over her head, she let the tears flow.

She found solace in the pump-house down by the river despite the tales of strange creatures lurking nearby. Those stories she believed spoken of, to ensure the Nicolson children stayed away, but in all the years she ventured along the path, she had never seen any sign of such things. She called the tiny room her musing place and wished she could go there now, but night eclipsed the estate. Curling into a ball, she resolved to look for a chance in the morning.

♫♪ ♫♪

The minute the sun peeked through the window Catherine was awake, the annoying events of yesterday abated. She had planned to dash out to the stable to pat the horses at daybreak, as she wanted to be up and out before the young ones woke and needed a hand to get ready for the day's activities.

Inspecting the dress her mother chose for her to wear, she smiled. It was her favourite blue pinafore. As was her habit each evening, Catherine's mother laid out the children's outfits on their beds. There was no doubt Willowbank's mistress fussed about the family's clothing which she designed and stitched herself. She made no secret of the fact she expected her children to be well attired and modest, and often said, as the young ladies and gentlemen of the landed gentry ought to be.

Catherine set the pinafore aside, dressed in her house-frock and passed through the kitchen plucking a carrot from the vegetable basket on her way to the stable.

'Best not be taking too much time, I've almost got the porridge at the boil, and you wouldn't want to miss breakfast.' Sarah grinned, mindful Catherine enjoyed her food.

Catherine chuckled. It was pleasant to hear the servant girl's inflection. She passed by Sarah's father, Mister Edward, as she referred to him, on her way to visit the stables. Propped up against a hay bale, he suckled a lamb. She bent to pat the creature, its skin soft.

'I found the weakling down by the creek, standing beside its dead mother,' he said.

Catherine frowned, sorry for the poor little mite, but in her old friend's good hands, the lamb would thrive.

According to Evelyn, who seemed to know most everything, Edward Jackson's story was enthralling. The servant of her Majesty's saga began when, transported from London following a conviction for stealing, he served four years of a seven-year sentence. Edward was responsible for encouraging the men in his work gang to cooperate with the constable. As a result, he received a governor's pardon, gained a ticket of leave and was released for good behaviour. Catherine's uncle, the officer in charge of the chain gangs, evidently considered Edward a reliable man and recommended him to Mister Nicolson, who employed him as a farmhand. Within the first month of his service, Mister Nicolson assigned him the care of his entire stock, having observed Edward's gentleness with the horses.

♫♪ ♫♪

Catherine found her father attending to the animals.

'Can I help feed the horses?'

'Certainly, you may, but we'll keep the carrot for later.'

Her father brushed a lock of hair from his face, his forehead wet with perspiration. Catherine picked up a spade and began filling the box with oatmeal, and Father filled the water trough.

They sat down to rest, her father's ruddy complexion intense due to the amount of energy he had expended. He inhaled and pursed his lips, sounding a whistle as he exhaled. Shuffling closer, Catherine laid her head on his chest and measured the steady pulsing of his heart.

'I understand you hit Stuart yesterday, Catherine. Is that correct?'

She lifted her head, her chin in a defiant tilt. 'No, I didn't. He punched me, look.' Catherine bared her arm to reveal the bruise. 'He's always fighting with me, says I boss him.'

'I think it would be a good idea to let Mother do the bossing from now on.'

'She doesn't see the naughty things he does, and she says I

tittle-tattle.'

'Oh, I reckon she sees plenty. I want you to let your brother be. He's very young, and you must be fair.'

'Fair? He's the pet.'

Her father, refusing to enter her argument, stood and held the carrot out to her.

'Here, Catherine, you can feed the foal now. Then, it'll be time to go back and change. You've only a few minutes until breakfast, go now, and help Mother dress the young ones.'

Catherine threw her arms in the air, snatched the carrot, hurled it toward the foal and marched off.

'Mind your attitude, young lady.'

She flung the kitchen door against the wall and slammed it behind her. Sarah looked up. Catherine hopped onto a kitchen stool beside the bench where a large pot of porridge plop, plopped. Sarah repositioned a stool, stood on her tiptoes and retrieved a delicate, china jug.

'Pass the milk please, Catherine, me brother brought it in earlier.'

It was Sarah's brother Thomas' habit to deliver a pail of milk each day and leave it by the kitchen door. Sarah tipped some into the jug and Catherine poured a glass, guzzling the lot.

'Hard work out there with your father this morning?'

Catherine wanted to say it was a battle to get her folks to realize they baby Stuart, but even to her, the complaint sounded churlish. How she wished she were not so quick-tempered.

'No, I just love the creamy flavour, that's all.'

Catherine watched as the young woman went about her chores while singing. Catherine liked spending time in the kitchen. Sarah had often made extra dough for Catherine to roll and cut-out, when Catherine was little. Did Sarah know Catherine's mother before she married Mister Nicolson? Did she wonder why Missus Nicolson treated her mother like a sister?

Sarah interrupted Catherine's reflection, 'You'd best run along, miss, breakfast is ready, and I'm about to ring the first warning bell.'

Catherine dashed out—the youngsters would be waiting to dress— and bumped into Betsy.

Straightening her large white bonnet, Betsy said, 'Woo, missy.'

'Sorry, Missus Betsy.'

'Wouldn't want me huge basket of laundry getting in the dirt now, would I?'

'Suppose not.'

Betsy stepped through the doorway humming a tune.

Catherine took the stairs by two, stopping on the first landing. She was pleased she was born a Nicolson, a well-heeled family, and not like Betsy's penniless family—she could not imagine the drudgery of being a laundress. She would never marry someone like Thomas, who, with his sister, had lived on the estate before Catherine's birth. When he was of age, her father contracted him to assist with the milking, the planting, and the harvesting of crops. The bond between the two families on the Willowbank Estate was unlike the relationships she observed between the workers and the landholders on other properties. Deep down she had an inkling regarding the curious rapport. Regardless of their servant family's amicability, Catherine would be sure to find a husband of her ilk. She could not subject herself to the toil expected of the Jacksons.

♫♪ ♫♪

Discovering her younger sisters and brothers were almost ready for the day's activities, Catherine hurried to her room and pulled her blue pinafore over her white blouse. Father liked the family to be prompt to the table, and she had best not exacerbate her earlier impudence.

'The puffy sleeves and embroidered collar on this blouse are a bit fussy, don't you think, Miss Evelyn?'

'Very feminine, I'd say.' The governess helped her tie the straps in a bow at the back.

Catherine hoisted herself onto the stool in front of the mirror, and her governess dragged the brush through the thin blond hair.

'I'm pleased you've helped dress the little ones, Miss Evelyn. I'm thoroughly sick of taking care of them.'

Evelyn grimaced but refrained from replying. She was far from her composed self. Instead of the usual neat knot, her mousy-brown hair fell lank and looked dull. Her cheeks were sallow, accentuating her deep-set chocolate-brown eyes.

The bell sounded for the family to gather in the refectory. Catherine, conscious she had but a few minutes until the second bell, tidied the shelf beside the large Elizabethan-style cot she shared with her sister, skipped by the bedroom occupied by Adele and on to the young ones' rooms. There she tied her brother's shoelaces and assisted Celeste and Louisa by plaiting their hair.

'Hurry up, Stuart. Off you go downstairs, now, or you'll be late for breakfast.'

Stuart poked out his tongue and leapt away before she could retaliate.

The coast clear of all but her youngest sister, Catherine looked around—should she slide down the highly polished banister? She did not, as the previous day she landed on the mat at the bottom and was subject to Evelyn's disapproving scowl. Instead, she chose a more responsible action becoming of a big sister, and took Louisa by the hand guiding her down.

Catherine revelled in the meal times—the family gathered around the long oak table in the dining room. She rubbed her hands together, glad of the wood fire in the large brick fireplace. She felt the warmth on her back and wrinkled her nose at the smell of pinecones crackling in the grate. As was her father's habit, he bowed his head, the signal for the family to pause and recite the morning grace in unison.

Mother tinkled the small silver bell beside her, the signal for Sarah to deliver bowls filled with steaming porridge. Sarah returned to the kitchen and brought in a pretty china teapot with a matching milk jug on a silver tray. Betsy followed her, balancing a platter of hot buttered toast. She set her load down on the oak-duchess and scampered out, leaving Sarah to pour the tea.

A sharp blow stabbed Catherine in the leg. Stuart sneered at her across the table—her brother was such a knavish creature. She wriggled further along her seat, anxious to preserve the harmonious mood. Her father helped himself to two lumps of sugar and tapped her hand as she reached for a piece. Stuart lifted his chin and looked down his nose. She crunched her lips tight, knowing the rules, and did not need extra, tasting the golden syrup Sarah added to the porridge. Stuart licked his lips, his demeanour like that of Ginger the cat when she caught a rat.

Her father signalled Mother, and she jingled the small bell, issuing in Catherine's favourite part of the day. Her father invited the servants to join the family each morning as he read a short passage from the Bible. A scripture he often read was from the Psalms, the writer confident, no matter the trouble he faced—God walked with him. As young as she was, Catherine questioned the significance of the reading. They did not have problems. Her family was well-off. She looked around, firstly at the John Glover landscape that took pride of place above the dresser, and then at the gilt-edged mirror above the mantelpiece. She swivelled and set eyes on the lush garden through the giant, picture-window. That Scripture would not mean anything to her family.

Glimpsing at Mister Edward in the mirror, she bit her bottom lip. He was smiling at her mother. He was aware of the significance of the verse—his family were poor. Willowbank's servant-family did depend upon the goodness of God and indeed the kindness of Mister Nicolson. They retreated, not delaying in returning to their chores following devotions. Her father often told Mister Fraser, Edward and his kin were loyal, diligent workers, a fact consistently borne out.

♫♪ ♫♪

Evelyn and Sarah discussed the verse from the morning's reading, and Catherine listened in.

'You'll understand it better by and by, girlie,' Evelyn said, her broad Scottish accent stronger than ever.

If only she could siphon just a little of Mister Edward's temper into her veins, she might remain composed when her brother riled her. Recalling Edward's soft glance in her mother's direction, to be sure indicating she was also a beneficiary of God's goodness. Catherine sighed. Did he know about Mother's past, or was Betsy alone privy to the mystery?

Chapter Three

Catherine woke early, drew the drapes and flung the shutters back allowing the sunlight to stream into the bedroom.
'Close them, Catherine, my eyes hurt.'

Catherine faced her sister, and with her back to the open window, yanked the curtains closed in front of her. She spun to look toward the river, foliage in every shade of green covering all but the shingle roof of the pump-house. There must be a way to get there today, re-read her memoirs and add to her notes. She would like to quiz Betsy about Mother's family, but Father's constant reminder of the importance of preserving reputation would not allow it. Besides, if the old servant had no knowledge of Mother's background, the query might cause her to suspect a scandal. Catherine screwed her nose—her hunch flimsy.

Her eyes followed the row of willows delineating the river's course. If she walked along the edge, she would come to the shallow ford, and once across the river, she could follow the track to her Uncle Cameron's Myrtleford property. The Cameron Nicolson's were due to return from England soon. Leaning on the sill, she pictured her cousin, Florence, with whom she longed to spend time. They played together when they were young, dressing up, Florence always choosing the blue silk gown, pretending to be duchesses captured by pirates. In her imagination, Catherine tiptoed behind Florence as she crept down the bluestone steps and entered a dark chamber, deep within the bowels of the great house.

She caught her breath, adrenaline shooting through her veins. Entangled, she wrestled the clinging drapes, her terror as real as the day the cell door snapped shut. Unravelling herself, she stepped away from the window, her temples throbbing.

Lucille sat up and flung the covers off. 'What in the world are you doing?'

'Nothing,' Catherine wheezed. Too often, her overactive imagination excited strange notions. Maybe even her mother's apparent secrecy was mere fancy.

Laughter echoed. Catherine pushed the curtain aside and leant out the window. Sarah, the servant girl and her brother, Thomas, stood at the end of the veranda of the shearing shed nodding their heads. A dark-haired youth, the same height as Thomas, conversed with them all the while twirling a tweed-cap upon his finger, a swag jammed between his legs.

She had not seen the youth before, though the friendliness on display by Willowbank's young servants gave the impression they knew him well. Perhaps they had met at the General store in Evandale when they shopped for supplies, or maybe he had taken a shine to Sarah and had come seeking permission to court her.

The visitor flicked the bedroll up with his feet, slung it over his shoulder and adjusted his cap.

Thomas thumped him on the back and said, 'It was good to see you again. You can come and stay anytime.'

Catherine did not catch the name. The young man swished by, right under her window. Apart from his wavy, black hair and apparent agility, there was nothing remarkable about him. Then again, Catherine did not get a good look. She would enquire regarding him. If there were another romance to keep an eye on, she would be on hand. If Sarah were of age to consider a follower, then maybe Catherine's turn would not be long in coming. Besides, she found the flirtations of her sisters Adele and Lucille fascinating, and even her parent's marriage had retained its spark despite the apparent disparity of their social origins.

♫♪ ♫♪

It was stupid to be couped-up in the upstairs drawing room on such a fine day. Most days at Willowbank began in the same manner for the four eldest Nicolson children under the tutelage of Evelyn, the family governess, learning English, history, and mathematics.

Catherine slumped on her desk, her chin cupped by her left hand and her pencil poised in her right. Evelyn's drone barely penetrated her consciousness, something about God saving an ancient mariner from fiends and an albatross. Catherine tapped her pencil. The reader's eyes signalled, don't do that. Her stern countenance would make the bravest recoil. The small brown, beady eyes penetrated one's soul. A mole sat right in the middle of her elongated nose, and her thin, mousy hair, pulled into the tightest bun, caused an already severe face to look more austere.

Evelyn stepped behind her students. 'Write three sentences about the parable.'

Catherine chewed on her pencil and gazed out the window. Mother sat in her white-wicker garden-chair, a sketchpad on her lap and a charcoal stick in her hand. Undoubtedly, she was drawing a picture of the grand magnolia in the centre of the lawn, something she regularly did. The young ones played nearby catching butterflies and making daisy chains. Catherine murmured. It was fun when she was little, playing catch and chasing small skinks.

'Catherine, please look at your work. You're not concentrating.'

Evelyn's scolding was savage. Catherine snapped her head around and stared at her governess, her face burning.

She whispered, 'I'd rather be outside.'

A gasp hissed. Catherine spun—her sisters' mouths wide open.

'I'm not deaf. You're far too sassy for your own good, young lady,' Evelyn said.

Catherine dropped her eyes and bit the inside of her lip. Evelyn's voice hummed on and on. Catherine squirmed, recollecting her father's lecture when she grumbled about having to sit in the stuffy drawing room from the January following her seventh birthday, the age each child commenced studies.

Evelyn exhaled noisily and said, 'Collect your easels and follow me.'

'Hooray!' Catherine squealed. 'We're moving outdoors.' She scraped her chair across the floor, thankful Evelyn's love of biology and art meant the class ventured outdoors for some lessons.

Evelyn frowned and said, 'Catherine, you are uncooperative.'

Catherine chuckled at the new word Evelyn had used. The class had learned to spell it during the lesson, though it was one Catherine had heard a time or two before. She mouthed, 'Sorry.'

Once outside, the governess' charge skipped, lessons no longer a trial to endure but an exciting adventure, and painting a favourite past time.

'Catherine, don't run ahead, or you'll not be allowed to paint.'

A pair of yellow wattlebirds birds shot from the bush screeching a cacophony—"Look out, miss, look out, miss!". Catherine stopped in her tracks. She wished the others would hurry up, but she was aware her familiarity with the path would be rather too obvious if she hit upon the head of the trail too soon.

'You all dawdle so. We won't have enough time to finish our creations. Come on.'

They set up their work at a spot a hundred yards downstream from the pump-house, Evelyn handing out paint and brushes for them to experiment. 'Look at the view across the river. Notice the golden plains and the blue hue of Mt. Ben Lomond in the distance,' she said.

Indeed, the familiar scene did provide a picturesque landscape to capture on their canvasses, Catherine dabbing her brush in the red-brown ochre pigment and replicating her hideaway, the shape prominent in the foreground of her painting. Immersed, she jumped when the house bell jangled indicating it was time for lunch.

'I'm starving after our hard work this morning,' she said and handed her sheet to Evelyn, folded her easel and ran toward the sound.

'Make sure you leave enough for us, Catherine,' Lucille called after her.

♫♪ ♫♪

Catherine rolled her eyes. She ought not to complain about Mother's expectation that the children would rest in their rooms for an hour in the afternoons. After the morning's play in the crisp air and partaking of the usual fare of fresh ribbon sandwiches and glasses of milk, they needed a quiet hour.

'I don't have to sleep, do I, Mother? It seems such a waste of time.'

Her mother moaned and pointed to the stairs, her countenance dark. 'Not if you're quiet, but I need a few minutes of peace.'

Catherine pushed passed and scurried to her room. Her mother made it clear she enjoyed the private moments at her loom, the hour's quiet-time giving her the opportunity to relax since she was pregnant again. Catherine did not lie down, instead, reclined in a chair by the window, waiting, flipping through pages of a *Penny Illustrated*.

Lucille's soft rhythmic breathing suggested she was asleep. Catherine retrieved her tiny brass key, crept down the rear stairs springing over the last step to prevent it from squeaking. She made her way along the backside of the hedge to the clump of trees hiding the path. A rustle, just as she reached the side of the forbidden structure, caused her to jump. Her breath caught in her throat. She squatted, silent—everything still—and eased around toward the front of the hut. She pulled the door, the hinge grating. Letting herself in, she secured the latch.

A sweet scent, mixed with the musty smell of the damp floor, greeted her. She stalled, her eyes growing accustomed to the dim light filtering through the gap at the top of the wall, a window of sorts that did not extend to the roof. She stood on her toes to fetch her notebook and graphite pencil from the high shelf, and unwrapped the canvas bag lined with camphor-paper, containing her jottings. Unlocking the book, she flipped through until she found the dogged-eared page and scribbled, but not for long, incase someone missed her.

She stretched to return her precious compendium to its hiding place, yelped and snatched back her hand. Blood oozed from her little finger. What bit into her skin? She dug for her handkerchief tucked inside her sleeve and held the cut tight. The gash was not from a bite, but try as she might, she could not see what her hand had struck, she was not tall enough, and had nothing on which to stand. Certain that the rest hour was over and she was required to entertain her younger sisters, Catherine fled to the house, stopping to rinse the sleeve of her bloodstained housedress and her handkerchief in a bucket of water in the laundry. Tiptoeing upstairs, pleased to have escaped notice, she wrote cards and delivered them to her sisters' rooms, inviting them to sit with her. She set the small table and chairs for a tea party, using the real porcelain tea-set given to the girls by their grandmother. Grabbing her favourite cloth doll, the one with straw-coloured hair Mother had made, she dressed her in the outfit sewn from leftover scraps of material—she and her doll attired alike in their white muslin, sporting a sky-blue bow.

Lucille stirred and read her note. 'I'm too old for such babyish games,' she said.

'Please yourself. Dolly can have the fourth chair,' Catherine said, as her younger sisters scurried to their seats. 'I am the lady of the house. Welcome to my high tea.'

'Oh, Catherine,' Lucille put on her most affected voice, 'your imagination runs away with you sometimes, my dear.' She flounced from the room, the sisters giggling.

Catherine could hardly wait to come of age and be hostess at bona fide parties like the ones her aunts organised from time to time. However, there were aspects of being an adult, Catherine was not ready to embrace, such as mending. Mother required her to tackle the task when the womenfolk gathered in the parlour in the late afternoon for their craft session.

♫♪ ♫♪

'That's my favourite pattern, Mother,' Catherine said, admiring her mother's exquisite salmon and sage-green panelled quilt draped over the sofa. 'Can I make one like it?'

'Certainly, you may, when you're more accomplished.'

Catherine, already proficient at chain stitch, had completed a duchess-set that graced the dining-room sideboard. She looked forward to the latter part of the craft session, because after mending, she would learn the new crochet knot-stitch from her sister, Adele.

Mother lay bolts of fabric down and set needles, thimbles, and various coloured strands of cotton on the table.

'Miss Evelyn's not here.'

'She'll be along soon,' Mother said.

Mother instructed Louisa to complete some simple stitches, while Adele cut patterns to sew new dresses for Catherine and Celeste.

Evelyn approached carrying a roll of her pupils' latest, completed artworks. 'All dried,' she said.

'We'll finish here first,' Mother said, picking up a shirt from the pile and handing it to Catherine. 'Hem this please.'

'Oh, but that's not interesting. I wanted to try the knot-stitch like Lucille. She's making pretty flowers.'

'We've all had to take our turn at mending, Catherine. If you finish the shirt first, perhaps Adele can teach you,' Lucille said.

Catherine's nimble fingers zoomed in and out, in and out, and she bit off the thread.

'Finished.'

'As rapid as a wattlebird's tongue,' said Evelyn.

Mother tilted her head and cocked an eye.

'Our lesson this morning, Missus Nicolson,' Evelyn said.

In unison, the girls mimicked the bird's harsh sound and laughing, collapsed on the settee. Mother joined the throng, and Father appeared and leaned upon the lintel. He feigned a severe look, and Celeste jumped away—the twinkle in his eye, disguised by the wire spectacles balanced on the end of his nose, not missed.

'I could have been mistaken, but I thought I heard a gaggle of geese.'

Celeste yelped, ran and locked her slim arms around his trouser legs. His spectacles flew off and skidded across the polished slate but somehow remained intact.

Mother cleared her throat and pointed to the pattern in her needlecraft-journal. 'Catherine, look at the picture. Adele will teach you to follow the steps.'

Catherine's elder sister, Adele, was patient and willingly demonstrated the stitch, allowing Catherine to try her own, and within a few minutes, she became adept.

'See, I told you it would be worth it.' Lucille clapped. 'Well done, little sister.'

'Now let's reward Miss Evelyn by displaying your landscapes,' Mother said.

Catherine scooped up her paper and stepped behind the settee. Her sisters showed off their paintings to exuberant exclamations, met with smiles and words of appreciation.

'Let me see yours, Catherine.' Mother beckoned her.

'I gift mine to you, Mother,' Catherine said and pushed by Lucille, flashing a cautionary eye at her sister's wry grin, her conscience cut to the core.

'I've things to do and places to go.' Lucille folded her handicraft, placed it in the camphor chest and swished from the room with her painting tucked under her arm.

Evelyn corralled the others and shooed them out.

'Here,' Catherine said, holding the painting toward her mother.

A crinkle of eyebrows and a finger held against quivering lips posed an unasked question. Mother's eyes flittered, wandered across the page searching the busy scene. Her gaze settled upon the central feature—a ray of light streaming through the canopy of tree branches highlighting an ibis hovering above the pump-house roof.

'It's beautiful, dear.' Mother met her eye. 'I imagine the ibis guards hidden treasure.'

Catherine's brow puckered. Treasure—yours or mine? 'Or, maybe divulges a message to a poor maiden,' Catherine said.

'Daughter, those fairy tales have you utterly beguiled.'

Catherine and her sisters had thumbed through Hans Christian Anderson's, *The Marsh King's Daughter*, most days since receiving the book in the post from Florence.

Mother was clever; a guarded enigma. However, the time would come when the ibis would speak.

Chapter Four

Warm summer days had given way to the cool of autumn when leaves traded their vibrant colours for crumbling dry mulch. Grey skies settled over the plain, and the women gathered beside the crackling fire to undertake their handiwork, indoor activities having replaced those outdoor. While Catherine missed her sister, Adele, after her marriage to Captain Robert, the sewing bees continued to be enjoyable experiences for other reasons. As the women's needles bobbed in and out of their material, Catherine gleaned crucial information she wanted to add to her almanac.

Evelyn told the story of her sea voyage to the colony when she was a small child. She stopped sewing, rubbed her forearms and chewed her lip, the faraway look in her eye incomprehensible to Catherine. There was no doubt the spinster considered it a blessing to be part of the Nicolson family, invited by Mother to be governess when her parents died. Evelyn's candour prompted Mother to divulge her tale.

'I too, was lonely without family until I came here,' she said.

Evelyn lifted her head, though familiar with her mistress' story.

Catherine leaned forward. Mother, born in Scotland, sailed as a youngster and became an orphan when her mother perished at sea. A hush descended like a mist. Mother leaned back and closed her eyes. Why did Mother not have other family members living nearby? What had happened to her father?

Sarah's entrance with tea and Betsy's freshly baked scones relieved the melancholy mood.

'Ooh, Devonshire tea, my favourite,' Catherine said, scooping her sewing pieces and stowing them in the camphor chest.

Sarah spread a cloth and served from the low table where the girls had been working. Catherine piled more cream onto her scones than the gentry considered polite, her well-rounded figure testament to the fact. Lucille patted her sister's tummy and waggled her finger.

On most days, after the sewing bee and before dinner, the sisters had approximately an hour to spend in any manner they desired. Catherine chose to read. She perused the shelves of the parlour lined with dozens of books, purchased by her father and transported on trading ships along with the other goods from the mother country. Sometimes Evelyn read to the girls, but today she retired to her quarters complaining of a headache. Mother excused herself, bound for the stables. Mister Fraser had brought his horse by to be re-shod by Edward.

Catherine picked up Celeste's favourite book, *The Goody Two Shoes Picture Book*, and invited her sister to sit beside her, point to and enunciate the letters.

'I can't wait to read well enough to try the other books you speak of written by *Jane Austen*. She must be your favourite.'

'That she is, Celeste. Her stories are so real, almost making you think you're one of her characters.'

'And your big sister, Celeste, is most assuredly most like the contrary, Miss Bennett.'

'Ah, ha, Lucille, but in as much as your dapper Mister Harry Butler fits Darcy's likeness, is it not you who plays the heroine of the Midland Plains?'

Lucille's cheeks coloured at Catherine's jest, and she curled her legs beneath her chin locking her gaze upon the flames dancing within the grate.

Catherine selected another picture book for Celeste and set her to reading, whispering close to her ear, 'I'll be back soon.'

She slipped out the back door, meandered toward the hedge—no one in the yard could see her behind the foliage—ran to the river-path and headed for the pump-house. It was many months since she had ventured to her little nook. She must make a new entry with respect to her mother's tale while it was fresh in her mind.

Stepping deftly over the rocks, she wished she had changed into her boots; the earlier drizzle making the path slippery. She reached for the trunk of a tree to balance and scraped the mud from her dainty shoe. A flash of yellow caught her attention, and then it was gone. Was it one of Father's creepy creatures? The awful guttural squawk of a yellow wattlebird broke the silence, "Look out, miss, look out, miss!" She hurried through the pump-house doorway.

Once inside, she grappled for the shelf to find her canvas wrapper—it was easier to reach, she was taller than on her previous visit. She groped about, touched something cold and pushed the article toward the edge. A metal box, the size of a jewellery case, teetered. She grasped it with both hands to keep it from falling and placed it on the floor.

The insignia engraved on the lid was one she had seen before. She ran her finger over the raised design and traced a shield. Except for a large "F" on the bottom left side, the eroded wording was difficult to read. That the banner was quite rusted, given the moisture in the hut, was no surprise. She fiddled with the padlock, but it would not give. Should she force the lid? No, but the next time she came, she would examine the contents. Returning the box to the shelf, she retrieved her canvas bag, made an entry of two pages in her notebook and retreated to the path.

She entered the house via the rear door, but not before stopping to scrape her shoes free of mud, and slipped up to her room to hide her key. Squatting on her stool to change her shoes, she noticed a movement near the hedge and watched. She would have followed the person slinking past the scrub near the pump-house if, at the time, it was not so close to dinner. The figure resembled Betsy, but what reason might the woman have for entering the machinery shed? It was not the first time, and most often following a stopover by Mister Fraser, when Catherine sighted the Willowbank servant loitering in the vicinity. Perhaps it was fortuitous she had returned to the house earlier.

The parlour hushed, Catherine's sisters, so engrossed in what they were doing, had not noticed her absence. Evelyn, quite recovered from her headache, came to remind them to go upstairs and change for the evening meal.

'Hurry, girls, your grandmother is arriving very soon. Adele is also coming.'

'It is hard to believe, she's been married a whole year?' Lucille said.

'I miss her,' Catherine said.

'We all surely do, she's such a genteel soul,' Evelyn said, her eyes censuring Catherine.

Adele coincided her visit with Grandma Kate's, making no secret of the fact she loved her family. Since marrying Captain Robert Davenport, she had resided in Launceston but visited Willowbank at every available opportunity.

Catherine clapped—Grandma would be sure to bring the letters received from family in England and Hobart. Of course, she would also repeat her stories of historic-clan happenings. Why tales from bygone days were of such interest to older folks was a mystery, but tonight, in the hope of picking up a clue to solve her puzzle about her mother, Catherine would stay by Grandma's side. Vigilance would be her friend.

♫♪ ♫♪

The smell of cooking wafted through the house.

'Oh yum, Sarah's preparing Grandma's favourite meal, roast lamb dinner and apple pie.' Celeste had poked her head into her elder sisters' room.

'I prefer a beef-roast with Yorkshire pudding followed by golden syrup dumplings. Definitely my favourite,' Catherine said.

'Will you tie my bows, please?'

Catherine lifted her young sister onto the stool, turned her to face the mirror and obliged her.

Donning her own costume, Catherine buttoned her soft-blue silk blouse with the delicate, white lace-collar, and tucked it in at the waist of her velvet skirt.

'If only you were as lady-like as you look, Catherine.' Lucille examined her sister's outfit.

Catherine glared and stepped toward her. Lucille jumped and bounded from the room.

'Don't get mad at her, Catherine, you might be sent to your room instead of staying up with the grownups.'

Catherine stroked Celeste under the chin, 'You are a sweet princess.'

Her little sister skipped out and down the hall. Catherine, twisting her hair into a tight knot, and attaching a matching blue bow to hold it in place, stole a glance in the mirror satisfied she would meet her grandmother's approval.

The doorbell sounded as she reached the bottom landing.

'I'll get it,' she called to Sarah. 'Welcome, Grandma. Adele, come and see what we made today.'

Sarah arrived and reached to help Kate Nicolson out of her woollen coat. Catherine waited, hopping from one foot to the other. Taking Grandma and Adele by the hands, she led them to the parlour.

'My, this handcraft is worthy of adorning any of the palaces of Europe.'

'Oh, Grandma, you always say that.'

'Grandma, you may have some of my work.' Lucille presented the older woman two crocheted doilies.

'These delicate pieces shall grace my hall-table for all to see, thank you, Lucille.'

Not to be outdone, Catherine offered her a set of embroidered cloths.

Mother burst into the room. 'It's remiss of me, Kate, not to greet you. I lay on the bed to rest awhile and went sound asleep.'

'Are you quite well, Arianna? You look a little pale.'

'Just tired, Kate, just tired.' Mother leaned back into the settee.

Sarah carried in a tray filled with teacups and served from the hall-table.

Grandma Kate sipped tea from her delicate cup and smiled. 'Ah, this is a welcome courtesy after the dusty ride from the Nile.'

'Your pansies, Catherine, is that a new stitch you've mastered?' Adele asked.

'Ah, Adele, but of course you know. It was from you I learned it, and even Evelyn reckons they're nearly as pretty as yours.'

'I'd have to agree. Let me have a closer look.'

Celeste skipped in and squatted on a stool next to Grandma's chair. 'Did you bring us any surprises, Grandma Kate?'

'I certainly did.'

All the Nicolson children counted on Grandma Kate to bring goodies when she came—that was her way. Aware sweet delicacies were a rare treat for the family, she brought jars of raspberry jam from the Perth Village General Store.

'The jam was produced at the new Peacock's factory in Hobart Town. Aunt Elizabeth discovered it when she moved to Hobart and recommended it.' Grandma Kate opened a jar and spooned some into her saucer. 'Have a taste, Arianna.'

'Perhaps after dinner.'

'I will.' Catherine said, keen to try the concoction. 'My tummy's rumbling.' She rubbed her belly. 'Yum, it tastes as good as any homemade jam ever did.'

A door slammed. Stuart skidded into the parlour. 'I'm starved. Dinner smells good.'

'Wash up for dinner, Stuart, and then come and greet Grandma and Adele,' Catherine said.

'Yes, miss bossy britches,' Stuart said and stomped up the stairs.

'Dinner's ready, Missus Nicolson,' Sarah called from the doorway.

'Ring the house bell, please, Sarah.'

Sarah retrieved the jars of jam, carried them to the kitchen pantry and jangled the great brass bell.

Adele threw her hands in the air, 'Gracious me, I'd forgotten how loud that gong was. There's no mistaking that clang. I remember hearing it as much as half a mile away,' she chuckled.

'Sarah's ready to serve the roast. Let's be seated in the dining room,' Mother said, grasped Grandma's arm and took her across the hallway.

Father met them at the door, holding out his elbows. His wife threaded her hand through one arm, and his mother did similarly on the other. He led them to their seats, his animated chatter indicative of the pleasure he felt in his mother's company. Everyone loved Grandma.

Catherine savoured the delicious dinner and watched Adele,

mirroring her every move—holding her fork in the same manner and patting her lips with her serviette. Even brother Stuart tried to impress, sitting tall and exhibiting his best behaviour.

Grandma Kate raised her glass high and offered a toast. 'To Willowbank, Tasmanian lamb sought after in the mother country, and I do declare, Nicolson's lamb is the best to be had.'

Catherine loved the way her grandmother honoured her sons, Grandma Kate unashamedly proud of her sons' prowess as sheep graziers.

'To the Nicolson families, thanks be to God.' Father clinked his glass with Mother's and swilled its contents.

'Not only is the meat excellent, but the governor has praised our colony's fine merino wool, saying it's the best in the known world,' Adele said.

'Certainly, our recent shipment of fine wool fetched a handsome price in Scotland,' Father said.

The youngest children began to squirm. Mother looked along the table and jingled her small table-bell. Catherine licked her lips, and her mouth watered as Sarah served the dessert of apple pie topped with lavishes of fresh cream.

'This is delicious, Arianna. Your cook excels herself.'

'Indeed, she does. It's Betsy's specialty. I'll pass compliments on.'

'Apples from our orchard,' Catherine said.

The dining room hushed as the family tucked into their pudding. Grandma's teeth clunked-clunked on her spoon. Stuart grinned in Catherine's direction, but Catherine desperate to ignore him scraped her bowl clean with her spoon. It would not do to laugh at Grandma's expense. Stuart swiped his finger across his plate. At that point, Catherine could no longer contain her chuckle and collapsed into a fit of giggles, her laughter contagious. Soon all the children chortled, the earlier decorum dissipating.

Her father coughed and looked stern. 'And, miss, just what tickled your fancy?'

Catherine tensed her shoulders and stammered. She must spare her brother on this occasion.

'We're all scoffing pudding down like it's our last meal and we're off to the gallows.'

Her father wiped his mouth with his serviette and said, 'Children, finish your pudding. Mother and our guests shall retire to the drawing room along with me.'

Catherine caught her mother's sideways glance as she left the room, approval of her daughter's deflection. With a frantic clinking of spoons upon china bowls, followed by the scraping of chairs, the remainder of the group retreated and sat in a circle near Grandma Kate's chair, anxious to hear more of her news.

'Catherine, please take the younger children upstairs. They ought to go to bed,' Mother said.

'Please, Mother, can't I stay?' Catherine tilted her head.

Mother looked at Father, and he said, 'Yes, all right, you may. Evelyn would you be so kind as to oblige?'

Evelyn glanced at Catherine. Her eyes narrowed, and Catherine wilted.

'Go with Evelyn, children,' Father said and lifted Simon from his lap.

Evelyn spread her arms and shooed the young ones up the stairs, while Catherine leant her head on the arm of Grandma's chair.

'How is your mission progressing, Grandma?' Adele said.

Grandma Kate reported on her charity work, ministering to the ordinary folk. She told how she and Aunt Rowena produced all manner of handicraft items and preserves to sell to their well-to-do friends, to raise funds, to distribute to the poor.

'Perhaps we could donate our sewing and produce too,' Mother volunteered.

'You could, and we'd welcome the help. However, we've got an even more exciting thing happening. One of our ladies recently suggested it might serve the folk better if they learned to sew and cook.'

'Doesn't everyone do that already?' Catherine swivelled her head to look at Grandma.

'Some poor folks don't own more than one dress, Catherine,' Adele said.

'The ladies in our society have taken to teaching them to read too. Most ordinary folks haven't attended school. We use the Bible, and that's way they learn of Jesus,' Grandma said.

'I want to be just like you, Grandma, when I grow up.'

The old lady smiled. 'It would please me immensely, Catherine, if you chose to serve the poor.'

'Undoubtedly, it's our Christian duty, we're so blessed to be without want ourselves,' Adele said.

The pucker of Grandma's forehead was curious. Did she wish to differ with her eldest granddaughter? If her thoughts were at odds with Adele's, Grandma did not say so.

'I believe, contentment is found in a mission that inspires you, and this is my desire for you all.'

Hushed murmurs indicated Grandma's motto had stirred her audience. Catherine imagined a room full of deprived girls, their eyes fixed on her as she demonstrated the making of a chain stitch. Her skin tingled—teaching young women handicraft would thrill her heart.

The conversation switched to news of the Nicolson relatives' activities. Grandma unfolded a letter she had received from her daughter, Elizabeth. Apart from her recommendation of Peacock's jam, Elizabeth described the first performance of the Tasmanian Philharmonic Orchestra.

Grandma read, 'The orchestra played Brahms and Chopin, in addition to Liszt, all my favourite pieces. The occasion provided an opportunity for the government officials and wealthy citizens of the city to parade their finest apparel. I wore my cream, chiffon gown with matching shoes and gloves, but compared to others I felt somewhat underdressed.'

This piece of information brought smothered laughter from Lucille, 'I am very sure Aunt Elizabeth would never have allowed the other officers' wives to outshine her,' and her sisters snickered with Lucille.

Aunt Elizabeth was the most proper lady Catherine had ever met. As she listened to the description of the grand events, a tinge of guilt washed over her, for she hoped one day to enter the society described by her aunt and had expressed such a desire in her secret notebook. Did Aunt Elizabeth also help the poor? She sounded so high and mighty, Catherine did not think it likely.

Lucille voiced Catherine's sentiment. 'Ooh! I'd love to be gussied up and attend an operatic concert.'

'Hobart is gaining quite a reputation as a high-quality arts centre,' Adele said.

Grandma Kate laughed, 'How sophisticated we've become. I was a slip of a girl when growing up in Sydney Town. The colony was barely twenty years old, and with no more than five thousand people, the population mostly made up of convicts. Suitable wives were scarce, many officers marrying recently pardoned prisoners. The women had little option, had to adapt to their new situations, most of them relieved to be rescued by their menfolk.'

Catherine glanced at her father. He remained in the room with the ladies but seemed to be thinking of other things, his eyes focused upon Mother who sat on the outer circle. Their eyes met, and a wistful smile creased her mother's mouth.

During her treatise, Grandma Kate alluded to the fact her father had married a woman from the ordinary folk, but no one probed the veiled reference. Catherine learned early, such facts remained hidden to protect family reputations, but her cousin Florence spoke of a skeleton. Florence informed Catherine, a skeleton was Grandma's term for a juicy titbit. Her cousin had a knack of wheedling information from people. Catherine wished she were as bold, she so wanted to ask more questions, but with a glance at her father, changed her mind.

Except for Mother, the impromptu history lesson kept everyone engrossed. Mother fidgeted, a frown etching her brow, and reaching for a handkerchief she patted her face. A look of alarm crossed Father's face, and he nodded. Mother jingled the tea bell, and Sarah rushed to her side feigning breathlessness. Catherine's brows puckered. Sarah and Betsy had hovered in the hallway most of the evening.

'You called, ma'am?'

'Sarah, please bring tea and some of the butter cake.'

Grandma Kate glanced in Mother's direction and smiled.

'Go on, Grandma, tell us more.' Lucille shuffled her chair closer.

'The images portrayed by my parents, of life in England, were hardly imaginable, and except for having seen the drawings in the few books my father brought with him, I'd not have believed them. As bad as transportation to Australia may have been, many were glad to leave the old country.'

Sarah popped the supper on the sideboard, whispered to Mother and withdrew.

Mother stood and stretched her back. 'If you don't mind, I think I'll go to up to my room,' she said and retreated to the hallway.

Catherine shrugged, and tucked into a couple of pieces of cake.

'We've come quite a way since the early days, what with our very own concerts and plays in the Theatre Royal,' Adele asserted. 'Even in Launceston, I have the opportunity to attend plays and orchestral evenings.'

'We shall have a performance right here, daughters,' Father said.

'I'm certain Grandma and Adele would like you to recite the poems Evelyn taught you.'

'I'll go first,' Catherine said, swallowing her last bite of cake.

'*The Boy and the Butterfly* by *John Bunyan*.' Her tongue was like a runaway horse as she quoted the verse. Breathless, she flopped on the settee.

''Tis as well we know the poem, Catherine. For one moment, I thought it was you stung by the nettles,' Adele said laughing.

'I believe Lucille has learned *Daffodils* by *William Wordsworth*.' Father directed her to stand.

Grandma clapped her hands, 'I'd love to hear it.'

Lucille bowed to her audience and quoted the first verse with all the dignity it required.

'Beautiful,' said Grandma Kate. 'And to think, he could have been describing this very place instead of England.'

The evening concluded with a favourite hymn, an unaccompanied rendition of *The Lord is My Shepherd*, with Grandma singing alto, Father bass, and the remainder warbling soprano. Catherine skipped to the waiting carriage to say her goodbyes while her sisters waved from the steps.

Edward sat atop the seat ready to depart. 'Ah, it does warm the cockles of me heart to hear ye singing. The music rang out all the way over to me cottage.'

Catherine giggled, how blessed to have such a family. As the carriage disappeared down the track, she looked back at the house—she ought to begin by loving those living under the same roof if she desired to serve the poor. Her heart skipped with joy due to her effort to get along with Stuart tonight.

Chapter Five

Catherine welcomed the distraction of Evelyn's tutorials since Mother had taken to her bed most days for the last few weeks. She missed her mother's chatter, the house quiet but for Betsy's clatter in the kitchen and Sarah's cooing as she attended to Simon. Wide-eyed, Catherine had listened and learned about the life cycle of the green frogs, and on occasions had collected tadpoles from the pond observing the changes as they developed.

Hurrying to the garden ready for a fresh lesson, she tapped her forehead trying to recall the unusual word Miss Evelyn had written on the blackboard.

'Metamorphous—I must find a cocoon,' she said, bobbing under the row of bottlebrushes.

'Come here, Miss Evelyn. Look what I've found.'

'Ah, well done.' Evelyn carefully lifted the chrysalis, a brown and orange creature, struggling to free itself.

Stuart scurried over to check out the discovery and snatched at the cocoon, 'I'll help you out, Missus Bug,' he said.

Grabbing his arm, Catherine yanked it back and snapped, 'Don't do that, Stuart. It must get out on its own. Isn't that right, Miss Evelyn?'

'Yes, I know you wanted to help, but it's the struggle that makes the butterfly strong, lad.'

Catherine rolled her eyes. Evelyn was too forgiving of Stuart. Why was it a colossal effort for her though? Nevertheless, she would not forget Evelyn's words—*the butterfly becomes stronger through struggle*. Oh, for a chance to visit her secret place and enter the saying in her notebook, along with the Bible verse containing a similar thought, her father quoted yesterday.

The governess' lessons were interrupted by the arrival of Fraser's buggy. Andrew, handing the reins to his father, leapt off the seat and ran toward Stuart. The boys could almost pass for brothers, alike in appearance with slight frames, the same shade of red hair and freckly noses.

Mister Fraser greeted Thomas, retrieved an enormous bunch of roses from the carriage, rushed up the steps and through the open door. No one in Catherine's acquaintance appeared as comfortable with the Nicolson family as Mister Fraser. However, it struck her as strange, Missus Fraser never accompanied her husband on the visits.

Evelyn threw her hands in the air and said, 'Enough for today, you're all free to go.'

♫♪ ♫♪

Catherine hummed as she trekked by the hedge and started along the pump-house path saluting nymph, 'Watch over me, my guardian angel,' she said, ducking through an opening.

A hooded figure sprung from the hedge, clutched her arm and twisted it behind her back. 'Caught you.'

Catherine squirmed to free herself. 'Let me go … I know it's you, Betsy.'

The assailant dropped her captive's arm and removed her disguise revealing a floury apron. Catherine jutted her chin.

'Snooping does you no good. Messing in other's business, it'll cause you sorrow.'

'What are you talking about, Missus Betsy?'

'The forbidden pump-house … you think nobody knows you sneak off, but you're wrong.'

'There's nothing there but a bit of noisy old machinery. What can be the harm?'

Betsy's scar twisted; her grotesque expression meant to be a smile. She looked more like a hobgoblin. Catherine screwed her nose.

'Do as your father says, then you won't git hurt,' Betsy said and headed toward the back door.

Catherine skirted around to the front courtyard where Mister Fraser and Andrew were climbing aboard their vehicle.

'Hello there, Catherine. I hope you are a good girl for your mama. She could do with a hand with her toilette. I couldn't find Betsy, so would you please ask her to take some lavender oil to your mother's room.'

Betsy was the last person Catherine wanted to seek out, the woman's last words shook her to the core. With what business was she supposed to have interfered? Did it concern the battered old tin box? Betsy had not found her compendium, or she would have mentioned it. Besides, Catherine had locked the book, and even if Betsy broke it open, she could not read it.

Chapter Six

In the early hours of the morning, Catherine awoke to a commotion in the hallway. Snatching her dressing gown, she dashed out the door only to bump into Evelyn.

'Slow down, missy, you won't be wanting to go in there.'

Catherine baulked.

'Your father sent Edward to town earlier in the night to fetch the doctor. Your mother had trouble giving birth.'

Catherine covered her ears and shook her head from side to side.

Her father stepped from the room, 'Go back to bed, Catherine,' he said, patting her on the head, 'The ladies can see to your mother.'

Catherine stood her ground—her reluctance met with Evelyn's stern glare. She retreated, her heart pounding.

Lying still and straining her ears to catch every sound emanating from the hallway, she glanced at Lucille. Her sister had not stirred. What could have happened? She listened, waiting for a baby's cry. Instead, a galloping horse passed through the rear yard—the doctor had left. On hearing a shuffle, she leapt from her bed and jammed her ear against the door. Through the crack, she saw Evelyn emerge from the attic stairs with a bundle of towels.

'The boss, he called for me. The doctor said the child is dead.' The distraught voice belonged to Betsy.

Betsy's words shot a wave of nausea over Catherine, and she clasped her hand over her mouth, a tight band squeezing her temples.

'Shush, take hold of yourself, woman,' Evelyn said, 'You need to clean her up.'

'Who, the baby, or ma'am?' Betsy asked.

'No, the doctor, wants you to bathe Missus Nicolson. She haemorrhaged.'

'He knocked at the cottage door, said Missus needed me. I don't know. I can't.'

The panic in Betsy's tone caused Catherine to hang back, not daring to leave her room.

'Bring more towels and warm water, and I'll sit with her.'

Sliding under the covers, Catherine waited. The sound of Betsy's feet padding up and down the hallway, to retrieve the water and fresh linen, and the odd murmur the only noises she heard until daybreak.

As the first ray of light filtered into the rear courtyard, Catherine rested her chin against the windowsill, watching. Her father carrying a bundle wrapped in a sheet entered the stable. He, Edward and Evelyn emerged in the cart and drove toward the grove of Myrtle-Beech trees, down by the river, doubtless to bury the unnamed child. Catherine eased her trembling body onto the chair.

Lucille emerged from under the counterpane, 'Whatever is the matter with you, Catherine?'

♫♪ ♫♪

Catherine attended to the young-ones, taking them to the nursery while Lucille went into her mother's room. It was not long before the funeral party returned, and Evelyn's footfall sounded in the downstairs hallway.

'Sarah, where are you?'

'In here, Evelyn, I'm coming.'

Evelyn caught sight of Catherine and said, 'Stay with the others a few minutes more, I want to speak with Sarah.'

Catherine tipped a bucket of wooden blocks onto the nursery mat, and the children scrambled to snatch the pieces. Tiptoeing to the door, she sat at the top of the stairs to listen to Evelyn's report.

'Sarah, your father went out early, dug the grave and placed a cross there.' Evelyn sniffed. 'Tell your mother the solemn ceremony was short. Mister Nicolson quoted Job, you know the verse about the Lord giving and taking away, and then he threw a shovel of dirt into the hole.'

'Poor ma'am.'

'An unseemly business indeed.' Evelyn blew her nose and ascended the stairs.

Catherine scurried into the nursery. There was no further mention of the incident, and though Catherine questioned, Evelyn hushed her without explanation. Mother withdrew to her room for days and tearfully grieved alone. Would she ever return to her cheerful self?

Catherine snapped at her sisters and brothers. Nausea engulfed her, and her stomach cramped as though a knife pierced her gut. The gloom crushing her spirit pervaded the entire Nicolson household, and while she gritted her teeth complying in every way possible to the demands made of her, she worried. Evelyn had said to Betsy—the mistress teetered on the edge of the cliff of despair.

'Catherine, please help pack up the new nursery clothing,' Sarah said, setting the items aside.

Catherine picked up a pair of wee booties and rubbed them on her face—so soft.

'Trust in God, Catherine. He is merciful and knows all about your troubles,' Sarah said and began folding a tiny nightgown.

Mother came, stood at the door and on seeing the article, snatched it, hollered and tore it to shreds. Poor Sarah, she staggered back, her mouth gaping open.

Catherine ran into the hallway and yelled. 'Father, please come.'

He bounded up the stairs.

'It's Mother.'

Wrapping his strong arms about his wife, he held tight until her screams became sobs, and after what seemed like hours became intermittent sniffs. He carried her to the far side of the bed and stroked her hair. Though she faced the window, Catherine noticed her panting gave way to an even rhythm. She had entered a blessed sleep.

Father instructed Edward and Betsy to collect the baby's clothes, the bassinette and take them to Evandale for distribution to the needy.

Father trudged down the steps, his face grave, and no matter what Catherine tried, she could not raise a smile.

'Catherine, you simply cannot fix everything, just let them be,' Evelyn chided.

Catherine raced after her father. He flopped onto the garden bench as Edward guided the dray, loaded with the baby trappings along the driveway.

Catherine snuggled close, resting her head on his lap and prayed, 'Dear Lord, help my dad.'

Lifting her head at the sound of hooves, she sighed. Grandma Kate's carriage pulled into the courtyard—the old lady had come to offer her help. Father walked her into the house and rang the bell.

'Sarah, please find Miss Evelyn and bring a tea-tray to the parlour.'

Father withdrew to the adjoining room and directed Catherine to the big armchair next to his desk.

He turned to the Psalms and, caressing the old family Bible, mouthed the words, 'The Lord is my shepherd.'

While china-cups clinked upon saucers, Evelyn's words hummed, no doubt reporting the sequence of events of the last week. Catherine picked up but a snippet of the conversation until Grandma raised her voice.

'How could the girl understand his desperate loss and the subsequent withdrawal of succour from her mother?'

It was uncharacteristic of Grandma, but she sounded somewhat peeved. Father coughed, warning the women he was within earshot.

'Catherine, go in and let your grandmother know she may visit Mother. I'm going out to the barn to look for Mister Edward.'

His slow gait and rounded shoulders, weighed down by his broken heart caused Catherine's nausea to resurface, her hope, that Mister Edward's deep faith might reassure Father of God's care. While Grandma did not stay long, Catherine learned her visit soothed Mother, as she promised to let her near-neighbour, Mister Fraser, know Mother would appreciate his company. In no time, the old man arrived carrying a bunch of fresh roses, his son Andrew riding with him.

Catherine popped up to chat with her mother after Fraser's coach pulled away, expecting the visit had cheered her, but when she poked her head in the doorway, her mother's form shivered under the covers, and the sound emanating was like that of a calf. Even Mister Fraser could not console Mother. Would a sense of solace ever return to their household?

Catherine tiptoed out, pulled the door and met Betsy, carrying a fancy jar, the whiff of lavender potent. The gift was one of a variety of moulded scented candles Betsy made in the copper boiler in the laundry. If anyone could comfort Mother, Betsy, her mother's old friend, was that person.

Catherine slipped away, pleased Betsy was otherwise engaged, and scribbled one short paragraph in her hidden notebook. A strong sweet smell permeated the hut signifying Betsy had already made her trek, but Catherine did not feel inclined to pry or stay too long, not because she thought Betsy might find her, instead because she felt ill, yet again, with an upset stomach. No mystery was worth pursuing while Mother lay languishing.

♫♪ ♫♪

Betsy and Sarah served, beyond obligation, to ensure Catherine's family received physical support while Mother was in mourning, and Evelyn made sure she maintained the household regime. The woman completed the many tasks for which Mother commonly assumed responsibility, such as organizing the children's clothes and planning the weekly menu. Catherine cringed at Evelyn's bossiness. She was not at all like Mother. Catherine clenched her fists, the added restrictions and rigidness, entirely unsuitable, however, she submitted and made sure the other children did too.

Lucille's exasperation boiled over, 'For goodness sake, Catherine, we can see what needs to be done without you also telling us.'

Most often, Evelyn arranged outdoor activities for the children, though the weather, like the mood of the estate, was dismal. In the months before the baby's death, Mother had assigned a small patch of ground to each of the children to plant vegetables or flowers of their choice. She had said, 'Feel the soil under your nails as you dig, drop the tiny seeds and wonder as the first buds appear. That should give you an appreciation of the Lord, our Creator.'

Betsy took it upon herself to supervise and encourage her charges as they weeded their patches. When the first shoots appeared, Catherine and her sisters ran to tell Mother, but she had no interest.

♫♪ ♫♪

Father hung his hat on the hallway hook and strode to the dining table. Young Simon followed his father, mimicking his every move.

'Me is just like Dad.'

Mother laughed loudly at his cute antics. 'Yes son, just like your father.'

'It's wonderful to hear you laugh again, my love,' Father said, leaning over to brush his lips across Mother's cheek.

Catherine twirled around and looked at her little sisters, their smiles as wide as a couple of chimpanzees. Lucille's eyes sparkled with the teardrops washing over her pupils. Father sighed, relieved. Simon's impersonation had instigated a change in the atmosphere. Mother regained an interest in her young son, and was soon her cheerful self and once again took charge of the household routine. Moreover, Catherine's stomach cramps vanished after a single dose of Betsy's foaming brew.

♫♪ ♫♪

As the cold winter days of sleet one day, and frosts another, gave way to warm breezes, new life was evident in the paddocks. It was time for Mother to inspect the children's plantings. Catherine clutched her hand and pulled her through the hawthorn hedge to the vegetable patch to show off her herbs and flowering bulbs, yellow heads dancing in the breeze, while her younger sisters ducked and weaved under their linked arms. Celeste pointed and giggled at the lambs skipping along, shaking their tails.

She ran to the fence and called, 'Look, Mother, in the paddock.'

Newborn calves suckled at their mother's teats.

Celeste dashed off and jumped up and down in her patch of the garden until Mother came. 'See my carrots planted in a row, Mummy. You can see the green tops.'

'I have lettuce, beetroots, and radishes.' Louisa pointed to her rows.

Catherine indicated a section further over, 'Mine's the herb garden. I have mint, parsley, and basil.'

'We're going to have quite a feast when all this is ready.'

Mother glanced skyward, and Catherine followed her gaze, a huge black cloud rolling over the Western Plains threatening.

'Time to get back to the house,' Mother said, 'Mister Fraser is coming by today.'

She wheeled around and balked, transfixed at the tiny mound with a wooden cross poking out, the grave covered in mauve flowers.

'Oh, Betsy,' Mother said and bowed her head in prayer, ''Tis in his loving presence I find my peace. Tumultuous tempest in my heart does cease. His promise is sure. He disappoints never. I will be with you, now and forever.'

Mother glanced at Catherine and her sisters, smiled, waved them on, and they cut through the apple orchard, the trees laden with blossom. 'Betsy and Sarah should have a good bottling this season.'

Her mother's pleasant lilt remained. Catherine's heart skipped, and she bent to pick the few daffodils blooming at the base of a tree.

'Baa, baa.' The sound of ewes caught her attention, and with newborns at their side, they grazed in the clearing beyond a rock fence.

'The poor little lambs are out in the open,' Celeste said.

'I'll let Thomas know, they ought to be in the home paddock,' Mother said, stroking her daughter's hair.

Catherine grasped Celeste's hand, and they skipped back to the house. Mother and Louisa arrived much later, arm in arm.

That week the family celebrated the spring festival in the tiny chapel on the property. A variety of floral arrangements made a colourful display, the daffodils spectacular. Catherine added her voice to the singing of God's praises affirming her trust in the Lord's bountiful supply. She glanced behind at Edward's family, surprised to see their young friend with the black wavy hair had joined them. He whispered in earnest to Sarah and slipped out the door. Betsy peered at Catherine, Catherine unable to comprehend her expression.

Though Willowbank felt safe again, an unidentified conundrum lingered. Catherine opened her duchess drawer and picked up her diary key. Twisting it about, she repositioned it in its hiding place, confident her Lord would settle her uneasiness and calm her fears.

Chapter Seven

Catherine leant her head against the mare's silky coat as she gave the mane one last stroke. She loved helping to take care of the estate horses. A clatter of hooves on the cobblestones resonated, her father's curricle circling and stopping at the stable door with Mister Fraser's vehicle arriving in tandem. The friends were back from town after the monthly meeting of the Pastoralist's Society. Catherine ran to greet them, swerving as Thomas stabbed the pitchfork into a bale of hay and hurried to take care of the Braeside sulky, while Father walked his stallion to the door and handed the reins to Edward. Catherine rested on a three-legged stool in the stall watching Edward unbridle the horse and wipe its sweaty flank with a towel. He picked up a brush, began to groom the horse's rump and jumped away as it pooped sloppy dung.

'Pooh! That stinks,' Catherine said and scurried off the stool.

Edward snatched the shovel and hoyed the mess out of the barn. The horse turned its head in Catherine's direction as though to say, 'What did you expect?' She giggled.

'Achoo! Fresh hay. Achoo!' She swiped her nose with her sleeve.

'Bless you, Catherine Rose.' Mister Fraser ruffled her hair.

She looked into his laughing eyes and wiggled as he twitched his auburn handlebar moustache. Mother appeared at the stable door and made her way to the rail next to Catherine.

'I heard you come in, Francis. Any news from town?'

'Indeed, we do, Arianna.'

'To be sure, there is,' Mister Fraser said. The older man's lilting Scottish tone always intrigued Catherine, his accent strong, though having lived in Tasmania for some years. 'There's to be an Agricultural Show this year, our first ever. They're calling it the Morven Show.'

'A bit of competition for Campbell Town then?' Mother said.

'Those who enter stock there will also come to Evandale. I want to promote our premium wool, enter a ram, a ewe with her lambs and exhibit a fleece.'

When Father mentioned his intention, Mother's eyes twinkled, 'Our own show, isn't this a boon?'

'Andrew's been training our Archie. He's sure to outshine the local sheepdogs in the trials. We'll enter him into the Campbell Town Show first,' Mister Fraser said and moved behind Mother. 'Felicity will be beside herself with excitement having another occasion to socialize with her friends.'

Mother twisted to face him, her lip curling. His brow crinkled.

'Dear Mister Fraser, you are right, of course, a perfect occasion for the ladies to mingle,' Mother said, her face colouring.

Catherine glanced at her father. His eyebrows had shot up to his hairline. He looked toward Edward and then at Mister Fraser.

Mother laughed and turned to go. 'Come in soon, Catherine,' she called over her shoulder.

Mister Fraser went to his vehicle, retrieved something and followed her to the house.

Catherine continued with her task. Father and Edward struck up a new conversation, and it seemed, unaware of her presence.

'Edward, you'll remember we entered livestock into the Northern Agricultural Society Show in Longford on a previous occasion, with great success.'

'I do, sir. Won second place, beat up the competition all over the Midlands, only lost to the Deloraine entry owned by one of the Carrick brothers.'

♫♪ ♫♪

Catherine raised the subject of the show again during the evening meal. 'Mother, tell them about the fair to be held in Evandale.'

'Catherine's right. A committee is planning the event to be held later in the spring.'

'Can I go, Father?' Stuart's eyes shimmered, something Catherine rarely saw.

'Yes, to be sure, and you can help us show off our Willowbank livestock.'

Catherine huffed at Stuart's haughty gape, but she bit her tongue.

'What about us girls?'

'You can all go, Catherine. The committee intends to create a grand family event,' Father said.

Catherine retired to her room, right after dinner to browse through the fashion magazine she put on the bookshelf when she tidied this morning. She had noticed several new dress patterns perfect for the spring show. Flopping onto the seat near the window, taking advantage of the twilight to read, she was surprised given the late hour, to see her mother and Betsy slink by the hedge and make their way along the path toward the pump-house, Betsy carrying a wad of paper. Catherine rushed to follow, but Stuart blocked her at the foot of the stairs, not because he was aware of her intention, rather because he had waited until their parents were out of earshot so he could brag.

'Catherine, it's such a shame you're not a boy. Think of all the benefits you'd have if you were a favourite son, such as riding horses or showing animals.'

'Stuart, you little monster, let me make myself clear, I would not wish to be a boy for all the wealth in England.'

'You'd better treat me good then, cause one day I'll be your benefiter.'

'I'll ensure you'll be no such thing. Anyway, the word is benefactor, silly.'

'You're such a sourpuss. You reckon you want to help others to follow the Good Book, but you're not even nice.'

Catherine prickled at her brother Stuart's reminder—grumpiness was not virtuous. She scowled, wished she didn't let him needle her so. The rear door closed—her mother had returned.

♫♪ ♫♪

Catherine thrilled at the flurry of activity as her mother unrolled the new bolt of emerald-green poplin and spread patterns on the schoolroom floor. She watched Evelyn's precision with the shears as she cut the material. Her penchant for accuracy proved advantageous for this activity, even if on other occasions the characteristic was irritating.

'The dresses are identical except for the colour,' Mother said.

'I choose the blue then, to match my eyes.' Catherine held the blue against her cheek.

'Lemon for mine,' Celeste chimed.

'Celeste, if Mama shows you how to thread the ribbon through the eyelets on the bodice, it'll look like shirring,' Lucille said.

The feverish needlework in the weeks leading up to the show culminated in fetching outfits for the women of the household. Mother used the pattern on a previous occasion, Catherine grimacing at the memory. Felicity Fraser insisted Andrew escort Catherine from her carriage into her friend's home. She had blushed when the woman enthused about the design of the frock she wore. If only Missus Fraser was more discreet with her compliments and had considered the impropriety of outshining a friend on her birthday. An embarrassing hush descended upon the hostess' crowded foyer, and Catherine had wished she might vanish.

Catherine jolted into the present—her mother insisting the girls try on their gowns.

'You do me proud dressed in all your finery.' Mother exuded praise as her daughters pirouetted in their new creations.

As the family gathered for dinner, Father jangled the bell. 'Shush girls, it sounds like a barnyard in here.'

'Father, your chest will burst. You'll like our outfits.'

'So, your mother has you all trussed for the show has she, Lucille?'

Catherine frowned. The wry grin on Lucille's face, a puzzle. She would ask her sister about it later.

Mother held her head high. 'As is becoming of the ladies of the Willowbank household, Mister Nicolson. What about you, Francis, have you made your selection yet?'

Father confirmed he had chosen a large ram, a ewe and her lambs and a large merino fleece to be transported to the showground and added, 'Our estate is making a huge contribution to the Morven Show. It should get off to a strong start indeed.'

♫♪ ♫♪

Three carriages rolled through the gate on the morning of the show and travelled the newly-gravelled road to Evandale. Edward's family had the day off. Betsy reneged.

Mister Nicolson paid a handsome sum at the gate. 'Generous to a fault,' Evelyn said.

'We're thankful, sir, it's very kind,' Sarah called over to the lead carriage and leant toward Evelyn. 'Mister Nicolson is good-hearted. Would you agree?'

'Without a doubt, he treats us well.'

'Entirely my pleasure, Miss Evelyn,' Father said.

Catherine smiled—her father generous to include the hired hands in the day of fun.

The men parked the carriages and tethered the horses. Evelyn left the group with Lucille in tow, but Catherine chose to stay and help her mother.

'We'll divide the young ones between us, so they don't wander away,' Mother said, assigning Catherine her charges.

Little brother Simon jumped up and down on the spot yanking his mother's hand. 'Me want to look for our baby lamb.'

'We have to wait for the tour,' Mother said, straining to hold him in check.

Catherine squatted so she was at his eye level. 'Simon, look at all these people. If you run ahead, we might lose you. Hold my hand, and you'll see lots of stuff.'

He placed his little fingers in her palm, and they checked out the pavilions. He and Louisa squealed with delight at the proud cock and its crown of feathers, the cute yellow chicks, the prancing lambs, the unsteady calves, and various breeds of yapping puppies.

'Ooh, a gigantic tractor,' he said and tore away.

Stuart and Celeste raced past the younger children to see the farm equipment, the exhibits including the latest farm cart and a newly invented plough.

Catherine's attention diverted to the manufacturers who proudly demonstrated their scythes and axes, Mister Fraser also watching with interest. Catherine shivered at the flashing of the sharp instruments and stepped away, but on turning, almost tumbled into someone. Her eyes widened. The fellow she collided with wore a patch over one eye. Sitting on a wooden stump, he held an axe in one hand and a sharpening flint in the other. Had she ever seen anyone as ugly in her life?

'Look out, little girl, the Campbell Town woodchopper will cut off your head,' he said.

'Ooh, you are a horrid man,' she shrunk back causing him to cackle like a barnyard chook.

'Beware, lest prying leads you…'

Catherine ran, stumbling to her mother's side, her knees trembling, 'Where's Father?'

'Watching the field machinery, let's catch up.'

Catherine did not wait for her mother but bolted away dragging Simon and Louisa with her. Seldom had she encountered a person who emitted such an air of evil as the creature who wielded the hatchet. She wanted her father to take them home, but he stood, shaded his eyes, engrossed in the ploughing competition.

'See the straight, clean-cut furrows,' he said pointing, and when the tractor came to a standstill, bent to examine the locally made implement.

Catherine rocked from one foot to the other. Mother came up behind with Evelyn who had re-joined the group.

'Lucille slipped off to speak with her friend, Douglas, and his mother,' Evelyn said.

Catherine grimaced—the family would not be leaving the showground any time soon. Mother and Evelyn turned their attention toward Father, laughing about his enthusiasm.

'Mister Nicolson seems to think Edward's boy would produce a greater yield per hectare if he were to employ a double-furrow plough, such as the one he's investigating. He's also interested in purchasing a threshing machine,' Mother said.

'It would be a boon if it increased the production of crops for the stock,' Evelyn said.

An exhibition of whip cracking interrupted their conversation, the men clapping and cheering at the ear-splitting sound. Disinterested, Catherine watched the farmer under the tarp behind them. Thomas chatted to the man, who sat on a bale of hay platting fine strands of leather, his kindly smile in stark contrast to the nasty axeman's leer.

In the afternoon, Evelyn took the younger children to revisit the baby animals, while the ringside activities held Catherine and her mother's attention. A sheepdog-trial enthused the crowd in the stands, cheers heard from the Fraser family of Braeside. Their dog, a Smithfield, won the event and received the Champion's cup, Mister Fraser's bold prediction realized.

Andrew Fraser patted his dog, 'Good girl, you're the best.'

'Congratulations, lad.'

'Thanks sir, Mister Nicolson,'

Andrew, a favourite with Catherine's father, loaded up with fresh vegetables to take home whenever he visited Willowbank.

'How's your mother, Andrew?'

'Doing much better, sir, but she remained at home seeing as it is but a week since her bout of influenza.'

'Pass on our best to her then, please.'

Andrew nodded and raced off, his red hair flying in the breeze. His dog strained at the leash, pulling him at break-neck speed toward the sheep enclosure.

'Now, there's a fine young man.' Father nodded in Andrew's direction.

Catherine giggled at her father's statement. Why should she care? Catching sight of her mother, she made off toward her. Mother appeared to be engaged in serious discussion with Mister Fraser. He placed something in her opened palm, enclosed her hand about it and caressed her elbow. On seeing Catherine approach, he gave a slight wave and turned on his heel.

'What did he give you, Mother?'

'Mister Fraser gave me money to buy you all a treat.'

'But, Father has plenty. There's no need, and Mister Fraser knows it too.'

'He's a kindly old man, Catherine Rose, and likes to endow gifts, that's all.'

Catherine's mother took her arm and guided her between the stalls. They found Evelyn with her charges in tow.

'There's Missus Herbert with a new carriage,' Evelyn hurried to greet her friend and Mother followed.

'How's your new baby?' Mother popped her head under the bonnet of the baby-wagon.

'As cute as could be, don't you agree?'

Mother stalled and stepped back, her face ashen. Catherine looked in the carriage, the infant wearing the ensemble her mother had crocheted for her baby who had passed. Father had sent the outfit to the church for the disadvantaged. How could someone as well-off as Missus Herbert acquire a gift from the charity box?

Evelyn whispered to Catherine, 'She's thinking upon her recent loss.'

Mother sighed, seeming to gather her composure and moved away.

On the way to meet with the rest of their party, they passed by a tent where men ringside watched a well-known pugilist in a boxing bout. It was common for the local men to challenge him to fight.

Catherine cringed as she overheard the taunts. 'Hey, low blow. What a cross? Break the clinch, you moron. He's out cold. Git off the deck, you got a glass jaw?'

Catherine's mouth hung open—Thomas engaged in conversation with the Campbell Town axeman.

'Go, go!' Mother hurried the group by the ring. 'No need for us to witness the distressing activity.'

'Sarah, come here a minute, I want to talk,' a young man beckoned.

Catherine hung back, waiting. Sarah stepped into the shade of an awning. The youth removed his cap revealing a head of wavy black hair that fell over his eyes, the same lad Catherine had seen at Willowbank.

'Not seen you in anything but black, Sarah,' he said, 'That's a nice yellow dress.'

Sarah smoothed her skirt, 'Yes, Missus Nicolson made it for me.'

'Is Thomas here at the show?' The young man's mellow tone was just audible.

'He's here somewhere, near the ring, watching a bout or two. I saw him a minute ago talking to cousin.'

Catherine frowned. The Campbell Town axeman, cousin to Thomas and Sarah?

'That's good. I got to find him, not seen him in a couple of months.'

The young chap glanced in Catherine's direction, or was she mistaken? He flipped his hair away from his face. She lowered her eyes. He headed toward the boxing ring, jiggling his cap over his curls until it covered all but a couple of loose strands of hair.

'A family friend, Sarah?'

'Ed, yes, Thomas and me has known him since we was nippers.'

'He has gorgeous hair, so wasted on a boy.'

'A nice fellow too … Thomas says he could trust Ed with the king's gold.'

'You like him, Sarah?'

'Could be I do. Oh, never mind. Let's catch up to the others.'

Catherine, not often put off by her servant friend, raised her brow. However, there was a caution in Sarah's manner preventing her from pursuing the conversation. The girls ran to catch up to their party. Lucille had re-joined the group for lunch.

Afterwards, the young children sprinted to get into the line for a ride on the Shetland ponies. Simon, not satisfied with one turn, threw himself on the ground and kicked his legs. Mother pacified him agreeing he could have another ride. Catherine clenched her lips, Lucille shaking her head, her tacit counsel checking Catherine's temper.

Celeste bounced on her toes, pointing. 'Look at the funny dolls.'

Simon squealed, his attention diverted. He giggled, mesmerized as he watched the Punch and Judy show, laughing at their jerky movements.

'I loved the rainbow coloured outfits and what clever lines by the puppeteers,' Catherine said to Lucille when the show finished.

'Even more cheek and chit-chat than you hand out, sister of mine.'

'I admit you saved my hide,' Catherine laughed.

Lucille tipped her bonnet.

'Though, I think Mother spoils the boy, Lucille.'

A stall-keepers shrill voice tempted, 'Iced gingerbread-men only one penny today.'

Catherine's mouth watered.

Mother hesitated and chuckled. 'Why not, and I'll have one too.'

'Umm, Mother. They're delicious but so very sweet,' Catherine said, extracting the sticky biscuit from her teeth as she followed a couple of clowns to the games area.

A couple of boys tried their hand at skittles and quoits and won, receiving prizes for a perfect score. The lad who had stopped Sarah earlier, stood hands in his pockets and looked on. He pulled something from his pocket, glanced at it, grimaced and walked away.

'Please, please, Father, may I try,' Stuart said, pulling on his father's sleeve.

Father gave him instructions, 'Aim the ball at the centre skittle,' and Stuart managed to knock down all ten skittles.

He bragged about winning a ticket to the evening concert. 'I won! I won!'

'It's time for a spell.' Father directed the family to join the crowd perching on the wooden risers and told Stuart to find the show convenor since he was to take part in the main parade.

Catherine looked across to Thomas in conversation with Sarah's curly-haired friend, their discussion animated. What could be so interesting? How well did they know one another? She shrugged and turned her attention to the activities taking place on the paddock. Farmhands led animals to the far side fence.

Lucille moved along the bench next to her. 'Now here's something to watch.'

Outside the shearing-shed across the paddock, Stuart held fast to the Nicolson's prize ram. He lined up with the handlers, and they began to guide their charges around the perimeter of the grounds. All went as planned until one of the collie dogs pulled loose from its owner.

'Oh no!' someone yelled from the fence-line.

'Careful,' Lucille grabbed Catherine's arm, 'looks like trouble now.'

The collie snapped at the heels of a large Hereford bull just behind Stuart. Stuart glanced back. The bull charged. Stuart let go of the rope and ran to the post and rail fence. Father leant over, gripped him by the jodhpurs and hauled him to safety. By then chaos reigned—animals loose and owners running in every direction trying to catch them. Everyone on the paddock ducked and weaved to avoid the charging bull. It ran, first one way and then the other. Two riders mounted horses and got into the action and with the help of a lasso and a blue heeler. They corralled the bull into the holding area, where Thomas' friend, opened the gate. Teetering on the top railing of the fence, he wobbled. Catherine caught her breath. He jumped down, slammed the gate shut, and the crowd cheered and doubled over, laughing.

One or two owners angrily remonstrated with their charges. 'Go easy fellers, no harm done.' Catherine gasped—the axeman—and he stood beside Mister Fraser.

'Funny as a circus,' Mister Fraser laughed along with the man.

Catherine chuckled. Her title for the next class essay Miss Evelyn would be sure to assign—The Main Event.

Late in the day, the committee held an auction in the main pavilion to sell off equipment and produce. Catherine rubbed her hands together when her father bid for a handsome, black stallion. A concert followed, to raise funds for the show society, featuring many talented performers, Catherine noting a singer around her age.

Lucille leaned toward Mother. 'She has the voice of an angel. Who is she?'

'The Chapman's daughter. They own property near Perth. Aunt Rowena knows her mother well. They have a son around your age, and he's being schooled by his uncle to take over the hardware store in town. A nice-looking young man, I'm told.'

Catherine smirked at the knowing glance her mother fired at Lucille.

In return, Lucille shot an accusing look at her mother. 'You don't like Harry, do you?'

Catherine looked over to Thomas who leaned against the wall. His friend with the wavy hair chatted with Harry, all three ogling at the

Chapman girl.

Catherine rolled her eyes. 'Boys.'

♫♪ ♫♪

The clip of the horses' hooves echoed as the carriages made their way home in the fading twilight.

'What a wonderful outing it was, Francis,' Mother said, her sentiments evoking an avalanche of enthusiastic impressions about the show's events.

Father relayed some news, saying the gossip of the day revolved around the recent visit of Prince Alfred, Duke of Edinburgh to Hobart Town, where a grand ceremony had taken place. 'I read about the occasion, the laying of the foundation stone for St. David's Cathedral, but of interest locally was the news he had turned the sod for the new Western Railway.'

'Well, of course, dear, you might have given them a blow by blow account since you were there as a guest.'

'And you, my dear, had you chosen to accompany me.'

'An attempted assassination was made upon his life when he visited Sydney.'

Mother gasped, 'Never.'

'I heard it too,' said Evelyn. 'It took months for him to recover before he was able to continue his Royal Tour.'

By the time the coaches reached the driveway at Willowbank, Catherine's brothers and sisters had succumbed to their fatigue. Catherine, however, stared into the starry night. In her mind's eye, the curly-haired young man wore a smile meant for her alone.

'Best of all,' Father lowered his voice and leant toward Mother, 'catching up with relatives, our long-standing friends and meeting new ones, has made it a very worthwhile day.'

'If not somewhat expensive,' murmured Mother. 'Francis, I'm pleased Missus Fraser wasn't there.'

Father patted Mother's hand, 'You worry so, Arianna.'

Catherine shuffled, and her mother glanced over, her jaw tightening. Catherine held still, squeezing her eyes shut.

'It's a pity, Amelia and Cameron's ship had not arrived. They would have surely attended the show,' Father said.

'And probably scooped up all the prizes too.'

Catherine wriggled to make herself comfortable, happy to know Florence would be home soon.

Chapter Eight

Uncle Cameron Nicolson and his family returned from England for an extended stay on their Myrtleford Estate. Catherine, keen to spend time with her cousin, planned to quiz Florence about her adventures in the Old Country. As was their custom, Uncle Cameron and Aunt Amelia sent invitations to the surrounding property owners and the local government officials to attend a garden party at their Myrtleford estate. In accordance with etiquette, the despatch forwarded well in advance of the day, ensured the guests had ample notice and would reply in time to cater for the grand occasion.

'Arianna, please send an acceptance immediately,' Father said.

It seemed Catherine was not the only one happy to revisit the estate.

Due to Mother's habit of sewing costumes during the winter months, the family's summer wardrobe was complete. 'Francis, wear your light-grey pants, white shirt and the matching waistcoat.'

'Whatever you think, my dear.'

'Daughters, I want you to wear your organza dresses, and decorate your straw sunhats with matching ribbons.'

Catherine screwed up her nose. 'They're a bit frilly don't you think, Mother? I'd rather wear jodhpurs, then I could ride.'

She had been practising a walk, trot and canter routine on the new stallion, Ebony, and wanted to show-off to Florence.

'There'll be no riding on the day. You know how formal Aunt Amelia's garden parties tend to be.'

Catherine did not recall, only having attended one very flash gathering at Myrtleford, at least since she was old enough to remember. However, aware her heritage was akin to nobility, not of the English kind of course but to that of the new country, she must behave as such. How tiresome. She would much rather run across the paddocks and climb trees.

♫♪ ♫♪

The morning of the garden-party was a somewhat misty day. Catherine swung her bedroom shutters wide, low cloud hovering over the plains. Her mother, undeterred, set out the summer outfits on their beds. If rain prevented outdoor activities, her aunt and uncle had ample room indoors for their guests, whether in the drawing room or the conservatory.

Mother's voice echoed along the hallway, 'Lucille, would you please help your sisters into their frocks and your brother into his jodhpurs? There's a vest to go over his white shirt.'

'Catherine can. I've still to fix my hair.'

Catherine huffed, but she hurried to find the youngsters, Willowbank household too charged with excitement to be argumentative. Usually, Evelyn stayed behind to care for the younger children on such an occasion, but because this was a whole of family invitation, everyone would attend.

Catherine returned to her room, put on her frock and ran to check her reflection in her mother's duchess mirror.

'Stop hogging the mirror, Lucille.'

Lucille huffed. 'There's room for you too, Catherine.'

Catherine twirled. Her outfit of soft sky-blue complimented her blond hair and fair complexion. Her younger sisters shuffled in beside her. The deep shade of pink of Celeste's organza suited her dark hair and Louisa's cream her freckly skin.

'We all look the part at least, but aren't we prissy?' Catherine said as she curtsied.

'You're all very lovely indeed,' Mother said as she entered the now crowded room.

'My, Mother, you look smart.'

Mother pirouetted and paraded in her sea-foam, crepe frock adorned with a lace-inset bodice and matching bonnet.

Father's voice echoed up the stairwell. 'Please be sure everyone has eaten, my dear. I do not wish for any uncomplimentary remarks about my children's impolite manners on this grand occasion … and no squabbling.'

Catherine grimaced, sure the remarks intended for her and her brother, Stuart. She stepped on the top landing to object, but Father waggled his finger at her. Surely, he had noticed how improved and ladylike her conduct was of late.

'I'm off to the stables to arrange our transport,' he said.

As soon as his footfall silenced, Mother said, 'Your father's a good man and is proud of you all. Don't disappoint him.'

The air of excitement escalated during the early lunch, and at eleven o'clock sharp, the family assembled ready to climb aboard the carriages. Edward and Thomas had excelled, the horses' silky coats brushed and the vehicles polished. Thomas handed the reins to Father and walked toward the stables. His friend, the lad in the tweed-cap, leaned over the railing of the horse enclosure. Thomas spoke and pointed. Catherine could feel the boys' eyes upon her. Thomas must have invited the lad to visit, because, except for Edward who would drive one of the vehicles, the servants were excused from regular duties, the family away for the day. Catherine supposed the young Jackson pair had planned their own party. Perhaps Thomas promised the youth a ride on one of the horses, or—she caught her breath—maybe he had called to walk-out with Sarah. Catherine looked away. She hoped for some pleasant male company of her own. It was possible she would meet a prospective young man at her uncle and aunt's function today.

'Sir, they're all set,' Edward said.

'Is everyone here?' Father seemed anxious to be on the way.

'Everyone, except Stuart,' Catherine said.

'Where is he?'

Her mother looked toward the upstairs window.

'Evelyn, would you mind searching for him? He must still be in the house.'

Evelyn stepped from the carriage just as Stuart rounded the corner, covered in mud from head to toe.

'What have you been doing? Where have you been?' Mother said.

'I fell in the pond, collecting tadpoles in a jar. I wanted to take them to show cousin John.'

'Well, that was a fine time to go off, just when we were all ready,' chided Catherine.

Mother cringed.

'You, shut your mouth. You're not my mother,' Stuart yelled.

'You knew we were about to leave.'

'Evelyn, please take him to wash and change. We're leaving in five minutes,' Mother said.

Evelyn grabbed him by the ear and marched him up the steps.

'Your constant bickering is maddening, Catherine.'

'But, Mother.'

Mother, lips pressed shut, was clearly tired of her children's arguments. Tears stung Catherine's eyes, and she dug her fingernails into her palms, wishing she had not mentioned Stuart was missing. He deserved to stay home with Thomas.

Catherine pretended to take an interest in the scenery as the carriages began the journey. She had tried so hard to ignore Stuart's mischief in the past weeks, their strained relationship getting her mother down. Chewing over Mother's words, she sat stone-faced. Her brother took delight in blaming her for all sorts of misdemeanours, real or otherwise. First-born boys were spoiled brats.

Staring across the plains, she drew deep breaths, the smell of the wet grass teasing her nostrils. The horses followed the track across the South Esk River ford while excitable chatter of youthful voices sounded out across the plains.

Catherine caught sight of a family of wallabies grazing, her mother seeing them at the same instant.

'Look, over there. The mother has joeys.' Mother pointed toward a flyer.

The wallabies startled, bounded across the paddock, Catherine straining to see where they went but the forest swallowed them up. Not five hundred yards further along, an echidna waddled across the road into the path of the lead carriage. Edward grabbed the reins, steered the horses to the left and the coach lurched. Everyone in the carriage slid across the seats, Catherine's shoulder crunching against the door.

'That was close.' Edward wiped his brow.

Catherine readjusted her position and smoothed out her dress. 'It's as well Edward's such a good driver.'

Mother was quiet, her face drained of colour, except for a circle of rouge she had dabbed on each cheek.

'We're nearly there,' the youngest Nicolson children chorused.

The horses trotted down the long lane and through the Myrtleford rear gate, the carriages pulling into the circular driveway. Uncle Cameron waved as Francis Nicolson's family arrived at the grand mansion. Aunt Amelia, their cousins and a few friends gathered in the courtyard.

'Welcome, Francis and dear Arianna. How lovely to have you all with us.'

Catherine smiled at her Aunt Amelia's contrived greeting.

'You certainly have a colossal brood now, brother.' Uncle Cameron nudged Father in the ribs and assisted the youngsters from the vehicles one by one.

Catherine alighted, her brother Stuart, immediately behind her. He snatched her hat, sent it flying and ran off as fast as a native hen, disappearing behind the hawthorn hedge bordering the driveway.

'Stuart, you're an evil little troll. Get my hat back here, now,' Catherine said, waving her arms in the air. 'You, make me so mad.'

How she resented him causing her this indignity, she so wanted to impress the present company.

As the hat came spiralling back across the hedge, red-haired Andrew Fraser saved the day, scooping the bonnet up mid-flight and presented it to Catherine.

'Here, my dear, there's no harm done. You do look lovely today, Miss Catherine.'

'Thank you, Andrew,' Catherine said, rearranging her accessory.

Father was right. Andrew was a fine boy and kind as well.

The family traipsed through the archway, overladen with a profusion of mauve wisteria, and entered the rear garden. Introduced to the other guests by name, the Nicolson sisters were received in order of seniority. Lucille smiled, waved and made her way to the garden seats on the far side of the lawn.

Catherine heard her name announced, 'Catherine Nicolson.'

Now fourteen years old, Catherine could join the adult activities, the younger children cared for in a separate garden where they engaged in games: drop the hanky, quoits, and marbles, all organised by Myrtleford's governess.

Catherine caught sight of Adele and Captain Robert. 'Hello, big sister.'

Adele pecked her on the cheek, smelling of her sweet baby.

'Adele, you look lovely in your apricot coloured dress and bonnet.'

Adele pressed her skirt with her hands. 'We arrived early. Our baby boy needed feeding, and I wanted to settle him before you all arrived. Meanwhile, Myrtleford's governess whisked our little Margaret off to the nursery.'

Father came alongside and hugged his eldest daughter. He shook Robert's hand firmly and leaned over the baby carriage, doting on his new grandchild.

'Why don't you accompany me, Robert, and I'll introduce you to our neighbours? They'll be keen to learn more about the recent events occurring in Europe. You've heard more, I take it, via the telegraphic cable between here and the mainland.'

Father and Captain Robert wandered off across the expansive lawn toward the gathering of gentlemen. A gurgling sound emerging from the baby pram reclaimed Catherine's attention.

Adele's face puckered. 'You had best join the others, Catherine. I'll be there shortly.'

Catherine spied Lucille seated on a garden bench in animated conversation with a gentleman in a top hat, but not the young Mister Butler. Aunt Rowena chatted with several other women under the oak tree, an excellent vantage point, from which to watch the younger set play croquet. Catherine made her way over.

A lady, sporting an elaborate hat complete with a pheasant feather, addressed her. 'What is your name, young lady?'

Surely, the woman could tell she was a Nicolson. Catherine looked so much like Grandma Kate, and everyone knew Grandma.

Catherine twirled and bowed. 'Catherine Rose Nicolson, born on the tenth day of November, one thousand eighteen hundred and fifty-six,' she said.

The woman's eyebrows shot up, and she frowned in Aunt Rowena's direction. 'Insolence.'

Shuffling along the seat, the matron turned her back and engaged her nearest neighbour in conversation. Catherine shrugged and gazed about, and Rowena tugged on her sleeve, patting the chair next to her.

Ignoring her aunt's chastisement, Catherine said, 'What a splendid crowd from around the district, Aunt, all enjoying Cameron and Amelia's hospitality.'

'It's Uncle Cameron and Aunt Amelia to you, cheeky miss. Catherine, I wonder if you are ready to be in our grown-up company.'

Catherine gritted her teeth. She had overstepped the mark.

'I see Mother. I'll join her,' she said and scurried to the garden bench and settled beside her mother.

'Who's the lady in that elaborate hat, Mother?'

Mother clenched her jaw her expression severe. She tucked a loose red curl beneath her bonnet—usually allowed a curl or two to protrude to soften her face. Why was she hiding her pretty hair?

'You know Missus Fraser, and though you might be surprised, I've personally never met the woman and have no wish to become acquainted.'

Catherine flinched—she had not recognized the lady, but why had her mother spoken so vehemently of a person she did not know?

'You don't like her, Mother? I grant you she's snobbish and not at all like Mister Fraser.'

'You spoke with her?'

Catherine nodded. Her mother's face flushed, and she patted her brow with her handkerchief.

A maid approached with a tray of cordials. 'A glass, madam, you look a little warm.'

Catherine lifted two glasses passing one to her mother. 'Mother, why—' her mother held up her hand cutting her off.

'Have you seen Florence yet?' Mother lifted her head in the direction of a group of young people.

Catherine's eyes followed. 'No, she has many others with whom to renew acquaintance.'

A game of lawn bowls underway, Andrew Fraser stood on the sidelines watching. He and Florence unacquainted as she was on the voyage to England when he and his family moved to Perth from Campbell Town. Catherine waved, and her cousin signalled an acknowledgement before picking up her lawn-bowl and hurling it. Using more force than necessary, she knocked every competitor's bowl, including the chuck, into the drain running alongside the garden.

One of her companions screeched. 'Oh, Florence, you've spoiled our game.'

Florence ignored the criticism and flounced over to Catherine's seat. 'Hello, Aunt Arianna, Catherine,' she puffed. 'It's so good to have you here.'

Catherine, a year younger than Florence, relished her cousin's friendship developed while they played together as toddlers. 'Nice to see you, too.'

Florence sucked in the air. Catherine waited. The maid returned, refilled the glasses and offered Florence a cordial.

Florence guzzled the drink in one draft. 'Ah, I needed that, thank you.'

She linked arms with Catherine and said, 'Come up to the house. I've gossip galore.'

Catherine glanced over her shoulder. Mother had blanched, looked like a rabbit searching for somewhere to hide. Catherine hesitated. Father hurried across the garden toward Mother, and she waved Catherine on. Catherine sprinted after Florence—she loved the old sandstone place and had missed exploring the chambers while the Cameron Nicolson family lived in England.

Chapter Nine

Catherine followed her cousin along the path beside the brick fence separating the garden from the stables and the servant's quarters. Would Florence's gossip involve her life overseas? Catherine, keen to hear but, should her news be about a local delicacy of interest that would be better. She might even tell Florence about Sarah's new companion.

Florence drew Catherine's attention to the evergreen azaleas, planted around the fountain in the centre of the lawn. 'They were shipped from the Orient last year. Aren't they beautiful?'

'Impressive, but these red roses are my favourite and their perfume delightful.'

'Quite the young lady now, aren't you, Catherine?'

'Not as sophisticated as you, cousin, and I'm dying for you to tell me what it's like living in England?'

'Far more exciting than here, and I've absolutely no intention of settling in Tasmania when I can see the premier plays, visit the opera and mix with real nobility.'

'We've many elegant parties here on the plains too.'

'Phooey, unless you've had the privilege of being absorbed into English society, you could never understand.'

'I guess not.'

On reaching the top of the stairs to the rear entry, Catherine turned to take in the garden scene. Adele had joined Mother and Father on the bench under the giant elm, and Mother cradled Adele's baby.

'Nor do I want to,' she breathed.

The picturesque setting, beautiful dresses and family and friends all happily engaged in conversation, and the tranquillity of the river winding through the plains beyond the fence, made her quite content to remain in her beloved Tasmania.

From the rear hallway, Catherine and Florence entered the large drawing room with its tall window shutters pushed back, the sunshine streaming in creating a pool of light on the highly polished floor. Catherine gazed about, adoring the enchanting atmosphere.

'Indulge me, Catherine, be my guest.'

'Pleased to do so, my dear countess.'

Always ready to role-play, they laughed.

'Here we have my mother's rosewood grand piano, in the centre of the room, beneath the Florentine crystal chandelier.' Florence waved in an elegant sweep. 'The mahogany bookcase in the corner is father's choice piece, and beside the fireplace, the carved walnut display-cabinet contains Grandma Holbrook's fine china.'

'Beautiful,' Catherine sighed.

She caught Florence and her reflection in the gilt-framed mirror above the mantle, their likeness unmistakable, their well-rounded figures identifying the inherited Nicolson genes.

'Tarred with the one brush. Don't you agree, Florence?'

'We have Grandma Kate to thank for that.'

'Except, I've one or two freckles on my nose while your skin is peaches and cream.'

'Of course, my complexion is more like that of the English now, and if you'll pardon me, it seems you spend far too much time outdoors, Catherine, your skin looks quite leathery.'

Catherine winced, but she could not refute her cousin's remark, her slightly tanned skin betraying her.

'A mahogany-regency chaise, is it new?' Catherine said as she fanned her skirt and settled.

'How did you know?'

'Grandma described exactly the one, belonging to Aunt Elizabeth in Hobart.'

Selecting an English magazine, Catherine thumbed through the pages advertising the latest in fashion, soft furnishings, craft, and recipes.

'I like the new designs. They flatter the figure.'

'Come, see the new evening gown I purchased in London. You'll love it.' Florence beckoned, and she turned toward the stairwell.

Catherine closed the magazine and followed.

The blue-chiffon gown with its dainty frills was as lovely as any Catherine had ever seen. Where would one wear such an outfit in the Midlands?

'Our family is invited to the annual Thanksgiving Service and Charity Banquet, to be held in Launceston,' Florence answered as though Catherine had asked aloud.

'Grandma Kate is the guest of honour at the dinner in recognition of her ministry to the ordinary folk. Why don't you come with us?'

'I'd love to. I'll ask Father.'

Florence led Catherine to the window seat. 'You know, there's a reason Grandma's devoted to helping the low-born.'

Florence's tone contained a note of duplicity, and before Catherine responded, Florence said, 'Grandma was born to a convict woman.'

Catherine gulped. 'Surely not.' It was inconceivable her Grandpa, Reverend Philip Nicolson, would have married the daughter of an ill-reputed woman. 'But Grandpa ...'

'She attended the church in his parish.'

Catherine pulled a face. Her cousin appeared to have no compunction about spilling the family scandal.

'You haven't spoken of this to anyone else, Florence? Mother says those kinds of stories can be damaging to our family's reputation.'

'Grandma Kate doesn't think so.'

'Let's go downstairs.' Catherine gave Florence no option—she had no desire to discuss further idle rumour, and Florence's tale was not one she planned to speak about, ever.

However, Florence was not ready to quit. 'Father said, he believes there are more family secrets to tell, but he forbids us to pry.'

Catherine's armpits began to perspire, and she looked for somewhere to sit and plopped on the nearest couch.

'I'd best mingle,' Florence said, and left Catherine to contemplate what other damaging pieces of information might become known.

Catherine's desire to continue exploring the mansion dissolved completely, she no longer wanted to revisit the catacombs housing the servants, or visit the dark corridors and cells in the lower quarters after the chatter about convicts. She retreated to the garden for fresh air.

'Afternoon tea is ready, ladies and gentlemen,' the butler announced.

Taking a deep breath, Catherine followed the other guests to the conservatory situated on the northwest side of the residence. Her eyes opened wide. The refreshment area was a picture, its round tables covered in white linen cloths. In the centre of each, there was a small silver vase with a single pink rose. The most delicate bone china completed the setting. How quaint it all was. She eyed off the cubed smoked-ham, cheese and gherkin, and fresh salmon sandwiches served on silver trays. She would enjoy herself and forget about Florence's stupid disclosure.

The servants, in their black dresses, white aprons and caps, passed to and from the kitchen. They bobbed in and out among the guests, almost invisibly, topping up trays and filling teacups from silver teapots, leaving Catherine intrigued. The diners' appetite for sandwiches waned, and sweet cupcakes, pastries filled with raspberries topped with cream, and Scottish shortbreads on triple-tiered platters were served.

'May I?' Andrew Fraser interrupted as he dipped his head politely and pointed to the empty seat beside Catherine.

'Oh! Yes,' Catherine stammered, trying to think of an excuse to say no, but all thoughts eluded her.

'The salmon sandwiches are my favourite, I must have eaten half a dozen. It was a great idea to introduce fish to our rivers and lakes. I imagine, it should be a profitable enterprise when it gets established,' Andrew said and reached for yet another sandwich, prattling on and on. 'I'm going to take over my father's estate soon, and I plan to make it the best merino wool producing property in the colony. I'll be as rich as King Midas.'

'You'd have to compete with the Saxon merino from the Winton Estate. It won first prize at the Campbell Town and Morven Shows this year.'

Andrew did not respond, distracted. Catherine followed his gaze.

'Who's that girl over there with the blonde hair?'

'Oh, that's cousin Florence, part of the host family.'

'Please, introduce me,' Andrew said.

A relieved Catherine signalled to Florence, confident she had just escaped a net. She did not want Andrew to be her beau. She had thought him charming, but really, he was a snob just like his mother.

'Florence, please meet Andrew. He's from Fraser's estate near Perth.'

As Andrew and Florence became acquainted, Catherine took the opportunity to excuse herself, escaping to the garden once again, noting as she exited, her mother seated behind a large urn and engaged in conversation with Aunt Rowena. Just as she reached the door to the rear garden, a virile gentleman entered the hallway. He removed his top hat revealing a mop of unruly white hair, his laugh disarming her. His eyes, however, did not smile. A muscle jumped in her cheek.

'Excuse me, miss. The name's Patrick Callaghan. Where should I look for Mister Cameron Nicolson?'

'He's in the conservatory with his guests, of course.'

'A sassy one, eh?'

He brushed by her, his coattails slapping her hip. Every inch of her skin crawled, and she rushed down the steps. Alone, she shivered and looking about, sniffed the air, the smell of rain tickling her nose. She looked in the direction of the Tiers—menacing clouds rolled toward the plains. She rushed to alert her father to the pending storm.

On returning to the conservatory, she recoiled. The white-haired chap leant over the stair rail and across her mother's shoulder. Florence would call him a rake. Mother stepped away patting her face with her handkerchief.

Catherine found her father speaking with Uncle Cameron and tugged at his sleeve. 'Father, I think the weather's about to turn nasty.'

Father followed her to the door, agreed a storm looked likely, ordered the carriages to the front driveway and bid a hasty goodbye to their hosts. Uncle Cameron presented Father with a large box of

Cadbury's-Fancy-Chocolates brought back from England. With a wave to Grandma Kate, Adele, and the other guests, Catherine scrambled into the hansom driven by her father. Before they were through the gate, large drops of rain began to fall. The Nicolson party made haste knowing the gravel road became slippery when the district received more than half an inch of rain.

The horses reached the ford in good time, but as they crossed over, one of the carriage wheels became stuck on a rock. No matter how her father urged, the horses could not pull the vehicle free. Edward steered his cart to the other side and came back to help. Father and Edward tried to lift the wheel, but it would not budge.

'I want you to head for home, Edward,' Father said.

Before they left, Mother and the younger children transferred into the first carriage, Edward instructed to make haste and return with some tools to free the jammed wheel. As they sped off, lightning lit up the darkened sky and thunder roared, the rain turning to sleet. Father sprang into the driver's seat thoroughly saturated. He slapped the reins, but the horses made no progress. He groaned.

Lucille screamed. 'Try again, Father. We'll all drown.'

Father prayed. 'Heavenly Father, have mercy on our souls. Please help us in our dire need.'

Catherine added her plea, 'Lord, help Father.'

The river began to rise, water lapping at the floor of the coach. Catherine's stomach pulsated—she wanted to vomit. A foul odour rose, like that of a spooked farm dog. Her sister, Lucille, crouched in the corner, her teeth chattering.

Another crack of thunder sounded, startling the horses. They strained and struggled, the carriage lurching sideways knocking Father into the swollen river. Catherine screamed as the vehicle, now freed from the rock, pitched forward. She grabbed the reins, straining to keep the horses from bolting. The wheels bumped and bounced over the boulders. They reached the bank, and Catherine jumped out. She looked downstream in the direction of the current, swirling debris rushing along in the raging torrent. Running along the edge, she strained to see, but the black water offered no trace of her father.

The rain pounded, another flash of lightning, so close, she leapt.

Her body trembled, her wet dress clinging to her legs. She must remain in control. She fought the brush blocking her path, but it was no use. By now, Father had been dragged under, drowned. Stumbling a few yards further, she caught sight of him lying on the bank face down, clutching a willow branch. He must have pulled himself to the edge of what had become a wide river. She touched his face, and his eyelids flickered. He stared at her with no recognition and closed his eyes again. She waited. He reopened his eyes.

'Thank you for pulling me out, Catherine.'

What? She looked about. There was no one in sight. How had he gotten out? Who rescued him? He seemed confused. Now was not the time to argue—they could discuss what happened later. His breathing steadied, and he pulled himself to a sitting position.

'You're weak, Father. Do you think you can get back?'

He nodded, and she slung his arm over her neck and helped him along the track.

Struggling up into the carriage, he collapsed onto the seat.

'Father, thank goodness,' Lucille said and spread her dry shawl around his shoulders.

With a grateful smile, he handed Catherine the reins, and they started their journey home.

Edward met them along the track, Catherine gratefully wrapping herself in one of the woollen blankets he had brought with him. They drove through the gate, safe at last, a light shimmering through the parlour window. Thomas helped her from the carriage, stowed the vehicles and attended to the horses. Though she scanned the yard, she did not see the youth with the dark wavy hair.

Her father sat in his comfortable chair, his breathing still somewhat uneven. Catherine looked for Sarah, expecting her to be in the kitchen making hot tea, but all was still, and the lamp extinguished. Catherine opened the grate, allowed enough light to retrieve the warm kettle. She poured three cups of tea and huddled by the fire with her father and Lucille before she trudged upstairs and fell into bed. Sleep evaded her. Her leg muscles twitched, the ache excruciating.

The household had retired for the night, but Mother looked in on her girls.

'Mother, it was awful, Father almost drowned,' Lucille sobbed against her mother's breast.

Catherine lay quietly, hardly able to imagine what might have happened if her father had died.

The following day, he was absent from the breakfast table.

'Your father is unwell. I've confined him to bed. You must all keep quiet so he can rest.'

Father did not appear for several days. When he did, he looked pale and weak, seemed befuddled. Catherine would have to wait to clear up the misunderstanding regarding his rescue. He refused to allow Mother to send for the doctor and insisted all would be quite well in a day or so. It seemed he was right, for a week later, he had improved sufficiently to accompany Edward to the edge of the property to supervise the clearing of trees ready for ploughing. Mother sighed, sank to the seat at the parlour window and watched them leave. Catherine closed the library cabinet, having returned one of her father's books.

Mother sprang from her chair. 'I didn't know anyone was in here.'

'Sorry to startle you,' Catherine said.

Catherine frowned, not having seen her mother about the house much in the last few days, shocked at her appearance. Her eyes drooped and had dark circles around them.

'You look exhausted.'

'It's your father. He still has that incessant cough, and I've barely slept for days. I'm going back to bed. Please help Evelyn with Simon.'

♫♪ ♫♪

Catherine rushed upstairs to organise her wardrobe. Before her father left, she sought permission to travel with Uncle Cameron's family to the St. John's celebrations in Launceston, and he arranged for Thomas to drive her as far as Evandale in the curricle. Lucille sprawled on the bed reading. Catherine grabbed her hands, pulled her up and danced about the room.

'Why are you so excited?'

'Father said I may go with Florence.'

'I wish it were me. My Harry said he was going to Launceston with Andrew Fraser.' Lucille cuddled her pillow, her eyes glazed.

Catherine left her to her daydreaming and eased herself into the chair against the window. She looked toward the pump-house— she must find the time before going with Florence, to add to her compendium. Would it be wise to note her cousin's disclosure? She was not at all sure, but then her diary was lockable.

Ruminating set her to wonder about the youth with the curly, black hair. She had not seen him since she returned from Myrtleford. What was his real purpose for coming to see the Jackson family? She shook her head. Why the fascination with this fellow about whom she knew nothing? She ought to extract herself from the pages of Adeline Mowbray's imaginary world. Catherine had picked the book up from the floor where her sister had dumped it and found it difficult to put it aside once she began to read.

Chapter Ten

Thomas bowed, teasing as Catherine waltzed toward the curricle dressed in her finest travelling garb. He vaulted into the driver's seat. She would have been content to travel with him, but Mother insisted her brother, Stuart, escort her in spite of her protests. He tormented her all the way from Willowbank to Evandale.

Her fists clenched and her face wet with perspiration she exhaled, 'Stuart, you are irritating.'

'How were you invited to go to Launceston? I want to go.'

'For goodness sake stop whining, Stuart, you weren't asked. When the men make trips to town, you go, and we girls don't.'

'Boys are the most important in the family. We carry on the family name. I'll inherit Willowbank Estate, and you'll stay in line then, sweet pea.'

'I'll be certain to marry well, so I don't have to depend on you, little brother.'

'Not if you keep mixing with the ordinary folk, you won't.'

'What's so wrong in treating everyone kindly?'

'You sound just like Mother. She treats them like that because she was one of them.'

'That's not true. How would you know, anyhow?'

'It's true for sure. I heard Mother and Missus Betsy talking. They didn't know I was hiding in the cellar.'

Catherine lifted her nose, turned away from her brother and looked intently at Thomas. Thomas stirred the horses to a trot. He did not acknowledge her but stared straight ahead. Catherine's head began to ache, her troubling thoughts making her feel unwell. Stuart's claim, and the recent conversation with her cousin Florence, unsettling.

♫♪ ♫♪

The carriage pulled alongside Uncle Cameron's barouche at the Prince of Wales Hotel. His driver placed Catherine's small, leather case, dwarfed by the enormous trunk containing her cousin's fancy European clothing, in the luggage compartment. Mother did not have the time to help sew a new gown for her because Father was ill. She had packed the muslin frock worn at Myrtleford's afternoon tea, though it had a slight flaw. She had caught it on a branch on that fateful night, when searching for her father, and had to mend the tear.

'Hello, welcome aboard,' Florence greeted her cheerily.

'My, it's warm for an autumn day,' Catherine said, fanning her face.

'We'll get a cross breeze when we get rolling,' Aunt Amelia assured her.

Her window seat gave Catherine an unimpeded view as they spun around to head north. A loud wattlebird's warble reverberated between the buildings, "Look out, miss, look out, miss!", and turning, she saw a young man down the alley. Thomas circled and stopped the Willowbank curricle, and the youth leapt up to the seat next to him. Thomas leaned toward him, and the youth swivelled and waved his cap at the barouche. Lifting her hand, she lowered it and looked away. If only she had asked Sarah about the young man.

Florence gained her attention, and for a time they chatted about their anticipated visit to Adele's home. Soon tiring, Catherine rested her head against the cushioned seat back and scanned the landscape, the paddocks a vibrant green from the recent rain. On route, they came across a Guernsey milking herd grazing under the shade of eucalypts, several egrets accompanying them. The cows had worn a track around a dam and along the fence toward the milking shed.

'The property belongs to Douglas Butler.' Uncle Cameron pointed and added, 'He's got the best milkers in the district.'

Catherine scanned the property, soon to be Harry's inheritance, according to Lucille.

Some ten miles from Launceston, they passed by an orchard where straight rows of peach trees strained under their load. The travellers watched the pickers balancing on stacked wooden-crates to reach the fruit on the higher branches. The crop would fetch the farmer a reasonable price.

'That property belongs to the Carrick brothers. They're sending their peaches to Hobart to be canned at Peacocks and then exported to England.'

Uncle Cameron continued his commentary. It was apparent he was well-acquainted with the estate owners in the district.

'The Hollies,' Catherine read the sign flapping against the gate, as the horses cantered by an impressive white two-story Georgian house.

'The Hawke family operated a boys' school there for around twenty-five years,' Florence said,' Harry Butler's father attended the highbrow school.'

It seemed Lucille's connection with the wealthy family might advantage her prospects. Perhaps Mother's estimation of Harry was unfounded. Catherine lifted her head, a bell tolling in the distance, and at the Gothic chapel, an array of carriages were parked in the grounds.

'Must be the funeral of a prominent citizen.' Aunt Amelia sat upright searching the park. 'We're sure to discover whose when we attend the ceremony tomorrow.'

♫♪ ♫♪

The Nicolson party reached the brow of a hill on the outskirts of the city and made a rapid descent, approaching Launceston city via Wellington Street.

'Look at all the houses.' Catherine stretched her neck, unable to sit still, like a baby bird ready to try out its wings.

The barouche pulled up in Upper York Street in front of a two-storey Victorian home with wraparound verandas.

'Here we are, this must be the new home, commissioned by Robert … your abode for the next few days, girls,' Aunt Amelia said.

Adele's cook served an afternoon tea of club sandwiches and apple-cake on the front veranda. A waft of cinnamon reached Catherine's nostrils, and her tummy gurgled. Leaning back on the rattan and wicker seat, she rested her aching muscles and watched little Margaret stack building-blocks in an adjoining room. The new baby lay on a blanket, gurgling happy sounds. Catherine gulped her tea, but her thirst unquenched, she reached for another cup, Aunt Amelia's withering glare halting her mid-gesture. Catherine winced.

'My, what a magnificent view of Mount Arthur and the Tamar Valley you have, Adele, right in the city precinct too,' Uncle Cameron said, winking at Catherine, and she smiled.

'I am privileged, Uncle Cameron,' Adele said, gazing in the direction of the ribbon of water stretched along the valley. 'But I mustn't keep you. Take the programme and acquaint yourselves with the activities for tomorrow. Your driver is waiting to take your party to the Cornwell Hotel.'

♫♪ ♫♪

Catherine, drawn to the kitchen by the smell of toast the following morning, said, 'Just the thing to fortify our morning of exploring before attending Grandma's celebrations.'

'It's cook's day off,' Adele explained as she busied herself setting the table.

A curtain billowed against the open window revealing a layer of mist trapped in the valley.

'It's foggy. We'll have a nice day when it burns off.'

'Certainly, just like it does on the plains, Catherine,' Adele said.

Adele retrieved milk, butter, and cheese from the icebox in the pantry and set them on the highly polished oak dining table.

'Pretty,' Catherine said, examining the crocheted milk-jug cover decorated with green, translucent beads. 'A novel idea, the breeze won't blow that off.'

'I learned to make those at the Milton Hall craft group … we meet on Thursday mornings in the rear hall at the church. The women in the group are very clever, creating all manner of needlework, some of which we give to the benevolent society.'

It was plain to see Adele enjoyed her life in the city, and Catherine hoped she might be so happily situated.

'And to be sure, very prolific about the town gossip too,' Florence said as she entered the room.

Adele smiled at Florence's remark but did not comment. Catherine might have scolded Florence had she not felt a sudden tinge of guilt, her cousin's temperament too like her own. She reached for a dish, spread orange marmalade and a generous slice of cheddar-cheese onto her thickly buttered toast, and skulled a cup of Earl Grey tea. The existence of the elite suited her perfectly—she grinned, born to the privilege, town living agreeable, if only she might meet a comely young man.

Pouring another cup of tea, she said, 'My, this tastes good. Mother would like this. I'll have to buy a jar and take it home to her. Where do I buy it?'

'Johnstone and Wilmots.'

A loud knock at the front door interrupted the chatter.

'There's my neighbour, Muriel, now. She'll chaperone you while you're in town, and take you by the store on the way. Muriel knows every landmark of interest, and you have all morning to explore, a visit to Peoples Park worthwhile. It is looking delightful, the autumn leaves glorious.'

'We'll do our best, won't we girls?' Muriel seemed like a take-charge kind of person.

'Bye, Adele, we'll be back in time to get dressed for this afternoon's ceremony,' Florence said, the young ladies donning their comfortable walking shoes for their tour of the city.

♫♪ ♫♪

'You realize, we'll have to walk back up this steep hill,' complained Florence as they set off down York Street.

Missus Muriel talked as fast as she walked while navigating the city streets. Turning into St. John Street, they passed a row of stately Georgian homes and the newly constructed Victorian-style Town Hall building. On entering Johnstone and Wilmot's grocery store, Catherine strode to the counter, fossicking in her purse for a pound note.

'A one-pound canister of tea please, and may I have it in a brown paper bag?'

The shopkeeper handed the bag to Catherine and directed his attention to Florence. 'In town for the St. John's celebrations, are you?'

'Yes, here from Evandale for a couple of days and enjoying visiting your beautiful city.'

Muriel cleared her throat and waved her hand to indicate the girls move toward the door, 'We need to be on our way if we're to see everything.'

As the girls stepped onto the pavement, a well-dressed gentleman lifted his top hat and said, 'Ah, if it isn't the Misses Nicolson from Evandale.'

Catherine stared at his dazzling white mop, nodded and stepped back to let him pass.

'Hello, Mister Callaghan,' Florence said, and smiled broadly.

'Come, girls, we don't have all day,' Muriel beckoned.

'Good day, ladies,' Callaghan said, replacing his hat.

♫♪ ♫♪

'Muriel keeps up quite a brisk pace,' Florence panted as they passed by the Cornwall Hotel where the rest of their party were staying. 'Perhaps I'll stop in and visit Mother.'

'Florence, please don't bail out on me.'

Muriel turned into George Street, and the girls scrambled to keep up.

'You must be used to these hills, I guess.' Catherine cast a glance around, deciding no matter where you walked in Launceston, you would have to tackle a steep incline or two. Not at all, like the plains.

Muriel pointed. 'This is the church where I attend. We have an excellent choirmaster, and we are practising some marvellous pieces for our Easter services.'

'You're in a choir? That would be fantastic. How fortunate you are.'

'One advantage of living in the city, Catherine,' interjected Florence. 'That's why I'll be anxious to return to London where I can join in all manner of social activities.'

Catherine pushed the turnstile at Peoples Park main gate, marvelling at several species of trees. Deep-red leaves, fluttering from the maples onto the gravel paths, mingled with the multi-coloured leaves of the giant oaks and the yellowing elm leaves.

'Magnificent! I'm inspired to pen a verse. Evelyn would be pleased.'

Muriel walked ahead, inspected the rhododendrons and the blue hydrangeas covering the sloping banks.

'You gave the impression you liked Mister Callaghan, Florence. How well do you know him?' Catherine asked.

'He's a business partner of Father, deals in sheep and wool sales. He's always been a pleasant gentleman and stops by our home regularly.'

'There's something about him I don't like. He is too polished.'

'Catherine, you're truly fanciful.'

Catherine, her hands on her hips, gaped at Florence.

Muriel pointed, 'Look at these delicate pink cyclamens along the garden edges.'

'They're lovely. The garden is a masterpiece and so close to the centre of the city,' Catherine said, grateful for the diversion.

A slight breeze blew, scattering dead foliage about the park.

'We'd better be off, or you'll be late for this afternoon's ceremony.' Muriel led the way. 'We'll climb the steps to Brisbane Street and cut through Weymouth. It's quicker, though quite steep.'

Two young men, dressed in walking costumes, entered the top gate and approached along the path. As they drew near, Catherine recognized Andrew Fraser.

'How do you do, Miss Nicolson?' He swept his top hat from his red locks and bowed to Florence.

'Good day to you, Andrew Fraser.' Florence boldly stepped forward to allow him to take her hand and kiss her glove.

'Catherine, may I introduce you to my friend, John Carrick, of Relbia Park Properties. John and I are staying at The Grand as guests of Mister Patrick Callaghan.'

John Carrick's face lit up. He tipped his hat and gushed how delightful it was to make her acquaintance. Catherine threw her head back and laughed. He pushed an imaginary lock from his forehead and gave a lopsided grin. The introductions complete, the group discovered they were all in the city to attend the St. John's function. Why was Harry Butler not with his friends? Catherine did not ask in case they questioned her motive.

'We're returning to our quarters to prepare for the event, and we'll need to be smart about it. Good day to you, gentlemen.' Catherine tilted her head.

'We'll be delighted to make your acquaintance at the church. Until later then.' John Carrick touched the rim of his hat.

Florence gathered her skirts and huffed and puffed all the way up the hill.

'Honestly, Florence, you are far too delicate.'

On returning to Adele's, Catherine freshened up and dressed in her muslin walking attire and matching bonnet.

'All ready for the ceremony?' Adele's voice rippled through the stairwell.

'On our way.'

Chapter Eleven

Catherine entered the foyer at St. Johns and scanned the crowd for Grandma Kate and Aunt Rowena. She located them sitting near the front of the church and made her way down the aisle, surprised by the many ordinary folk who took up the rear seats. She passed by Andrew and his friend, John Carrick, seated halfway down the aisle. John winked at her. Dipping her head, she picked up her skirt and scurried to the front.

'Hello, Grandma, Aunt Rowena.' She slid into the pew next to Rowena. 'Isn't this a grand occasion?'

Kate and Rowena smiled their affirmation. Florence and Adele followed Catherine and squeezed into the second front pew immediately behind the government dignitaries. As soon as everyone settled, the bishop moved behind the lectern and began proceedings.

'Let us begin our Thanksgiving service with hymn number twenty-one.'

Catherine swivelled to look at the congregation during the singing of the hymn, enraptured by the sound of so many voices singing one of her favourite songs. Inspired, she lifted her voice with the huge chorus. When the organist modulated the key on the familiar last verse, the worshippers at the back sang even more robustly, the choir director waving his arms enthusiastically, looking as though he might soar to the rafters. When the hymn concluded, the crowd in the rear clapped spontaneously. Catherine smiled. The Bishop frowned, and his stance threatened a stern rebuke. Repositioning his eyepiece, he continued to read from his handbook.

The male choir's rendition of *A Mighty Fortress is Our God* was riveting, Catherine sitting transfixed. On the other hand, while the Bishop's address droned on and on, she fixed her attention on the vases of magnificent roses set on carved wooden stands. Her eyes wandered to the fresh produce stacked high on cloth-covered tables. There were large cabbages, hessian bags of potatoes, turnips, carrots, peas, beans, and silver-beet brought in by members of the congregation. The bottles of preserved fruit, jars of jam and crates of eggs, all arranged just as Catherine had seen at the Morven Show. Fluffy, yellow chicks pecked at the grain spread on the bottom of a small cage seated on the floor. The ladies' guild would distribute the produce to poor families in the Launceston area. Catherine's desire to help the ordinary folk intensified, but she was not sure how she might achieve her dream.

Florence tapped her on the arm, and muttered, 'Catherine, stand for the singing of the last hymn.'

How long had she failed to concentrate?

The crowd at the rear gave little regard to the Bishop's earlier rebuke, the crescendo during last verse nothing short of deafening. Catherine giggled at the contrast between the pious conduct of the posh and that of the ordinary folk.

Standing close to her grandmother while the older woman greeted friends in the Church's front courtyard, she perused the crowd.

A lady approached, 'I belong to The Women's Benevolent Society. Here is a collection for the poor in the Perth district,' she said and handed Grandma an envelope.

Without warning, the woman jolted forward due to a scuffle between two young lads behind her. A fistfight ensued. One lad yelped, blood pouring from his nose. Someone pointed and blamed the father of one of the lads, accused him of cuffing his son's aggressor. A well-dressed gentleman pushed through the crowd remonstrating with the offender, Catherine surprised to see Mister Callaghan. He tried to restrain the father, but a bystander punched him in the stomach.

'Somebody, please help him?'

'He don't need no help, leave him be,' another said.

Derogatory insults brought several others into the fray, and someone mentioned the Carrick name. Grandma grasped Catherine's arm and led her across the road to Princes Square, the remainder of their group scuttling behind. Catherine looked back. A constable from the municipal police arrived, brandishing a pistol, and soon had the scuffle under control. A man fell to his knees pleading for mercy, but the officer forced him away in handcuffs, leaving his young son in the arms of a distraught woman. The unpleasant experience confirmed to Catherine that the poor ordinary folk faced injustice, even when dealing with the law.

'Riff Raff,' cried Florence. 'Spoiling the day for everyone. At least Mister Callaghan attempted to settle them.' Florence lowered her eyelids and smirked. 'Perhaps, Catherine, he is a decent chap after all.'

Catherine cringed.

'We don't know what caused the fight, Florence, it may not have been the poor man's fault,' Grandma Kate said. 'It can only be imagined how some folks put up with accusations levelled at them. Besides, the strain on some men to provide brings them to a breaking point. I hope the court is not too hard on the boy's father. Come, let's sit beside the fountain for a while and enjoy the quiet of the garden.'

The party complied with Grandma's directive, and they had almost reached the bench when Andrew Fraser and a dishevelled John Carrick appeared.

'Blessed low-life socked him in the eye.' Andrew eased his friend to the seat.

'Oh dear.' Grandma moved to examine the young Carrick's eye. 'It is colouring already. Here Andrew, dip my handkerchief into the water. The young man should hold it against his eye and attend a doctor immediately.'

Andrew hailed his driver, and the fellow raced to attend. 'Sir, your carriage is ready, shall I give you a hand?'

'Yes, we'll take him to the hotel.'

Catherine watched as they climbed aboard. 'I hope he'll be all right.'

Adele flickered a look at Catherine.

'In England, the ordinary folk would not be allowed to attend,' said Florence, indignant.

Catherine bowed her head—of course, they should come. She felt sorry for John Carrick, but the constable ought to have questioned him—an image of the Ordinary man tied to a chain in the watch-house and pleading for mercy flashed across her mind.

'The poor were invited at my insistence, Florence. Now, where were we?'

'Grandma, you were saying, Grandpa Philip and you lived in Patterson Cottage.'

'Ah yes, in those days, the park was wide-open ground, often used for public meetings and military parades, and later for the celebrations at the cessation of the transportation of convicts.'

'The fountain has added interest,' Catherine said.

'Very much like the ones I've seen in England, Catherine,' Florence said, her nose tilted upward.

'It was bought from France. We're to be thankful to our horticultural society for the forward thinking in setting aside this ground and the many other selections we enjoy.' Aunt Rowena added her knowledge to the impromptu history lesson. 'Mind you, the work completed by convict labour.'

Adele moved to read the plaques at the foot of a row of young trees. 'Look at these oaks, positioned by Prince Alfred during his visit. Captain Robert and I were in the crowd when the planting took place. Think, girls, you may be blessed enough to see them when they are fifty years old.'

'Not me,' Florence asserted. 'I'll be a Londoner, admiring the oaks in Hyde Park.'

Catherine sighed. Florence was becoming quite the smarty-pants.

♫♪ ♫♪

'My, you do look elegant, my ladies,' Captain Robert tipped his hat as they boarded their transport to Grandma's honorarium dinner.

Catherine adopted the manner of a cultivated lady folding her gloved hands on her lap while the horses clopped along the pavement to Milton Hall for the celebration dinner. Though dressed informally compared to Florence, she was satisfied with her appearance in her ivory organza gown, a hand-me-down from Lucille.

A footman directed Catherine to the main table with Grandma Kate and Uncle Cameron's family. Andrew Fraser and John Carrick were conspicuous by their absence. She peeked across to a nearby table where several British Army officers sat chatting. Their boisterous laughter and rude pointing toward the Nicolson table warmed Catherine's face, and she lowered her eyes. A rumour was rife—the entire garrison would be leaving Tasmania during the year, and given their reputation for lewd behaviour, it was timely.

'Don't they look handsome in their red-dress uniforms?' Florence tugged Catherine's arm.

'Maybe you'll find yourself a worthy lieutenant, like Adele's Robert, when you return to London,' whispered Catherine.

'Excuse me.' A waitress, dressed in a starched, black and white uniform, interrupted their conversation.

She balanced a silver tray against her hip and set the dinner plates before the guests, the meal consisting of an entrée of scallops, a dinner of lamb with crispy baked vegetables, and glasses of apple juice. Catherine looked down at the array of cutlery. Which fork should she pick up first? Catherine hesitated. How could she enjoy such a meal while the prisoner shackled in the watch-house supped on a dry crust and gruel?

The master of ceremonies stood and gave honour to the charitable citizens of Northern Tasmania. He awarded Grandma Kate a plaque for her untiring service to the poor in Perth and its surrounds. Her acceptance speech, a spirited homily, encouraged the guests to be thankful for all of God's blessings, challenging them to extend grace to the disadvantaged ordinary folk.

'Need I remind you of Jon Bradford's adage—*There but for the grace of God, go I*,' she concluded.

'Bravo!' Catherine expressed her appreciation rather loudly, causing the soldiers to snort.

Aunt Rowena squeezed Catherine's hand, but other guests glared, their looks condemning. Catherine steamed with embarrassment. If only she could slide under her chair.

Still smarting when she returned to Adele's, she exploded, 'How dare they, they're so pompous! They don't care about the poor, they were just there for appearances.'

'There's a certain social etiquette, dear Catherine, and one of those conventions is to show restraint when applauding. You will learn, the more often you are invited to mix with the privileged.'

Florence's chiding did nothing to cool Catherine's temper. Her fingers twitched, she wanted to slap her cousin but instead retreated to the safety of the front veranda. Grandma, who had come to Adele's to look over her new home, followed Catherine outside and sat alongside for a few minutes, remaining silent.

'Grandma, why do I feel as though I don't belong to the privileged class?'

'Perhaps you are not of their ilk, dear Catherine, just as I am not. Though my mother reformed, she never forgot her woeful past and endeavoured to care for the factory women.'

Catherine raised her brows—so it was true, her great-grandmother was a convict.

'Jesus is our great example. Even though he was equal with God, he lived on earth as a common man, healing the sick and providing for the hungry. He showed us how to treat others with great compassion, and for all his good works, he was tried and condemned as a criminal.'

Catherine considered her grandmother's treatise.

'Catherine, I had a few minutes visiting Grandpa Philip's grave this morning at the Cypress Street cemetery. While there, I prayed for all my children and grandchildren, that they might come to understand how much God loves them, and has a grand purpose for each one of them.'

'Well, I know my purpose. I'm going to ask the Lord to help me take care of the poor, just like you do Grandma, and I've not forgotten your advice to realize contentment is found in a mission that inspires you.'

'I am happy to hear that.' Grandma Kate squeezed Catherine's hand. 'Just one other thing, in time, I hope you'll come to understand one's endeavour doesn't earn God's favour but is simply a result of already enjoying it.'

Catherine did not quite comprehend Grandma's assertion. She would think about it when she was not so tired. It had been a long day, but she would note her recommitment to the mission in her diary when she returned to Willowbank.

'Goodnight, Catherine.'

'Goodnight, Grandma.' Catherine hugged her grandmother.

Those few moments of discussion with her grandmother granted Catherine a sense of peace, and the following morning she sprang from her bed refreshed.

♫♪ ♫♪

Catherine mused, quiet during the return journey to Evandale, happy she attended Grandma's celebration. The remainder of the party cackled and sneered at the fashions worn by their colonial friends.

Travelling through Franklin Village, Aunt Amelia pointed and said, 'We found out the funeral at the church over there was that of Douglas Butler.'

Catherine's brow creased. Harry was too young to take over such an extensive property, but no doubt, he would try being a responsible kind of chap. He would need to take care of his mother, and his brothers and sisters.

'He died of a mysterious illness. There was chatter at our hotel of foul-play, something about a dispute regarding the servants from the next-door Carrick property.'

Catherine shivered, reached for her travel rug and wrapped it about her legs.

Uncle Cameron did not return with them. Instead, he had sailed to Sydney with Mister Callaghan, who had arranged for him to meet a trading merchant, Uncle convinced the business proposition was too good to pass up.

♫♪ ♫♪

Edward met her in Evandale with a load of produce from the general store on board. As they skirted the town, Thomas' friend came to mind. She would ask Sarah about him, but would it be wise to hope for an attachment? Their worlds were miles apart.

Catherine eased herself from the dray.

Lucille ran to meet her. 'Tell me all the exciting news.'

Catherine yawned and blinked, 'Not now, Lucille.'

'You look worn out.'

Mother came to the room and stroked Catherine's hair. Dozing, Catherine remained in her mother's embrace for a long while, comforted in the safety of her familiar environment.

Chapter Twelve

Catherine peered out the window to investigate the clatter below. Edward, head down, led a horse-drawn farm-cart into the rear yard. It was mid-afternoon, so she hadn't expected to see him. The old hedge gate stood open—he must have come from the north paddock where he and Father had been clearing for the past two months.

Her heart skipped a beat. 'No!' Her father lay motionless in the tray.

Catherine watched, Edward stopping in front of his cottage. Thomas appeared at the doorway, and his father beckoned him, and they lifted Father from the cart. Something was very wrong. Catherine hurtled downstairs to the drawing room.

'Mother, I think something awful has happened to Father. He's over at Mister Edward's cottage.'

Her mother dropped her handicraft to her lap. Catherine had barely finished her sentence when a loud knock rattled the front door. She ran into the hallway just as Sarah flung the door open.

'What is it, Dad?'

Edward pushed past his daughter, his face red and beaded with perspiration.

'Please find Missus Nicolson for me, Sarah.'

Catherine shrunk back, the gravity of his voice frightening her.

'She is in the drawing room, come through,' Sarah said.

'Missus Nicolson, I'm very sorry, but I am afraid your husband is ill,' Edward said.

Mother stumbled as though she would faint and sank onto the chaise. 'Oh! How? What happened?'

'Quick, Sarah, water,' Mister Edward ordered.

Mother sipped.

'He collapsed, likely weakened from influenza, and he's wheezing awful bad. My Betsy is damping him down with a cool cloth. You must come over, now.'

Mother rose, her legs wobbling, looking toward the door and back to the table as though she ought to find something. Edward strode out, and Mother followed, Catherine dashing after them.

She stopped and called over her shoulder, 'Sarah, tell Evelyn what's happened. I'm going too.'

Catherine tore across the yard. What if? She checked herself, envisioned her father crumpled under the willow tree. Why had she not thought to take a rug from the carriage to keep him warm on the night of the storm? Her legs quaked beneath her frame, her every instinct to run in the opposite direction. Censuring her panic, she pressed her back against the cottage wall—she must take hold of herself.

'Help me,' she prayed as she eased along. 'Surely, God, you would not have saved him from the raging river only to take him now.'

Grabbing for the door lintel, she paused, the sound of overworked fire-bellows confusing her senses.

'Catherine.' Betsy pulled her into the room and closed the door. 'Thomas has gone to fetch the doctor.'

Mother was on her knees beside the cot. The emaciated figure of her father panted, puffed and gasped, pain etched on his drawn face. A pungent smell like pure alcohol permeated the cottage, the smell secreted through his skin. Catherine stretched out across the foot of the mattress listening to the awful rattle of her father's chest.

Twilight gave way to blackness, a silver crescent arching across the expanse—in good times or bad, the elements continue their cycle, Catherine consoled by their perpetuity. Betsy and Sarah padded about making tea, changing bed-sheets, collecting fresh water until the visiting occupants of their tiny cottage succumbed to fatigue. Thomas had not yet returned.

♫♪ ♫♪

As morning light filtered through the small window, Catherine turned to look at her mother. Her frame straddled Father's limp form, one hand resting against his damp sallow skin and the other clutching a lace kerchief.

'Mother, are you awake?'

Mother stirred, stretching her stiffened limbs.

'Arianna, help me up. I want to move to our room,' Father's husky voice odd.

Catherine came alongside, and together the women eased him to the edge of the bed until his legs dangled over the side, and they assisted him to his feet.

'I'll fetch Mister Edward.'

'Don't bother, Catherine. He'll be busy in the stable.'

Mother slung his arm about her shoulder and Catherine moved to his other side, but he held his hand up. 'I can manage. You go on ahead.'

Catherine opened the door, waited until they moved out and headed toward the rear entrance of the main house.

A blood-curdling scream resonated through the quadrangle. Catherine spun—her parents sprawled on the ground. Mother moved, but her father crumpled, still. Catherine knelt beside him, searching ...

Mother cradled his head repeating, 'My Francis, my Francis.'

Lifeless eyes stared back at her.

♫♪ ♫♪

With Mister Edward and Sarah's help, Catherine and her mother stumbled to the drawing room. Catherine crouched at her mother's feet and gripped her hand.

'Sarah, please find Evelyn, and ask her to come to the drawing room at once,' Edward said.

The sound of pounding hooves echoed in the quadrangle, the door flung against the lintel.

'I couldn't bring the doctor. He was called out to attend to a fellow burned by a branding iron.'

Edward put his finger to his lips, 'Never mind, son. Mister Nicolson died.'

Thomas bowed his head.

Evelyn rushed into the room, Sarah behind her.

'I'll saddle one of the horses and speak to the rector in Evandale to organise Mister Nicolson's funeral. You take care of things here,' Mister Edward said.

Catherine helped her mother to her room, and Betsy, padding behind them, closed the door.

Mother threw herself on the bed and wailed, 'No! No!'

Thumping her pillow and thrashing about, she sat bolt upright, pulled great strands of hair from her scalp and rocked back and forth, tears streaming down her face. Catherine lowered herself onto the window seat, rested her head in her hands and closed her eyes. The gnawing in her stomach alarmed her. Would Mother survive another loss?

♫♪ ♫♪

A sombre atmosphere pervaded Willowbank throughout the days that followed, the children required to play quietly in their rooms. Stuart bellowed, but Simon and Louisa not old enough to comprehend the depth of the family's grief protested about their confinement to the extent Evelyn relented and asked Catherine to take them outside into the garden. This decision signalled the right for everyone to venture from his or her rooms. Stuart, eyes red and swollen from his hours of howling, ran toward the hay shed to seek solace—Catherine had found him there on other occasions when he was in trouble.

Evelyn approached Catherine several hours later, 'I'll take care of the young ones.'

Catherine looked about, checking for meddlesome eyes and started down the path toward the river. She squatted by the pond a stones-throw from the pump-house, where she had often retreated when she needed to calm herself. Early yellow daffodils grew along the water's edge, and wild ducks dived among the lilies looking for small insects—observing God's creation, an elixir for sorrow.

She looked up. Mauve coloured mountains in the distance looked solid and serene. The idyllic environment usually contributed a sense of safety, but her troubled soul was now in turmoil. She sobbed for a long time, groaning, until glimpsing a mother duck gliding, her babies lined up behind her—a reminder God would guide her if—

She recited a poem of comfort her Grandma Kate had written when her beloved Philip passed to Glory, the one Catherine had learned by heart and committed to her notebook.

'Oh! Lord, how much I feel my loss, I'm sad and sore perplexed.
The questions, countless, turn my mind they scramble all about.
Send aid I pray—my soul it quakes—disquiet, discord, and doubt.
Help me to see your hand in death or else my hope be vexed.

'My child, I see your hurt and tears, please hear my Word for you.
He is asleep. I'll care for you, and come again to bring you through.
You have a life to live on earth, a future in the Realms anew.
Trust in Me. I am your Peace, myself I gave, to atone for you.'

'I know it's true.' But fears tumbled in her heart. 'Lord, why did you take my father when we all need him so much?'

All at once, the depth of the poem's meaning struck her, and she clung to the words of the second stanza repeating them once more, 'I praise you, Lord. I know you will never leave me or forsake me, and I believe your promise. I will see him again.'

Regaining the path, the distinct trill of a wattlebird rang out, "Look out, miss, look out, miss!" Voices—she cowered. Betsy was speaking with someone. Catherine did not recognise the other person's voice, but it belonged to a male, the tone deep and authoritative. She could only pick up snippets but clearly heard the words trinket-box and drawing. The scuff of boots moved closer and stopped right beside her position.

'No one must find out, especially now. Missus Nicolson's secret must stay with us alone.'

'You can trust me, Edwin. You know she's been good to our family, and I care for her.'

Catherine crouched low until they moved away, not daring to enter the pump-house now. Turning toward the main house, she met Stuart on the path with Ginger cradled in his arms.

He yelled. 'Don't talk. Leave me alone. I hate you. I hate everyone,' and dropping Ginger, ran back to the house.

Catherine followed him to his room, but he had jammed the door shut.

She prayed, 'Lord, he needs your love. He's going to miss his dad.'

♫♪ ♫♪

Mister Edward brought the landau to a standstill in the front courtyard, its shiny exterior testament to the care he took in preparing it for Mother and Lucille to travel to the church in Evandale. The women, forlorn in their black mourning clothes, descended the steps. Catherine wanted to attend the service with her mother, but the Nicolson family considered it improper for children to witness funerals. That she was still considered a child at the age of fourteen irked her, but she dared not argue. She hugged her mother and grasped Lucille. Lucille clung to her sister, her body trembling and tears beading in her eyes.

'I don't think I can do this, Catherine, I'm terrified.'

'Mother needs you to keep her company, and you must, Lucille.'

Mother poked her head from the carriage. 'Lucille what's keeping you, we'll be late.'

Lucille broke from Catherine's embrace and fled to the house, Catherine chasing her up the steps.

'Wait, Mister Edward,' Catherine called over her shoulder.

♫♪ ♫♪

Catherine bolted out the door barefoot. She had changed into Lucille's mourning dress grabbing her black pumps on the way out, persuaded her sister to assist Evelyn with the younger children while she took her place.

Men from the district came to honour Father, crowding into Saint Andrew's Church of England. Grandma Kate, clutching a wreath of white lilies, waited in the foyer of the church with Adele and proceeded to the front pew with Mother and Catherine. Grandma placed the laurel upon the coffin.

Reverend Bates began by quoting a selection from *Thessalonians*. Catherine smiled at Grandma—they shared the hope conveyed by the verses. The strong baritone voices of the men's choir reinforced the message as they sang two of Father's favourite hymns. The Reverend's eulogy, describing Father's contribution to the prosperity of the colony, emphasizing the compassion he displayed to everyone regardless of his status, clearly heartfelt.

'Mister Nicolson Esquire has left a wonderful example, a heritage for all to imitate,' he said, the men in the pews nodding and murmuring in agreement. 'Human bodies, while temples of the Holy Ghost, are faulty earthen vessels but when Jesus returns renewed—like our Saint Andrew's with its ever-widening cracks, needs to be rebuilt.'

The congregation gasped in unison, Catherine covering her mouth. She glanced at her mother, Mother's eyebrows knitted in a deep frown. Grandma squirmed. Admittedly, the minister did not have to add his sarcastic remark, and during a funeral of all places.

The organist opened the stops during the recessional, and everyone turned and stared at the rafters. Sunlight shone through a massive crack in the masonry exposing the red bricks, an unspoken fear, the organ's vibrations might shake the foundations and cause the tower to fall on them, etched upon their faces.

In the twilight hour, the landau rolled into the Willowbank courtyard. Betsy took their coats, brought a tray to the parlour and poured cups of warm milk for Catherine and her mother as they relayed the events to Evelyn and Lucille. Betsy lingered, poking at the fire with a stick.

Mother touched her elbow. 'You may wait with us, Betsy. Pour a cup for yourself.'

Evelyn shuffled along the settee to make room for Betsy.

'It was a lovely service. My dear Francis, laid to rest near the row of South Esk conifers on the edge of the cemetery. God rest his soul.'

Betsy sniffed, and Mother reached for her handkerchief passing it to the older woman. She snorted into it like a nag on seeing a hay bag. Catherine bit her bottom lip. Usually, she would cackle if such a thing happened, but she did not feel at all jovial tonight.

'What's going to happen to us all now?' Lucille said, wringing her hands.

Mother's lip quivered, but she raised her chin and said, 'God will take care of us.'

♫♪ ♫♪

Though it was late, Catherine made her way to the pump-house but failed to take her usual precaution of slowing and checking for noises. Surprised, she found the door ajar. She peaked in—no one. Kicking the door with her foot, it slammed against the side. An involuntary 'Shush' escaped her lips.

Remembering the conversation when near the pond, she poked around the shelf to be sure its treasures remained safe. Her notebook, pushed to the back, scrunched between the tin and the external wall, just visible. She shuffled the jewellery-case forward, the insignia flashing in the shaft of light penetrating the entrance—she had forgotten to close the door. She took a stride and heaved it, but her cardigan sleeve caught on the edge of the box, and it tumbled to the ground spilling its contents—a few coins and a large envelope.

Prising the envelope open, she retrieved a folded sheet of drawing paper, and on it, a faded sketch of a woman and child. The background seemed familiar, so she inspected it more thoroughly and determined it was the billowing sails. Gathering the pieces, she returned them to the container and closed it. Something was different about the lid, the motto on the insignia now clearly readable the script in a foreign language.

She sounded out the words, 'Je Suis Prest.'

How odd. Catherine turned the container over to find the lock unfastened, unlike on her previous visit, but not broken. Who had opened it and why? Was something removed or added? Maybe the tin belonged to Betsy, the servant woman often trekking along the path in the direction of the pump-house.

Catherine placed the mysterious treasure-box back on the shelf just as before, made a note in her book of the date of her father's passing and wrote a couple of lines, recording Betsy and the young man's communication. She found a new spot to hide her precious chronicles. No one had read her jottings—they would have taken them or at least tried to place the bag exactly where it had been.

Outside the hut, the path was dark, for the last rays of sunset had faded behind the Tiers. A young wattlebird flitted about the heath and chorused, "Look out, miss, look out, miss!" Catherine inched along until she reached the hedge and ran her hand along the glossy privet to guide her. The clouds parted, and the moon hovered just above the hill lighting the rear yard. She exhaled. She had not realized she was holding her breath. She brushed passed nymph, the accusing face leering at her. Shuddering, she picked up her skirt and ran to the back door.

♫♪ ♫♪

Soon after her father's death, Catherine's Uncle Cameron wrote to Mister Fraser, asking him to advise Mother concerning her financial position.

'Uncle Cameron believes your brother Stuart's claim upon the property may be jeopardised if I married again.'

Catherine shook her head from side to side. Preposterous, Mother would not marry again.

'I reminded Mister Fraser of the legislation, recently passed in England, that has made it possible for married women to inherit and purchase property independently of their husbands. He said, he'd heard of the new laws but informed me, the politicians are somewhat slower to pass legislation here in Tasmania.'

Catherine failed to take in detail, however, raised her brow at her mother's comment, 'My papers of promise were retrieved. Your father gave them to me at the time of our marriage. I'm also given to understand Uncle Cameron wants the Willowbank trust to be temporarily transferred to his name until young Stuart reaches the age of maturity and can take charge.'

'Who's going to do all the work?' Lucille said, her tone expressing concern.

'Uncle Cameron proposed Edward manage the property for me, thinks it wise for him to continue caring for the animals and crops.'

Catherine, thankful there were few changes in the short term following her father's death, counted her blessings as she dabbled her toes in the pond. While she missed him, it was true—God had taken care of her family just as Mother said he would.

♫♪ ♫♪

After several months, the busyness of life without Father's steady hand evidently overwhelmed her mother. She was not at all her jovial self, her sadness pervading the entire estate—unable to manage the household, the younger children were cheeky and defiant. Catherine had always assumed her mother was an adequate organiser, if not a skilled disciplinarian, but it became evident, it was her father who had directed the household routines, as well as maintaining the discipline. If only Adele could come home to help.

There had been little opportunity to visit the pump-house of late, but Catherine would go when she completed her chores. Slipping out during rest-hour, she wrote a poem in her treasure book, and while there, examined the tin. No one had touched it—things still where they usually sat. She must get back. Pulling the hut-door open, she noticed a glint near her foot and bent to retrieve a small chain. On picking it up, more of it appeared from under the step. Attached was a tiny golden locket with an engraving on the front, identical to the one on the jewellery case. Leaning against the wall, she tried to snatch the fragments, weaving through her memory. Prising the pendant opened, she found an 'A' etched in the centre.

'Oh.' The pendant could only belong to one person, 'Mother.'

She wiped the chain with her handkerchief, stood and retrieved the tin. Unfolding the paper, she examined it more thoroughly. The tiny face of the infant animated, the eyes smiling, it was hard to tell. She scooped the necklace and placed it in the envelope with the sketch.

♫♪ ♫♪

Mother yawned and complained of a sore back during the regular handicraft session. Groaning, she put her knitting down. Until then, Evelyn had not interfered, but now she put forward ways everyone could contribute to the efficient operation of the household.

'Would you mind, Arianna, if I were to put some rules in place about bedtimes?'

'Of course, you may, Evelyn. After all, it is you who deals with the little ones most often.'

Catherine rolled her eyes—Evelyn in charge was not a prospect she relished.

'I could help keep the accounts in order. I'm handy at bookwork, and I can take over the sewing classes. I'll have the girls completing their dresses in no time.'

Evelyn's enthusiasm was contagious. Encouraging Mother to propose ideas of her own, her tone spirited.

'Sarah can teach the girls to cook biscuits and cakes. They could also learn to pick and preserve fruit from the orchard, and then Thomas could sell the cooking and produce to the travellers who drove by the gate on route from Campbell Town to Perth.'

At last, the household lifted out of the doldrums. However, not a month passed before Catherine regretted Evelyn's intervention. Mother increasingly depended on her friend. The governess asserted her authority, had them assist with the milking and the making of butter and cheese, though it was unnecessary since the Jackson family had always managed those chores quite well before. Evelyn also directed Stuart to lend a hand to care for the animals under the guidance of Thomas, the governess determined they should know how the ordinary folks toiled.

♫♪ ♫♪

The work, while hard, provided a positive outcome for Catherine, in that her previously well-rounded figure became agreeably slender. Still, she seldom refused the Devonshire tea Sarah provided during the handicraft sessions. She was pleased the activity continued, though so tired from morning chores, and often fell asleep in the chair. At other times, she snatched a few minutes, curled up on her bed, browsing through the London society magazines and various newspapers Florence loaned her, daydreaming of marriage. A more comfortable life as a lady of leisure just like the genteel ladies of London featured in the gossip columns, would suit her perfectly. She could marry the son of one of the wealthy district property owners, like Harry Butler. Lucille had broken her agreement with him. He was free. However, Catherine would not forget the poor, and especially now, she had experienced something of their lot. If only she could attend the district parties with Lucille, she might meet someone.

Chapter Thirteen

Toward the end of summer, Evelyn's anxious tyranny subsided somewhat, and the Nicolson children relieved of farming duties to attend lessons. The sisters' artwork showed enormous improvement in a few months, the warm summer months providing frequent opportunities for outdoor classes. Evelyn directed her class to the grassy mound near the pump-house and just above the river. Catherine sketched the weeping willows with glimpses of the yellowing plains in the background, the paddocks dotted with Merino sheep and grazing Hereford cattle.

'Catherine, I like the way your willow branches dip into the river. Lucille, you've captured the reflection of the clouds upon the water, and your trees are in proportion to the background,' Evelyn said. Her students responded enthusiastically to the encouragement. 'We are blessed to live in such an idyllic place. I'd not be inclined to leave when Simon finishes his schooling,' Evelyn's introspection implying her restless activity over the past her months due to a fear she would have to find another position.

'Mother would not want you to go, even when your services as a governess are no longer needed.'

'Would you care, Catherine?'

'Oh, yes, Miss Evelyn.'

The governess chin dipped, she looked down her nose at Catherine, 'It's time to pack up.'

Catherine wrapped her cardigan tightly around her chest to thwart the cool breeze that had sprung up. She shook her head. What an enigmatic soul Evelyn seemed. Her governess had a soft side but maintained a rigid stance. While her mother clearly enjoyed Evelyn's company, when troubled, it was Betsy, Mother sought out.

♫♪ ♫♪

'Saint Andrews church has announced a fundraiser show for church repairs, and I have decided we're going to attend.' Mother made the pronouncement at dinner, her year of mourning complete.

'Will they have prizes for entries before they do the auction?' Lucille asked.

'I believe they just might, and if so, I could enter one or two preserves and some vegetables as well.'

'I'll help you, Mother. We'll do sauce and apricot jam,' Lucille said.

'I'll enter a hand bouquet,' Evelyn said.

'I want to enter something too.' Catherine had in mind exactly what she would make.

The excitement of a new project lent a new lease of life to the household, and the buzz of activity ensured Mother's buoyant mood. On a trip into town to place the entry forms, Catherine and her mother stopped by at the general store to purchase the necessary supplies for the family's creations. After setting aside jars, bottles, wax, and sugar, Mother selected various shades of linen.

'Look, Mother, some new Peri-lusta embroidery and crochet cotton.'

'We could also stock up on those Jevon and Mellors wool skeins.'

The storekeeper approached. 'Missus, we have got a new edition of your favourite craft magazine, full of the latest designs.'

'Excellent, we ladies of Willowbank will sew new outfits for our big day out.'

Having purchased their goods, the ladies left their parcels with Thomas and lunched at the new teahouse. Mister Patrick Callaghan entered and tipped his hat. Catherine's eyes bulged, his white hair ghastly.

'May I join you, ladies?'

'We would be delighted, Mister Callaghan,' Mother said.

Catherine, gritting her teeth, shuffled along while he placed a chair between her and Mother. The hide of the fellow. Pressing her lips tight, she glanced upward and counted the number of motifs on the ceiling. In the corner, a black spider crept along its web and snatched at a moth. Surprised by her mother's laugh, Catherine whirled around and glanced at Mister Callaghan, the pair absorbed in conversation. He was charming, Mother's lively demeanour having returned. Catherine smiled. Mister Callaghan appeared a thorough gentleman, just as Uncle Cameron had affirmed repeatedly on his return from Sydney.

After paying the bill, he took Mother's arm and walked them toward their carriage, and slowing his pace, he waved Catherine along. He leant close to her mother and exchanged a few words before bidding her farewell, once again tipping his hat. Still, Catherine would reserve her judgement. There was something reckless in his manner.

♫♪ ♫♪

The women of the household were ecstatic when they examined the booty and applied their skills, their outfits soon completed and display entries well underway. Sarah helped Mother and her team prepare raspberry and crab apple sauce for the preserve display.

Catherine leant on the bench watching the proceedings. 'Let me help. I'll put the sugar in.'

'Be careful. You have to put in just the right quantity, isn't that right, Sarah?'

'It is, Missus Nicolson. Lucille has completed her sauce, and it's quite delicious,' Sarah said, 'How's your entry coming, Catherine?'

'I'm happy with it. I've sketched a picture of how I want it to look. Evelyn gave me some help to make improvements.'

'So, can I guess what it is?'

'Not yet, Sarah.'

'Evelyn said she was going to enter a flower design,' Mother said.

'She's going to raid your flower garden, the bulbs ready just in time, but the daffodils should look wonderful,' Catherine said.

♬♪ ♬♪

Edward and Thomas drove the Nicolson householders to the village on the day of the fete, St. Andrews a hive of activity. A hansom, various drays, and curricles parked on the kerb, and Catherine observed the Fraser, Carrick, and Butler families were all in attendance, their names imprinted on their respective modes of transport. Catherine put her finger to her cheek. The Fraser insignia, the same emblem as on the jewellery box, but the name not emblazoned on their everyday vehicle?

A ruckus caught her attention, and she spied Andrew Fraser and John Carrick. They were among a gathering of young people and had not noticed the Nicolson carriage arrive. She wandered toward the group, passing by several stalls to greet familiar friends on the way, stopping short on hearing her mother's name mentioned by John Carrick.

'You'd think the poor woman would have thought of that.'

The group collapsed in laughter. What might the content of that discussion entail? She would not speak with John or Andrew Fraser—they were beyond regard—and went in search of her mother.

'I'm keen to see how our entries compared,' Mother headed for the produce table with her entire party in tow. 'Look, I won second prize for my vegetable display.'

Missus Herbert had won the preserving prize and stood at the table rocking her baby carriage back and forth.

'Congratulations, Sybil,' Mother said.

'Indeed, also to you, my dear.'

Mother inspected her daughters' entries. Lucille had come third in the jam competition, and a ribbon and printed certificate announced Lucille's sauce had won first prize in its division.

'The consistency must have impressed the judges,' Mother said.

'Well done, Lucille.' Celeste clapped her hands and moved along to the floral display. 'Look, Miss Evelyn, you've won the hand bouquet competition.'

'I wonder where my entry is.' Catherine began to search.

'Over here, Catherine, see it received a highly commended … was surpassed by one other entry,' Lucille said.

A slight girl, dressed in a turquoise pinafore, giggled in front of the arrangement as Catherine approached.

'Is this your display?' she asked.

'Yes, it is,' Catherine replied, crestfallen by the young woman's chuckle.

'It's unique. I like it a lot.'

'Oh, you do?'

'It is rather special, Catherine,' Evelyn added, examining Catherine's entry, a table bouquet set in a cracked porcelain milk jug.

'But not everyone appreciates the beauty of the rustic form,' the other girl said.

Catherine saw the name on the winning arrangement and read aloud, 'Harriet Chapman. Is that one yours?'

'Yes, it represents a fountain,' Harriet said.

'Congratulations, an amazing display.' Catherine smiled, 'A clever design. Who taught you?'

'Miss Sterrit, my governess. She trained at Girton in Cambridge, last year. She has some interesting ideas.'

Harriet introduced her English friend. 'Please meet Miss Elena Sterrit.'

'How do you do, I'm Catherine Nicolson, and this is my governess, Miss Evelyn White,' Catherine nodded toward Evelyn and smiled.

Miss Sterrit linked her arm through Evelyn's, guided her to the benches and offered her a seat. Catherine, Louisa, and Harriet trotted after Evelyn to join the ladies. Stuart ran in, knocking into Catherine and slid toward Evelyn's seat.

'Stuart Nicolson, mind your manners.'

'I want, Mother. I need to go, quick.'

Mother, on hearing, grabbed his hand and dragged him to the door.

Harriet laughed. 'I remember him, that hilarious incident at the show years ago, the bull chasing the boy at Evandale.'

Catherine giggled, and Celeste joined in, 'Oh, yes, that's Stuart. It was funny.'

Catherine raised her brows—her little sister was growing up.

Lucille wandered over, and Mother returned, suggesting they might all go to the refreshment corner for tea and sandwiches.

'I'll be along shortly, Mother,' Lucille said and skipped from the hall.

'That's my sister, Lucille. Mother hoped she might meet your brother.'

Harriet frowned. 'My brother's moved to England, and I don't expect he'll return.'

Catherine linked her arms with Celeste on one side, Harriet on the other, and found a table where they could continue their conversation.

Harry Butler, plate in hand, sidled up to Harriet and said, 'Mind if I join the party?'

♫♪ ♫♪

The horses clipped along at a steady pace along the smooth, gravel road.

'All in all, a wonderful day, Arianna,' Evelyn said.

'Yes, it's been so long since we left the estate for anything as exhilarating,' Mother said.

'I had a stupendous time.'

'Now, Lucille, whatever happened to make you so chipper?' Mother asked.

'I was a guest of two of the most gentlemanly young men in the garden. They bought me cakes and cordial,' Lucille said, looking at Catherine.

'And who might they be?'

'Andrew and John, Mother.' Lucille giggled and smacked her lips together.

'Are you certain it was cordial the boys gave you? You do seem rather more excitable than usual.'

'Mother, I would never touch liquor.'

'Not knowingly, perhaps.'

'Where exemplary behaviour is concerned, those two leave a lot to be desired,' Evelyn said.

Mother knitted her brow. 'What have you heard of them, Evelyn?'

'It seems the local sergeant warned them about brawling at the Carriers Arms. I overheard Missus Beaumont at the craft table. She spun quite a story. I'm surprised though, as I've always found Andrew Fraser polite.'

'Gossip, all gossip, Evelyn. I do hope the Carrick lad is not a poor influence upon Andrew. It would disappoint his father,' Mother said.

Catherine weighed the exchange and bit her tongue. She would not forget the feeling of being ostracised by the popular set. That Mother assumed Andrew Fraser innocent, farcical. Catherine's lip quivered. Even Harry Butler had ignored her, and gave Harriet the new girl, undivided attention.

♫♪ ♫♪

Anxious to divulge her thoughts to her compendium, Catherine slipped behind the hedge, swung around the corner to the path and bumped into Betsy.

'Whoa, missy, you're in a bit of a hurry.'

'Betsy, I didn't expect to see you along here today.'

'And neither should have I expected you after our last meeting.'

Catherine frowned.

'Hey miss, your eyes are very puffy. Have you been crying?'

'Stupid boys, I hate them.'

'Come back to the house with me, and I'll make you a salve.'

Since she could not object, Catherine turned and followed Betsy and lay on her bed, a great wad of cloth covering her eyes. She would prove to her wealthy friends her family was more than capable of success in the face of adversity.

One day melded to another. Scorching summer winds rolled tumbleweeds across the plain. Autumn painted snow-like frosts, and winter lashed the fields with pounding rains. At last, the warm spring breeze drifted through windows flung wide, bearing the perfume of orchard blossoms and hope for better days.

However, each season was busier than the one before. Having

learned every task necessary to ensure Willowbank Estate thrived, Catherine's hands were often raw and bleeding after a day in the garden. Refusing to complain, she relieved her pain with a concoction of wool-wax recommended by Betsy. When would the drudgery ever end?

Her need for solace became desperate. She wanted to escape to the pump-house, add to her text and look at the drawing again. Having woken in a lather of perspiration following a dream of the drawing of a child's face, she wanted to confirm her suspicion, but on arriving at the out-building, she discovered a huge padlock affixed to the door. Perched on the seat beside the pond, she twisted the key to her compendium in her fingers, put it in her pocket, dropped her head into her hands and sobbed.

Chapter Fourteen

Catherine folded into her window seat and lazed in the sun, her shoulders aching from lifting bales of barley onto the dray. She and Stuart had helped the Jacksons with the harvest. One of her cousin Florence's fashion magazines lay opened in her lap. Glancing across the river toward Myrtleford, her mood brightened at the prospect of a possible reprieve from her never-ending chores at the invitation of Grandma Kate to visit along with her cousin. She would love a holiday, but how could she ask when Lucille had left home to nanny for the Butler family, and the bulk of her work would fall to Celeste and Louisa? Catherine twisted a lock of her hair.

Her mother's cheery laugh echoed up the stairs, and Catherine scooted into the hallway ignoring the urge to reconsider her action. 'Mother, I know it would be awkward for you and the girls, but do you suppose I could accept Grandma Kate's invitation?'

'Indeed, you may. You are sixteen now, and you've worked tirelessly of late. It's time you had some enjoyment.'

Mother assured her they would manage, and said she was pleased for Catherine to spend time with Florence at Grandma Kate's home during the summer break. The visit to Grandma's would be Florence's last before her family returned to England. Catherine could hardly believe it was three years since her cousin came home to Tasmania.

Florence arrived in the Myrtleford brougham to collect Catherine and her trunk. Catherine had stuffed it with pretty summer dresses, stitched while huddled near the fire with the other women of the household during the long winter evenings.

'Hello, Florence, I can't tell you how much I'm looking forward to this short stay. There's always too much to do around here,' Catherine said, accepting Charlie, the coach driver's hand.

He hoisted her into the vehicle and gathered up the reins. He had folded the carriage hood down. Catherine was content—she would enjoy the different surroundings.

Catherine breathed in. 'Nice perfume, Florence.'

'Paris, of course, Pommade Virginale,' Florence said, adjusting the travelling blanket to throw a corner over Catherine's lap. 'It's been wonderful to be back, so good to escape the English winter, and today is such a clear day. You can see for miles across the plains.'

'Indeed, as far as the Tiers.' Catherine pointed with her chin, and as the carriage rode over the brow of the hill, she distinguished the various browns of the escarpment of the jagged rock, highlighted in the sunshine. 'It's an amazing view, like a John Glover painted-landscape.'

'Undoubtedly beautiful,' Florence said.

Catherine sat up and gazed about, savouring the excursion, the rhythmic clop of the horses' hooves striking the dusty gravel road exciting her imagination. Once again, she was a debutante on her way to a grand social occasion.

The clanging of tools disturbed the tranquil scene—a noisy gang repairing the road. Dust kicked up from a horse-drawn cart, and the strong smell of sweat reached their nostrils.

'What a revolting stench,' Florence covered her nose with her linen handkerchief.

Catherine took a quick look at the sweaty, but well-defined, tanned bodies of the men as they bent over their tools. She winced. How beggarly, having to work all day in the sun. The men downed tools and gawked at the girls. Catherine turned her head away, but the men whistled loutishly as the carriage rolled along. She did not look back.

Shortly afterwards, they passed by Fraser's Braeside Estate. Catherine had visited the property once or twice with her father. She looked across to the rolling hills peppered by myriads of sheep, heads down, chomping on the lush, green grass. Andrew Fraser stood to inherit a grand property. As they neared the driveway to the main house, she peeked through the hedge.

'That's an impressive garden, so big one could get lost in it. Look at the magnificent floral display.'

'It's just like an English garden. You'd love our park, Catherine, the one in Stratford.'

Catherine acquiesced. Florence would always refer to a bigger or better whatever, no matter the subject.

'I understand Grandma and Aunt Rowena often call upon Missus Fraser. She gave them several damask-rose cuttings like the ones Mister Fraser brings to Mother,' Catherine said.

'I wonder if we'll get an invitation to visit them this fortnight.'

'Interested in Andrew, Florence?'

'No. Not at all.'

The driver eased the horses to a trot on the verge of Perth township and steered the carriage into Punt Road and around the corner into William Street.

'Whoa!' Charlie brought the carriage to a standstill at Grandma's house.

'Here at last.' Florence heaved a sigh.

As though it was her first visit, Catherine saw the house in a different light. She supposed now she was older, homes were of more interest, the residence perched on a sloping block providing a panoramic view of the South Esk River. The modest Georgian-styled, rubble-stone rendered building showed off French doors and had an impressive fanlight window at the entrance.

'Looks like some folks might be camping down by the river,' Florence said, standing to see over the low brush across the street.

'Probably the road gang we passed.'

Alighting, they walked under the giant magnolia tree gracing the centre of Grandma Kate's front garden, dwarfing all else.

A couple of spinebills chirped a happy song, and Florence pointed to the low branch of a bottlebrush. 'There they are, and a nest too.'

Catherine raised her eyes, drawn beyond the tree to the roses planted along the bluestone fence.

She gestured. 'What a splendid display? Most likely the damask-roses from Missus Fraser.'

Catherine stretched her back, her muscles already responding to the restful surroundings. She intended to explore the rest of the garden at her earliest opportunity.

Grandma Kate's maid greeted the girls and led them into the house. Catherine perched on a stool and unbuttoned her boots, dropping them with a thud onto the Baltic pine flooring. She glanced at the simple furnishings, the cedar panelling in the hallway and the taffeta silk drapes engendering a sense of opulence. However, it was not the trappings Catherine remembered most from having visited her Grandma, but the warmth of her hospitality.

'You'll be sleeping in the guest chamber, the room between your Grandma's and Miss Rowena's. I'll have your luggage brought in.'

'Much obliged,' Catherine said.

Florence traced her fingers along the four-poster bed in the guest room, covered in an exquisite white-lace quilt and decorated with mauve coloured pillows. 'Pretty,' she said.

Catherine flopped onto the bed, the folds of the quilt swallowing her up. 'And soft, filled with feather down.'

'I hope you don't snore, Catherine.'

Catherine swung her legs onto the floor, moved toward the window and touched the basket of fragrant violets upon the duchess cabinet under the windowsill.

She drew in a deep breath. 'Very nice indeed.'

Florence plonked onto the dusty-pink brocade chaise looking into the full-length mirror standing in the opposite corner. 'I look a little worse for wear. It's been a long day,' she said.

Catherine and Florence unpacked their trunks, hung their dresses in the robe and returned to the hallway. Catherine picked up one of her embroidered cloths from the console. Undoubtedly Grandma placed it there to encourage her.

'Welcome, dear ones,' Grandma greeted the girls, Catherine delighting in her grandmother's embrace. 'It is so good to have you here with me. I have arranged for your favourite, Catherine, Devonshire tea.'

'Oh, that is so sweet, Grandma,' Catherine smiled at her grandmother's remembrance of her partiality to cream.

Aunt Rowena emerged from the parlour and beckoned. 'Tea is in the sunroom.'

Catherine and Florence, keen to catch up on all the news of the district, asked the older women countless questions about family friends.

'Do you have news of the Fraser family?' Florence said.

'You'll be meeting them at Glenlyn. Mister and Missus Hanson have extended us all an invitation to a dinner party next Saturday evening. Mister Hanson rebuilt Glenlyn since the former house burned down.'

Grandma Kate had informed Catherine's family about the fire on one of her stopovers.

'I can't wait until you see it,' continued Rowena. 'It's a huge Mediterranean villa overlooking the river, decorated with fine cast-iron lace and it has the most beautiful terrazzo floors.'

Grandma Kate rose from her special chair. 'However, in the meantime, we have work to do.' She trotted to the kitchen and lifted the lid on pot upon the stove. 'Helen, have you added the sauces?'

'Yes, Missus Nicolson, the meal is ready to send around to the Murphy house.'

'Please ask the driver to take this too.' Even at eighty years of age, Grandma Kate continued her charity mission.

'No, ma'am, no,' Helen said as Grandma dropped a silver coin into an envelope.

'Now, girls, tomorrow being the Lord's Day, we will attend the service at Christ Church in Longford. At two o'clock in the afternoon, Rowena and I have some of the poorer children from town attend our Sunday school class here in the sunroom.'

Florence frowned. 'You mean the ordinary folk?'

'Yes, Florence, and we feed them before they leave. We would very much appreciate it if you would assist us. Since the downturn, many men have lost their employment and find it difficult to provide for their families.'

Florence dropped her eyes.

Before taking to their bed, the girls chose the outfits they planned to wear to the Sunday morning service. Catherine's soft pink dress with its overskirt was less colourful than Florence sky-blue outfit. Catherine studied the design of the cuirassed bodice drawing the eye to a bunched bustle and smirked. Florence hardly needed any extra padding in that region.

'Purchased at Bainbridge's in London,' Florence said.

The following morning, the congregation was out in force, and despite the concern articulated by Grandma about the declining economy worldwide, Christ Church pavement was a parade of high fashion. Aunt Rowena introduced her nieces to the young women from the district before they made their way to Grandma Kate's pew.

The pipe organ, accompanying the choir, lent power to the first song as it reverberated throughout the building. Catherine thrilled to lift her voice with such a throng, reassured in the uncertain times her family faced by the message of God's promise to provide. The service might have set the tone for the conversations that followed, but any consideration of comment vanished when Catherine noticed Harriet Chapman among the parishioners.

'This is a welcome surprise, Catherine. Have you completed any further fabulous floral arrangements?'

The friends exchanged stories of the intervening years since they had met at the church bazaar, Catherine relating how much life at Willowbank had changed.

Harriet expressed her initial angst about the recent passing of her mother. 'But I'm happier now, because Miss Sterrit, my governess, is going to be married to my father very soon.'

Catherine nodded and smiled, but she would consider it a betrayal if her mother remarried.

'I'm preparing to move to England to join my brother. I am enrolling at the university in Cambridge and am boarding with Miss Sterrit's parents.'

'What a fine prospect … you will return though?'

'It depends on whether I obtain a position here in Tasmania when I've completed my studies. There are very few lady teachers employed in schools in the colony.'

'Harriet, we're waiting for you,' Miss Sterrit approached.

'It's been pleasant to have met you again, Harriet. God's speed.'

'And you too, Catherine. Goodbye.'

Catherine bustled toward Grandma's conveyance.

'We've been waiting for several minutes, Catherine,' Florence huffed.

'It's been a stimulating outing.' Catherine laughed.

'Like a creature returned to the wild.'

Catherine pirouetted, her shoe making a small circle in the fine gravel, she had no argument with Florence's summation. Seldom had she the privilege of attending regular Sunday services with such a crowd. Catherine stepped up and settled into the seat beside her cousin.

Chapter Fifteen

Catherine climbed the stairs to the front door of Grandma's house and turned to take in the view of the Narrows on the bend of the river. The campers frolicked on the riverbank. Taking it in turns, they swung from a rope attached to a willow branch and splashed into the deep water. They looked to be having terrific fun.

'Members of the road gang.' Aunt Rowena nodded in their direction. 'They have camped down there for weeks.'

Catherine strained to see. Was it the same team she and Florence passed the day before? There was no time to linger because, following a quick lunch, they needed to prepare the sunroom for the Sunday-school class.

The children of the town assembled, some sitting on the squat chairs Rowena had lined up along the wall, and others on the rug. Catherine gagged, the smell of sweaty bodies potent. Moving toward the door, she took a deep breath.

Grandma Kate began the lesson. 'Today we are going to learn about a great flood that covered the whole earth.'

'Hurrah!' Noah's Ark was apparently a favourite story.

'I saw a flood, a long time ago here in Perth. It damaged the bridge and washed away many sheep and cattle. The water came right up to my front fence, and that was in 1841.'

Grandma Kate's knowledge of local history prompted her young pupils, and they contributed their own stories.

'My grandpa told me someone drowned in the river,' one of the pupils said.

'Yes, that is unfortunately true. Now, let's pay attention to Aunt Rowena.'

Catherine joined the class, squatting on a tiny wooden footstool.

Rowena re-pinned a stray strand of hair and opened her Bible. 'God called Noah to build an ark,' she said.

The children listened intently as Rowena related the story of God's provision of salvation for Noah and his family and their need to get aboard the ark.

Reaching over to the table, she retrieved the craft activity prepared for the children. 'Children, Catherine and Florence will help you to draw an ark and paste pairs of your favourite animals.'

'Me want some giraffes.'

'I want lions and elephants.'

Others chose horses, cows, and dogs, and while the children worked, the maid prepared an afternoon tea of sandwiches, cupcakes, and raspberry cordial, setting the spread on the sunroom table.

'Yum! I love coming here!' exclaimed a little boy.

'Hush!' whispered an older girl. 'They'll know we only come for the food.'

Catherine smiled, warming to the children of the ordinary folk.

♫♪ ♫♪

As the children left through the side gate, a loud ruckus sounded at the front entrance.

'Missus Nicolson, the lags have come asking for food. They heard they could get a feed of good tucker if they stopped by the Nicolson's house.'

'Invite them in, Helen. We'll serve them sandwiches and cake.'

Helen, along with Rowena, Catherine and Florence, prepared the light meal while Grandma Kate conversed with the young men.

'Mother is as happy as a pig in mud in this situation.' Aunt Rowena laughed.

Catherine carried in a jug of cordial and placed it on the sideboard, the maid following with a tray of glasses. Catherine beckoned Florence, but she ducked behind the kitchen door.

Grandma did not waste the opportunity to share the gospel message, and the young men sat, squirming, obviously regretting their decision to invade the Nicolson's afternoon tea. Their supervisor leant against the wall, his deep blue eyes following Catherine's every move. He was a well-built young man, about twenty, with black wavy hair. She had a vague idea she might have seen him elsewhere. As she held the tray of sandwiches out for him, their eyes met briefly, and he politely lowered his gaze. Catherine had not seen a man so attractive for a long time. Why did he seem familiar? She retreated to the kitchen, her face feeling flushed, wanting to talk with Florence, but Florence had run away.

Picking up a platter of cakes, Catherine returned, but before she took two steps one of the younger gang members snatched a cake from the plate.

The handsome one stood. 'Hey, Fatty, where's them manners.'

'Sorry, miss,' the lad said.

The men guffawed. The lad they called fatty was as thin as a willow switch.

'Fatty gobbles sweets like a honey-eating wattlebird.' Blue eyes twinkled.

Catherine served until the gang ate their fill and made a move to leave.

The supervisor nodded to Grandma Kate. 'Thanks for grub, Missus Nicolson,' his deep voice resonating in the confined space.

'Yeah, thanks missus,' chorused the others, and scooting out they sprinted along William Street in the direction of their camp.

Catherine stood at the front window peeking through the lace curtaining, the supervisor wrenching his cap onto his head and following his mates.

'Oh,' Catherine gasped, and he glanced back. 'That's Thomas and Sarah's friend, the youth with the black hair.' Catherine sunk into the cushioned settee to daydream, the events of the day awakening a particular desire.

She retired early for the night, almost too tired to undress. While brushing her hair, the smiling eyes reflected in the mirror expressed elation.

♫♪ ♫♪

The farmers and their wives came to town to do their banking and shopping on Fridays, and Rowena offered to chaperone the cousins to mingle with the crowds. Catherine bounced from the bed and hassled Florence to hurry. She leant on the banister, babbled incessantly and jiggled from one foot to the other until they set out. The first stop, the haberdashery store, excited Catherine further. While Rowena purchased wool and needles, Catherine perused the bolts of cloth, flipped through the pattern books on the counter and had her selections wrapped. She hoped the gift for her mother might cheer her some after the burdensome affairs of late. Catherine's heart was full—still glad for the respite at her grandmother's home—as they skirted Victoria Park and strolled along the riverbank. She looked toward the Narrows. The campsite was vacant. Her eyebrows knitting, she shrugged—better to remain prudent.

The toasty sunroom was the perfect spot for the ladies to pursue their task of making blankets for the poor. Florence reneged and curled up on the window seat to read magazines. Grandma and Aunt Rowena knitted coloured squares, and Catherine sewed the pieces together.

Catherine displayed a finished article. 'This should keep one little-one warm,' she said, calling to mind the children from Sunday's class.

Florence yawned and slipped behind Grandma's chair, putting her arms about the old lady's neck, and announced, 'I love you, Grandma. When we leave this time, we are going to England for good. Father's handing Myrtleford over to Alfred.'

Catherine's mouth gaped, and Rowena raised her brow.

'I knew this would happen eventually, for your father's merchant business has expanded rapidly,' Grandma said, setting her knitting aside.

'I'll miss you all terribly,' Florence said. 'It's a clear night, so let's climb the stairs to the observatory,' and gazing at the starry sky, she sighed, 'this may be the last time I see the southern skies like this.'

While the timing was unexpected, it was inevitable Catherine's eldest boy cousin would inherit the grand old place. It seemed Florence expected to make England her permanent home. Catherine would grieve the loss of her cousin's company.

♫♪ ♫♪

The embellished statues were silent observers as Catherine perched under the Laurel tree, reflecting by the pond, pencil and paper in hand. Inspired by watching the goldfish dart here and there and popping up to the surface to nibble insects, she wrote a poem. She enjoyed her moments alone in Grandma's garden and felt safe enclosed by sculptured hedges. The holiday was all she hoped it might be, and she dreaded having to return to the drudgery at home.

It was the eve of the Glenlyn party. Florence had talked of little else all week. She giggled as she donned her finery, a royal blue cloak, complete with a train enhancing her soft blue satin gown. Swooping her blond hair up, she held it in place with a jewelled clip matching her choker and earrings. Blue lace gloves and shoes completed the ensemble.

'You look stunning, Florence,' Catherine said.

Looking in the mirror with an approving glance, Catherine satisfied her gown suited her slender figure. The simple organza gown was ivory coloured with pink rosettes sewn into the shirring bodice and sported a ruffled skirt. She placed a band in her hair, clasped a string of pearls about her neck, and put on ivory gloves.

'I'm looking forward to meeting some old friends and new acquaintances.'

'The old crowd will hardly remember us, Catherine. We've both matured considerably.'

Sharply at five o'clock, the landau appeared in the driveway and, within a few minutes, pulled into the Glenlyn courtyard. The mansion was every bit as impressive as Rowena had described, and much bigger than Catherine imagined.

As soon as the butler announced Catherine and Florence, Andrew Fraser approached and took Florence's hand. Catherine grimaced, abandoned and relegated to spending the evening with Aunt Rowena. Grandma had remained at home.

'Enjoy yourselves,' Catherine said through gritted teeth.

She looked around at the over-embellished house with its painted ceilings, parquetry flooring, marble mantle, stained-glass windows, and gas light fittings. Her inquisitiveness got the better of her. She excused herself with the pretence of needing the restroom and found it at the bottom of the main stairwell. It was no less decorative than the hallway with its engraved glass panel in the door and hand-painted frieze above the hand basin.

On leaving the bathroom, Catherine noticed a second, smaller flight of stairs. She looked around to see if anyone was close by, and since no one was within sight climbed up to the tower. From her vantage point, she could see the extensive English-style garden, the flowerbeds containing all manner of species. Three magnificent trees adorned the central lawn, a giant oak, a weeping elm, and a birch. Beyond the garden, the river wound its way north.

Lost in reverie, she allowed her overactive imagination to have full sway. How many ordinary folk could she help if she were mistress of such an estate? She would establish a school. After all, education was the means of producing the ideal citizen. She could solicit funds if she could convince the well-to-do her ideas were valid, invite all manner of squires to her garden. They would assist her.

In her mind's eye, she entertained a renowned bachelor, her sponsor fit and tanned with dark, wavy hair and the bluest eyes.

She batted her eyelids. 'You will help me in my endeavour, won't you?' She twirled around and curtsied. 'How do you ...'

Encircled by strong arms, she froze, the air reeking of—he breathed into her hair. 'The pleasure would be mine, Miss Nicolson.'

She pushed him, but he grabbed her and pressed his body to hers, kissing her neck—the smell of rum revolting.

Lifting her knee, she scored. Yelping like a wild dog her accoster staggered back.

'John Carrick, you rake!' She bounded down the stairs.

All was quiet, the doors to the dining room closed. She dashed into the powder room. Her skin crawled, his scent lingered. How dare he? She folded her arms across her chest and squeezed. She felt dirty, molested. Splashing water over her face, she looked in the glass, her face blotchy red.

♫♪ ♫♪

She had missed the call to dinner, but she must get to her place without drawing attention. Poking her head around the door, she spotted a maid. The girl nodded, Catherine's face revealing her dilemma. She beckoned Catherine and led her unobtrusively to her place at the table.

'Many thanks, miss.' Catherine kept her voice low.

'Where have you been?' Aunt Rowena's chiding was unnecessary.

Catherine looked about and whispered, 'I climbed up to the tower. You should see the view of the garden.'

'Catherine, you must know it is impolite to go wandering uninvited through other people's private quarters. Do you want to disgrace our family?'

Thoroughly chastised, Catherine looked down, her face flushing. She most definitely would remain at Rowena's side for the remainder of the evening.

Fanning herself, she said, 'It's stuffy in here.'

Aunt Rowena frowned. Catherine was relieved when the servants appeared with the dinner trays, and she would avoid further scolding.

Fresh beef and Yorkshire pudding delighted the guests opposite if their compliments were any indication. Catherine smiled and nodded. John Carrick had not reappeared, and though her stomach churned, she did not knock back the compote of fresh strawberries and cream.

She leant close to her Aunt Rowena's ear. 'These strawberries are delicious. Certainly, my favourite.'

'Undoubtedly, from Fraser's garden.'

♫♪ ♫♪

The guests withdrew to a concert hall where a young woman treated the guests to an operatic soprano, and another gave a piano recital.

'Miss Catherine Nicolson will now recite her new poem,' the compere said.

Catherine's eyes opened wide, and she swung around meeting Aunt Rowena's gaze. Her aunt smiled and nodded. Catherine ought to have felt flattered her aunt approached the hostess to make the request. She must comply—could not embarrass Aunt Rowena. Shivering, Catherine stood, wobbling like a new-born calf—her legs might buckle beneath her. Her heart thumping and her skin clammy, she wanted to vomit. Gulping several deep breaths, she gripped the lectern.

'HOME ...
Home is where the heart dwells in peace and harmony.'
Her shaky voice frightened her. She sucked-in a great draft of air.
'We daily move beyond its walls,
To work, and learn and play.'
As she continued, her delivery became stronger.
'While forever deep within our soul,
We know we can retreat,
To rest, restore and be made whole,
Regain our strength, and dear ones meet.'

The resounding applause almost caused her to faint, but remaining composed, she sat down quickly next to Rowena, who enthused, 'Catherine, your poem was lovely.'

Florence and Andrew approached, 'Well done! I didn't know you wrote poetry,' Florence said.

Andrew gave a mock bow. He had spent the entire night wooing Florence, and Florence had flirted with him. They had tittered all through dinner. Catherine screwed up her nose—her cousin said she did not intend to form a long-term relationship since she hoped to meet a suitable young man in England and settle there. Sheep-headed Andrew was oblivious.

Catherine, relieved when the evening concluded, on reaching home, bid a hasty goodnight and retired to her room. She snatched a towel, dipped it in the water-bowl and scrubbed her body, desperate to cleanse John Carrick from her soul. She would not place herself in such a dangerous situation again.

Florence clopped up the stairs. Catherine dived under the covers and pretended to be asleep, in no mood to listen to Florence.

Chapter Sixteen

Early on Monday, Andrew Fraser came visiting with a groomsman and invited Florence to ride their stud horses at Braeside. Catherine was peeved, Florence did not ask her to join them, and stomped downstairs. She came to Grandma's to spend time with Florence, and her cousin had abandoned her. Reclining in the sunroom, her handicraft lying in her lap, she stabbed the needle into the pincushion, having no interest in embroidering the next flower.

She glanced at the sideboard, the loud tick-ticking of the sideboard clock irritating. Watching the hands go around, she huffed—they took ages, hardly moved. Rearranging her cushions and tucking her legs up underneath her, she grumped. Why should she care if her cousin permanently moved to England, the miss was so high and mighty nowadays?

Aunt Rowena padded up the hallway. 'I need to purchase some leatherwood honey from the general store.'

Catherine sprang to her feet. 'I'll come.'

'I want to collect a parcel. A telegram arrived from Adele last week to say some items completed by her craft group were in the mail. Adele sends the goods for Grandma to distribute to the ordinary folk. Let's walk via Victoria Square. It's a pleasant circuit.'

Catherine snatched her hat off the upstairs hallstand and caught up to Rowena who had set off at a rapid pace.

'There's a train due in at ten o'clock, on its way to Evandale Junction from Deloraine,' Rowena said.

♫♪ ♫♪

The engine shunted to a standstill, the passengers jostling their way into the railway station dining room, apparently ready for refreshments. The animated discussion about their journey caused Catherine to giggle—the sound like a company of parrots.

'This is the second stop since I boarded.'

'What about those fresh mutton sandwiches? Delicious with chutney, eh.'

'First-rate, even better than those at The Corners Station.'

Their conversation jogged Catherine's memory. She heard a guest at Saturday night's dinner discussing her January holiday, her intention to travel from Perth to Hobart Town by rail. On seeing the train, she agreed a trip was a jolly plan.

'Can we wait until the passengers depart?'

Not wanting to miss the amusement, Catherine plonked down on a bench and eyed a young woman who arrived at the ticket office carrying a large cloth bag. She watched the girl as she made her purchase and moved toward Catherine's seat. Catherine's eyes grew wide, realizing it was the Glenlyn maid who had rescued her on Saturday evening.

Shuffling along closer to the girl, she whispered. 'I can't thank you enough for getting me out of a pickle Saturday night.'

The lass smiled, her broken teeth catching Catherine unaware.

Re-gathering her poise, Catherine said, 'My name is—'

'Yeah, I know who you is. Me brother Edwin, he told me he saw you Sunday week ago at Missus Nicolson's place. He's taken a shine to you. I'm his sister, Mary Nelson.'

'Oh!' Catherine fanned her face.

'I'm travelling as far as the Corners junction, and then I'll catch a coach to Fingal where me family live,' Mary said.

'Fingal, but I've seen your brother a few times before. His friends,

Thomas and Sarah, are our workers.'

'They're cousins. Edwin sees them more than me, was closer, because he lived for a bit with relations in Campbell Town.'

Rowena coughed a hint, Catherine's interaction was unpalatable, too familiar. Catherine frowned, ignoring the caution.

'Well, goodbye, and may God go with you.' Catherine squeezed Mary's hand.

The stationmaster ambled onto the platform and blew his whistle.

'There's me signal to git aboard.'

Embers and soot belched from the train's chimney as it chugged away from the station.

'That thing must gobble up a mountain of coal, think of all the poor folks, dozens would use but a fraction to keep their fires alight,' Rowena said.

Catherine heard but did not respond—she smiled. Mary said Thomas and Sarah were cousins.

♫♪ ♫♪

Florence stood at the entrance to Grandma's house on Catherine's return, her agitation far from subtle.

'Catherine, I'd like to return home tomorrow if it is all the same to you.'

'Why? What's troubling you, Florence?'

Rowena reached out to comfort Florence, but she stepped away and said, 'Please, Aunt Rowena … I really don't wish to discuss it.' Turning, she dashed up the stairs.

Catherine did not follow, and Florence remained in her room for the rest of the day.

Leave, they did. On the return journey to Willowbank, Florence told Catherine, Andrew had asked her to marry him.

'You should have seen his face when I told him I was leaving Tasmania forever. I almost laughed, but the poor fellow looked completely bewildered.'

'Well, you did nothing but flirt with him all night on Saturday, Florence. What was he supposed to think?'

Florence groaned. 'I didn't think it would hurt to have a little fun.'

'I hope you've learned a lesson. You were cruel.'

'To think the Season opens in a matter of months too.'

Catherine tossed her head back. Florence was incorrigible.

'I'll be introduced to the best of society at a debutante ball in London. Mother's friend will be my sponsor, and I expect to meet many eligible partners.'

The cousins fell silent until the carriage came upon the road-gang they had entertained on Sunday.

'Good day, lasses,' a young man called and whistled before another gang member clouted him around the ear.

Catherine locked eyes with Edwin Nelson in an extended gaze. Florence huffed and turned her head away. Edwin's eyes followed Catherine until the carriage had pulled along the road some distance.

'Who was that?' Catherine winced, Florence's tone was insolent.

'His name is Edwin Nelson. I met his sister at Glenlyn, and they're from Fingal.'

'He's sure to be a government man then, so you keep your distance. You can do better, Catherine Nicolson. There are many pastoralists' sons who would love you to be their wife.'

'I'll be careful.' Catherine meant every word.

They turned into Willowbank driveway, and as they said their goodbyes, Florence gave Catherine a parcel.

'We'll be returning to England soon, and I want you to have the gown and accessories I wore to the Glenlyn dinner.'

'Oh, Florence, that's so kind, thank you, I love the gown.' Catherine leant over, hugged her cousin farewell, waved until the carriage disappeared around the corner of the house and hurried toward the front steps. 'Ah. It's good to be home.'

A whistle pierced the quadrangle. Brother Stuart strode from the stables and placed his hands on his hips.

'It's about time you got back to Willowbank and did your share of the work,' he spat. 'I've worked like a POM ever since you left.'

'Mother assured me you would all manage while I was gone. Anyway, I'm back almost a week earlier than planned.'

'I have news … Callaghan's here again. He's seeing Mother.'

'Ah, ha, so my sassy friend is back,' a male voice rang out across the quadrangle.

'Oh!' Catherine spun around.

Patrick Callaghan stepped into the doorway, his lip curling. 'It's a pleasure to meet you again, Miss Catherine. I'm sure we'll get on just fine.'

Catherine, aware her mother had bumped into Patrick Callaghan in town from time to time, was surprised he would make a special visit to Willowbank. Why should she need to get along?

Her mother appeared and cuddled up to him. Catherine frowned and took a step back.

'Welcome home, look whom we have here,' Mother said, looking up at Mister Callaghan.

Patrick Callaghan's intentions were clear. Catherine discovered the man, whom she had met on but a few occasions, had called by to propose marriage to her mother. Mother had accepted, believing she would have someone to care for her and her large family.

Catherine could hardly imagine what her mother saw to like about the fellow. Indeed, he appeared cultivated and fit of body, but his skin was as white as death. His light blue, beady eyes and shock of white hair repulsed her. She remembered her first encounter at Uncle Cameron's home, and another at the Evandale General Store where she had stared in horror until Mother tapped her on the arm and tutted.

Catherine feigned an excuse to leave and find Evelyn.

'Miss Evelyn, what do you know about the man mother is about to marry?'

'Edward informed me, Mister Callaghan is a recent widower and the father of two daughters. He owns a sheep property near Avoca. Mister Callaghan considers it advantageous to control Willowbank—the estate well positioned for some enterprise in which he's involved. It seems he's aware Stuart is the legal heir but says his business will be completed before your brother is old enough to take over the property.'

Catherine wanted to ask what enterprise Patrick Callaghan had in mind but thought better of it and went to her room to unpack her trunk.

Celeste perched at the dressing table combing her hair. 'You're back.'

'You don't sound pleased.'

'I've been sleeping in your bed. Mother said you wouldn't mind. This room is so much bigger than the pokey alcove I had to share with Louisa, and more private too. Besides, it's too near Adele's old room where Mister Callaghan has been staying. He snorts in his sleep.'

Catherine laughed at her sister's moaning, wheedling sympathy. She did not have the heart to send her back to her bedroom.

♫♪ ♫♪

Within two months of his first visit, Patrick Callaghan married her mother, Catherine perplexed about her mother's decision. Mister Smooth had weaselled his way into Mother's heart. She was as a bird trapped in his cage. The panicky twisting of her mother's hands, when she learned Patrick Callaghan ordered Edward and Betsy to the Avoca property, confirmed Catherine's suspicion.

Poor Sarah, inconsolable, her downcast countenance a perpetual reminder of her pain, the first time separated from her parents. Catherine ached for her. Catherine would not like to live so far from her mother. A vision of Edwin's blue eyes flashed before her. She gulped, she would be at risk of the family's ostracism if she pursued an association with him.

Sarah shifted into the cramped servants' quarters at the rear of the main house and Thomas, who had recently married a local girl, settled into the worker's cottage, his wife Marjorie assigned Betsy's duties.

Why was it necessary for Patrick Callaghan to make changes, to send Willowbank's trusted servants away? Whom would he employ to replace them? Catherine shook her head. Perhaps it was best not to jump to conclusions. Reputed to be a successful grazier, Callaghan's enterprise had flourished in Avoca. Maybe Willowbank would prosper too. Anything would have to be better than the backbreaking work they had done since her father's death.

Chapter Seventeen

Catherine stopped short, aghast at the ruckus in the parlour.
'I don't care, and forthwith, I terminate her employment,' Patrick Callaghan yelled.

Louisa flew into Catherine's arms. 'He said she no longer needed Evelyn's services.'

'Oh no, Mother won't manage without her,' Catherine said, rocking her sister back and forth.

Callaghan's frightful display of temper rumbled up and down the corridors of the big house. Louisa clutched Catherine, her pupils dilated and face contorted. He had treated Mother so well in the days leading up to the wedding, his present behaviour bewildering. Louisa begged her sister to take her upstairs to avoid hearing any further confrontation. They huddled under the counterpane, Louisa's teeth clattering and her incoherent babble ensuring Catherine's fear of Callaghan multiplied.

'He's the angel of Hades. He hollered at Mother earlier today too, calling her nasty names and swearing. I don't know how, but Evelyn has a black eye this morning. I think he attacked her in her quarters last night,' Louisa said.

Unwelcome thoughts tumbled. Catherine squeezed her eyes.

The next morning, Thomas wheeled the curricle into place. Louisa,

Celeste, and Catherine stood beside their mother in the courtyard.

'I don't want you to go, Evelyn,' Mother said, tears glistening in her eyes. 'You've become part of my family over these many years. Here's a letter of recommendation concerning your work here at Willowbank. I hope you're able to find another position soon.'

'I'm obliged, Arianna,' Evelyn said and climbed aboard the vehicle.

Mother stood, weeping, as the curricle disappeared down the track.

Turning back to the house, she linked her arm through Catherine's, 'Thank you for writing the reference for Evelyn.'

Callaghan rounded the corner of the house. 'That's enough wailing, Woman! Girls, finish your chores and, Catherine, after you've finished, help your mother tutor Simon, do you hear me?'

Catherine recoiled. Bile oozed from her glands. She wanted to spit but swallowed, shuddering—the taste bitter. 'Yes, sir.'

Clamping her lips, she glanced at Celeste, her expression unreadable. Louisa, on the other hand, snuggled close to Mother who stroked the young one's hair. Catherine grasped her mother's free hand, and they moved up the steps as one, Catherine's face set like flint.

A mood of sadness like a storm cloud hung over the house. Days turned into months of endless drudgery. Catherine's every muscle protested. Callaghan constantly altered routines and restricted the handicraft sessions, insisting Mother conducted them in the evenings when all other work was complete.

His ornery comment addressed to Mother in her daughters' presence, 'The only reason I permit you to continue this ridiculous activity is, it'll fetch a pretty penny from your pathetic neighbours with whom we have the misfortune to associate.'

Only once, did Catherine venture to the pump-house. It remained locked. She saw Callaghan on her way back to the yard, dived into a bramble bush and hid until he passed by, the close encounter enough to stop her trying again. The only person who ventured down the path other than Callaghan was Thomas. Catherine figured he still had access to the pump since managing the crops fell to him. Callaghan strode toward the stables, and she headed in the opposite direction, sped along the driveway determined to put distance between her and her stepfather. Finding a gap in the hedge, she crawled through and leant against a burnt-out stump. 'I'll not be found here. Why, oh why, is he such a brute ...', her erratic spiel tumbled between sobs. She must get word to Mister Fraser about the nasty man. He would help them.

Her face felt warm. She wished she had brought her sunbonnet. A wattlebird's curlew trilled beside her, "Look out, miss, look out, miss!" Another answered, and though she could not see them, the pair hid amongst the heath along the fence. The scene of Jonah sulking under the vine complaining to the Lord came to mind, and she laughed, lifting her sombre mood.

The deafening clatter of wheels and hooves pounded over loose gravel, her breath catching in her throat, 'Callaghan!'

Her stepfather's large frame loomed as the carriage thundered across the pavement. She waited until the hammering of metal shoes dwindled and ran back to the house.

He returned two hours later. A familiar voice tittered in the hallway, and Catherine scuttled down the staircase. Evelyn and her mother were in a fond embrace, and Louisa had wrapped her arms about the women. Catherine rubbed her younger sister's back, and the tension drained from her little body. Celeste stood by with folded arms, and Catherine eyed her, her sister's face betraying her. Celeste had cajoled Callaghan into reversing his decision. Mother smiled up at Callaghan.

He shrugged and marched to the parlour singing, 'Blow the man down.'

♩♪ ♩♪

Patrick Callaghan's temper assumed a friendly tone in the ensuing weeks, but with little provocation, he became odious once more. He began to divide his time between the Willowbank and Fingal properties. The home was like a ship gliding on a gentle breeze during his absence but when he was present like one tossed in a wild and stormy gale. He thought up all manner of ways to keep Catherine and her brothers and sisters working all day. Catherine and Stuart assigned yet another task, the sale of produce to travellers passing by the front gate.

Catherine learned of the new arrangement from her Mother.

'Thomas has informed Mister Callaghan, Friday is the best day to set up the stall. We know many pastoralists and farmers from the district travel to Evandale to attend to business at the bank and to buy groceries from the general store.'

Early on the first morning, the pair met in the parlour, dressed ready to start their trading, Callaghan's growl penetrating the walls. 'Catherine, Stuart, report to Thomas, now. He's ready for you.'

'Yes, sir.' Stuart was irritatingly compliant, his face resembling the frost covering the lawn, but understandable since Callaghan had threatened to give him a belting more than the once.

Thomas manoeuvred the cart, full of fresh fruit and vegetables, preserved jams, and handicrafts to the clump of gum trees and unhitched the horses. 'I'll be back later. Watch out for your sister, Stuart.' Turning he trotted the horses in the direction of the rear yard where he would hitch them to the plough ready for a day's work in the paddocks.

Stuart was sent to the front gate with Catherine to ensure her safety as there were often shady characters passing by. Mother protested to Patrick about her children assisting in this way. Apart from the one requisite, her objections rebutted, Mother unable to counteract Callaghan's aggressive nature. Nevertheless, Catherine agreed many people from the district would stop by to purchase their produce since the Nicolson's Estate had an excellent reputation for quality merchandise.

As Catherine and Stuart set up the heavy-laden wagon, they noticed a gang mending the road about a hundred yards away. Dust clouds billowed across the paddock. Catherine watched as a team of bullocks dragged a cart full of crushed stones. Two of the road-gang members shovelled the gravel evenly over the newly graded surface. Another couple of bullocks pulled a second vehicle transporting a water tank. The workers released a valve, the water pouring over the stones, and packed the surface down, the gang completing a section at a time.

A carriage approached from the north and the vehicle was redirected around the area. The driver stopped at the stall, and his companion dropped to the ground, selected a shiny plum and sunk his teeth into it.

'Hmm, I'll take the lot, please.'

Catherine ducked under the dray to retrieve a bag catching her hair-ribbon on a hook. She lifted her head, her bun unravelling.

'Please help the gentleman, Stuart,' Catherine said, twisting her hair and re-tying her bow, errant strands of hair tickling her face.

More travellers stopped, purchased preserves and a variety of vegetables. The buggies kicked up dust as they left, the grime sticking to Catherine's sweaty skin. She wiped her face with the hem of her dress.

Stuart collapsed laughing. 'You look like an urchin. Mother will have a fit of the hysterics.'

Mister Fraser's vehicle pulled alongside. If only Stuart were not here, she would ask him to advise her mother.

Their dear old friend bought fruit, gave Catherine an odd glance and said, 'Your bonnet will do you no good hanging down your back.'

Catherine shrugged and placed it firmly on her head.

'Is Mister Callaghan at home?'

Stuart snarled. 'Wish he wasn't.'

Mister Fraser turned his vehicle around and headed in the direction from which he had come, leaving Catherine stammering.

Around midday, one of the men from the road-gang approached the produce cart. Catherine looked for somewhere to hide but stood her ground. Stuart, though not fond of her, would do his brotherly duty.

'What do you want, mister?' Stuart demanded while the member was still some distance from them.

'I want to buy fruit for me lads. They've not had anything fresh for a week.'

His voice, though rough, had a deep rich tone. He was two yards away before Catherine recognized him and gasped—the man, Thomas' friend, the road-gang supervisor, she saw a year or so ago at Grandma's. Those eyes, she would always remember. She racked her memory for his name, but she did not have to wonder for long.

'Edwin Nelson, I met you at your Granny Nicolson's place in Perth. It was Catherine, wasn't it?'

'Yes, yes.' Catherine stammered. She looked down at her soiled frock.

Stuart made a face, puzzled, unsure what to make of the exchange and butted in, 'Well sir, buy what you need and then be off.'

Catherine ignored Stuart. 'What can I get for you?'

'That crate of apples and the bag of berries, thanking you, ma'am.'

Catherine smiled, Edwin too polite. Stuart snatched a bag to attend to his request.

Catherine engaged Edwin in conversation. 'How is your sister, Mary?'

'Ah, Mary. She got her first baby. Remember, you saw her catching the train? She was off home to marry her sweetheart.'

'I do. So, Mary told you I had met her then?'

His blue eyes crinkled. 'Yes, and told me about your scrape at Glenlyn.' He was teasing her.

'It was good of her to rescue me. I was grateful. It could have been embarrassing for my aunt. Etiquette is all important, you know?'

He laughed. 'I been here a time or two to visit Thomas, but it's a while ago now. He works here for your family still?'

Catherine nodded.

'His dad and mine, they was in the same gang many years ago, married sisters.'

Stuart interrupted. 'What do you mean, the same gang? You a governor man's son then?'

'Stuart, you're rude to Mister Nelson!' Catherine growled. 'I'm sorry.'

'No harm was done. I'll get going then.' Edwin dipped his cap toward Catherine.

Stuart scowled. 'I'd be telling on you, Catherine Nicolson, if it wasn't for the fact Callaghan would probably lock us both up for talking to a convict.'

'He's not a convict just because his father was.'

'You've heard it same as me. Once a bad egg, always one.'

'You respect our workman and know what Evelyn taught us, many of the convicts hardly committed any crime other than stealing food for their starving families.'

'Maybe some, but many were murderers and thieves.'

Their argument curtailed when another carriage stopped, the passengers buying up much of the remaining stock.

Stuart counted the gentleman's coins, examining one shiny piece. Putting the others in the tin, he glanced at Catherine.

'Don't even think about it, Stuart,' she said.

'Callaghan will likely gamble it all away anyhow,' he said, tossing the gold coin in the tin.

Late in the afternoon, Thomas came back to hitch up the cart. 'Wait here for a bit,' he said, leaving the horses in Stuart's care, and he went down to chat with the gang.

'Thought I'd seen the fellow around,' Stuart mumbled.

After a few minutes, Thomas returned and with a measured glance in Catherine's direction said, 'All right, we'll be off then.'

Toward evening, Catherine entered the house via the kitchen entrance. Sarah greeted her, passing on a message from Marjorie. The young woman asked if Catherine would visit the worker's cottage after dinner to teach her a new embroidery stitch.

Mother agreed Catherine could go, and she gathered up her sewing basket making her way across the yard. Catherine had not visited the bluestone, convict-built cottage since Marjorie arrived. The smell of lavender greeted her as the door swung open. Marjorie beckoned Catherine to a low table near the window where she was working, the area infused with the last rays of golden light.

Catherine took in the scene. The hut featured small windows of multi-panelled, cylinder glass. In the dim light, she could make out an oiled hessian cloth covering the wooden slab-floor, and various children's drawings stuck to the whitewashed walls. A bed stood against one wall, and on the opposite wall, a cast iron oven inserted into the brick fireplace. The chimney drew the eye to a shingle roof made of black-wood.

Marjorie cleared her throat. 'I is much obliged to you, Miss Catherine, for helping me with me embroidery. When laundering, I has noticed your pieces is real neat. I has trouble learning me some new stitches.'

'It's my pleasure, Marjorie … let me have a look.' Catherine gestured for Marjorie to pass her handiwork.

Catherine took care to demonstrate a new stitch in the same manner her mother instructed her. Marjorie mastered the technique so quickly Catherine smiled—Thomas and Marjorie were up to something.

The warble of a wattlebird sounded, followed by a light tap on the window. Thomas bounded to the door. Catherine's pulse raced. What if Callaghan was the caller? She watched Marjorie. Her eyes glued to the entrance showed no sign of fear, as though she was expecting someone.

'Come in, cobber.'

Edwin stepped over the threshold and swiped his cap from his head revealing his black curls.

Catherine's face burned—she dropped her gaze.

'I believe you two has met before,' Marjorie said.

Thomas pulled a chair from the table and placed it by Catherine's. She stammered. 'Yes, our paths have crossed a time or two.'

'Hello again, Miss Catherine.' A breathless Edwin thumped onto the seat.

'How dandy to have my old crony Thomas living right next to me work? It's a boon to get a break from camp.'

'Do you all have tea?' Marjorie pulled the kettle from the fire.

'That'd be good, black and a bit of honey, please, Marj,' Edwin said.

'Miss Catherine, how do you like your tea?'

'A little milk but no sweetener, thank you, Marjorie. Perhaps I could help?'

Marjorie pursed her lips, 'No,' and poured the tea serving it with shortbread biscuits. 'Sarah give me these, left over from the main kitchen.'

Catherine raised her brows, surprised at the depth of conversation, Edwin well acquainted with Willowbank's affairs.

'Enough.' Thomas pushed his chair back and said, 'Let's play charades.'

Catherine laughed and shifted her chair. She was not sure about playing games with people she hardly knew. However, were they going to get a better opportunity to become better acquainted? Agreeing with Thomas' proposal, she was amazed her Ordinary friends might play a game of charades and tittered. If only cousin Florence could see her now.

Edwin consented to begin. He swept the quilt from Thomas and Marjorie's bed, flung it around his shoulders and pranced around the room like a king. Catherine had never laughed so hard in all her life.

After several guesses, Thomas said, 'Edwin is imitating Joseph with the coat of many colours.'

Thomas acted out a bookworm to gales of laughter. Marjorie cleverly acted out *Sleeping Beauty*, though Catherine did not expect the servant to be familiar with the fairy-tale. The others yelped when Catherine acted out a spiderweb.

A rattle outside disturbed their antics, and the door flew open. Callaghan strode over to Catherine.

He grabbed her arm and dragged her from the cottage, yelling, 'How dare you mix with this riff-raff? Get home, and don't ever come here again.'

Looking back, Catherine said, 'I'm so sorry, but I had a lovely time.'

Callaghan lunged, slapped her across the face and sent her reeling to the ground. Edwin flew across the path and with one blow punched Callaghan in the midriff, so hard it winded him. He doubled over gasping for breath. Edwin turned and ran like a frightened deer in the direction of his camp. Catherine leapt to her feet, bounded upstairs and banged into Stuart. He grasped her arm to keep her from toppling.

'Quick, let me by, he's after me.'

Catherine, confined to the house, burned with resentment toward Callaghan. Her jaw ached, and her teeth were sore from grinding. Using a soft cloth, Sarah smoothed oil onto Catherine's bruised face.

'Catherine, talk to me, bitterness only destroys you.'

Catherine rolled over, not ready to discuss the incident. Callaghan may be able to confine her physically, but he could not stop her scheming. She would find a way to meet with Edwin.

Chapter Eighteen

Catherine thawed some during her detention when her sister, Celeste, offered to spend time taking turns on Mother's sewing machine. They drew patterns, cut and dyed linen fabric and sewed several day-dresses, all the while chattering—their longing to escape their stepfather's clutches and how they might accomplish the feat uppermost in mind.

'Celeste, Thomas' friend, Edwin, is so handsome and the nicest person you would ever want to meet.'

'I think you ought to avoid close contact with the ordinary folk, and associate only with those in your own crowd. I don't need to remind you of their meagre existence, and I assure you, you'd live to regret any decision to accept the hand of such a man.'

'Oh, Celeste, you're so stuffy, and anyway, think how many workers have done very well in our society. Consider Mother. She was Ordinary.'

'Mother is an exception, and she married well. Things are different for men. Folks could move up in society when the government offered land grants. They could clear a patch of scrub and eke out a living, but that no longer happens. Everyone is required to purchase property now, and the banks won't lend to anyone if there's a risk of default.'

'Ha, Celeste, so adamant a discourse. Evelyn has convinced you.'

Catherine dropped the subject. Feeling hemmed in, she longed to go to the stable, saddle up her horse, Ebony, and gallop across the plains in the fresh air.

When permitted to leave the house, she sought out her brother, Stuart, whom she had not seen for days. She found him shovelling horse manure from the stalls. He leaned on the spade as she approached.

'All the beast has done, is boss us about. I tell you, when I come of age, I'll inherit this place, and I'll be the boss!' He spat.

Staring at the large bruises on his legs, she asked, 'What happened to you?'

'Callaghan belted me up again, with a willow stick. I gave him cheek.'

'Oh, I'm really sorry.'

'You'll need to watch out for him, too. He's the rogue from hell.' Stuart pursed his lips and narrowed his eyes.

What was her stepfather capable of? She shuddered. Though she and Stuart made no secret of their dislike for each other in the past, a silent pact passed between them.

♫♪ ♫♪

When Catherine and Stuart operated the produce stall at their front gate the following Friday, there was no sign of the road-gang. The only evidence of their earlier presence was a black ribbon winding through the bush. Catherine's melancholy spirit surprised her. Where might the team be working this week? As soon as she could, she would ask Sarah to find out from Thomas.

Immediately before dinner, she accosted Sarah. 'Sarah, can you ask Thomas to get a message to Edwin for me? You'll need to be careful though. I don't want Mister Callaghan to know I'm enquiring.'

'You haven't heard?'

'Mister Callaghan beat Thomas for inviting Edwin to the worker's cottage, and he's sent him to help his dad to clear more scrub on the borders of the Avoca property.'

Stuart and Simon, forced to undertake Thomas' chores, worked from daybreak until dusk each day. It was three weeks until Thomas returned, and as soon as he did, Callaghan decided to go to the Avoca property to check up on Edward—a collective sigh of relief uttered right after he disappeared down the road on horseback. Catherine took the opportunity to speak to Sarah in the afternoon—she could trust her servant friend. Finding her at the foot of the stairwell, she pulled her into an alcove, not keen for anyone else to hear her request—anyone complicit in her defiance punished.

'Sarah, will you ask Thomas if Edwin's safe please?'

'I'll let you know as soon as I can.' Sarah grinned.

♫♪ ♫♪

Mister Fraser swung his curricle into the front courtyard, and Thomas came to attend to the horse. They exchanged a few words, and Mister Fraser carried a small parcel into the house. He greeted Catherine in the hallway. Mother ushered him into the parlour, shooed Catherine off and closed the door, Catherine retreating to her room.

A sound came from the yard below her window, and she pushed her curtain aside. Sarah hurried along the river path with a parcel under her arm—Sarah, her mother's confidant in place of Betsy. Mister Fraser's vehicle left an hour later.

It was a week since Catherine had asked about Edwin, when Sarah gave Catherine a note. She scurried along the track to the pond and read. Before she sat, she checked and found the pump-house still padlocked.

'Dear Catherine, my gang's working round Evandale. We're sealing the main road. Sorry to get you into trouble with your stepfather, don't want to cause any trouble, so I won't come back. It's better this way.'

Catherine stared at the words. It was unfair. What could be so wrong in wanting to be friends? She folded the note and tucked it into her bodice.

♫♪ ♫♪

Having completed her tasks by eleven, Catherine saddled Ebony, headed north through the forest and across the plains, a shortcut. The cool wind was a welcome relief from the heat of the sun—she had left without her bonnet. Crossing the river at the ford, and turning toward the township, Catherine dug her heels into her horse's flank and soon encountered the road gang.

Edwin looked up, cautioned her to wait, and came toward the clump of trees where she dismounted. He did not comment about her getup. However, his wry look conveyed his thoughts. The pantaloon costume she designed meant she could straddle the horse's back.

'What you doing, coming here?' Edwin wiped the sweat from his brow.

'Edwin, I wanted to see you were all right for myself and to thank you for defending me from Callaghan.'

'He deserved it, but reckon I'll keep my distance. Don't want any trouble.'

Catherine shook her head. 'I'll come to you.'

'Catherine, you mustn't.'

Tears beaded in her eyes.

He touched her forearm, 'Stop riding on your own, it's dangerous. Callaghan will lick you good if he catches you. Word up Fingal way is, he's a lowlife.'

'He's been gone for a while. I wish he'd stay away.'

'Don't cross him. I've heard …' Edwin twisted his foot in the dirt.

She glanced at him, 'Please Edwin, there must be a way.'

'Don't you see … if your cranky stepfather caught me, he would pay a magistrate to order a flogging or worse, gaol me. No, you'd best forget me.'

She had not considered the possibility of reprisal. However, having seen firsthand the poor man at the St. John's service dragged away by the constable, without reason, other than he was Ordinary, left her in no doubt Edwin was vulnerable. He looked toward his workers and groaned.

'I've kept you away from your gang long enough.' Catherine wrenched the reins.

'Be careful. I'm not sure Callaghan's still in Avoca. Some of the lads saw Slim, the scoundrel he hangs with, at the hotel where they play poker. He passed by this way an hour ago,' Edwin said.

'I'd best be going then.'

He hoisted her up to her mount and took her hand. 'Be patient.'

She held his gaze. Beads of perspiration formed on his lip—his longing eyes spoke volumes.

He stepped back. 'Give Thomas a message for me. Tell him me dad's going to be with the boxing troupe in Evandale in a couple of weeks. Ask him to come 'cause me brother, Dave, will be there too. Dad's training the boys for a match. He was a pugilist you know,' Edwin obviously proud of his father's prowess.

'That's awful. I hope you don't ever get in the ring, Edwin.'

'It's terrific. You should see the troupe wallop the battlers,' Edwin said, providing a colourful description.

'Not my kind of entertainment, but I'll let him know. I must get back before sundown.'

Catherine trotted her horse through the clearing and turned. Oh, how different their backgrounds, as honey is to lemon. Surely, women did not really watch men bash each other.

Edwin waved his cap. The salute had an air of acknowledgment regarding their alliance. Goodbye, Edwin. She had seen the look in his eyes—he would not change his mind—he would not risk his freedom, even for her.

She entered the bush, the canopy so thick it blocked the sunlight, the shadowy darkness penetrating her very being. Leading Ebony through the virgin forest in the direction of the river, she glanced about, her heart thumping.

'What was the name Edwin called him, a scoundrel? I'd better get going.'

On reaching the river, the horse picked its way along the bank.

A movement in the trees startled him. 'Whoa, boy.' Catherine gripped the reins.

A branch snapped. Balking, Catherine scanned the area. Was that bleating? Impossible, Willowbank's flock were in the south paddocks, miles away. A dark shape darted through the dappled shrubbery. She tensed. What was that? Animal, person or was it the Slim character? Perhaps his association with Callaghan was not only related to card games, and if so, he must not spot her.

Looking about for the quickest route home, she dug her heels into Ebony's flank and urged him into a gallop. The stables loomed—Thomas in the yard. He shook his head as she jumped from the horse.

'Be careful, girl. It's not safe to go too far alone.'

'What's to be afraid of?'

'There's rustlers on the run, stealing the local's cattle and sheep.'

Should she mention hearing sheep? No, Thomas would already be aware if there were any missing.

The dinner bell sounded, and after passing on Edwin's message to him, he shooed her off. 'I'll fix Ebony.'

She joined the family in the dining room thankful no one asked where she had been. It seemed no one had missed her. Everyone must have taken the opportunity to indulge in a favourite diversion while Callaghan was absent.

♫♪ ♫♪

'Catherine, how many times must I remind you to wear your sunhat.'

'Ooh!' Catherine sucked in the air—her face did feel a bit raw.

'Your nose is red as a beetroot,' her youngest brother said and clapped his hand over his mouth and sniggered.

Stuart skidded through the door and slid into his seat. 'Sorry I'm late.'

'And just where have you been all day?' Catherine was quick to draw attention to her brother.

'Exploring, that's all.'

Catherine ate a few bites and pushed her plate aside. 'Mother, I'm not feeling at all well, I'm going to bed early this evening.'

'You're probably a little parched from the sun. Drink a glass of water.'

Catherine's head throbbed. Was she suffering sunstroke or was she apprehensive about Edwin's reluctance to visit her again? He had asked her to be patient, but right now things felt hopeless.

She tossed and turned. Her pillow felt scratchy, and sleep evaded her. Her head felt like it was in a vice, her stomach nauseous. She crawled from the bed, reached for a wet cloth and dampened her face.

Finally, exhaustion overtook her.

♫♪ ♫♪

Catherine awoke to deafening screams, the sound coming from outside.

'No! No! Help! Stop!' Stuart bawled, 'No!'

She sat straight up. What time was it? She could not tell. The curtain at the open bedroom window swayed gently. She felt in the bed alongside her. Celeste was already up, or maybe she had not even been in bed.

'Patrick, stop! You'll kill him. That's far too many lashes.' Mother's high-pitched wail echoed in the yard.

'I'll teach you to disobey me you little b... I told you never to go to the north boundary.'

'Patrick, stop it, please? He's bloodied.'

'Get out, Woman, or I'll whip you too!'

Catherine lay perfectly still, pulling the counterpane over her head. Heavy footsteps landed on the stairs.

She could make out Thomas' voice in the hallway. 'Where shall I put him, ma'am?'

'This way, Thomas, his bed is in here,' Mother's voice rasped, 'and, Sarah, would you mind getting me hot water, ointment and bandages please.'

Minutes passed. Catherine grabbed her dressing gown, slung it over her shoulders and crept along the hallway. She gently knocked on Stuart's door and went in without waiting for a response.

'Get her out. She's the one who told Callaghan,' Stuart's accusing eyes penetrating Catherine's soul.

'No, I didn't.'

'He said you did. He said you saw me in the north paddock.'

'I didn't see you or even know you were there. Anyhow, I've not spoken to Stepfather. I didn't know he was back.'

'I don't believe you. Who else would tell? Get out. I hate you.'

'Mother, I didn't, cross my heart.'

'I know, Catherine. Go now and prepare for breakfast.'

As Catherine turned to leave, she glanced down at Stuart's legs and drew a deep breath. 'How very cruel. I'd hoped he'd never return.'

Was Stuart the dark figure she saw in the scrub on the way back yesterday?

The breakfast bell sounded. She bumped into Marjorie at the bottom of the stairs. The servant beckoned, and Catherine followed her into the laundry.

'Thomas reckons the young fellow, Slime, I mean Slim has bin hanging around—seems the man's got some business dealings with Callaghan. He may have ratted on Stuart.'

Catherine nodded.

'Slim was asking who the kid in the funny pants was.'

Catherine squeezed her eyes shut. 'Dear Lord.' Stuart had taken her beating. 'Do you know this Slim?'

'Son of a nasty chap bonded to the Carrick family in Breadalbane.'

Catherine raised her brows, unsurprised.

'Stuart told Thomas there were a couple of dozen lambs corralled in the north paddock. Thomas knows there's a gang stealing sheep—doesn't take much to add two and two.' Marjorie kept her voice low and pointed toward the dining room. 'Mister Callaghan's in there.'

Catherine, in grave danger should she try to visit Edwin again soon, would have to lay low. She would look for a chance the next time Callaghan went away, though she would have to watch out for the Slim fellow. There was little doubt Callaghan had engaged him for some suspect activity.

Chapter Nineteen

In the few days since Callaghan's reappearance at Willowbank, a fearful and apprehensive mood descended upon the estate. For months, everyone tiptoed about the place, and even Simon lost his playful spark. Mother looked pale, rarely smiling. Catherine itched to get out of the house. Hemmed-in she longed to abscond but feigned illness and kept her distance from her stepfather. She could understand how convicts must have felt in the grip of sadistic masters.

She was even more desperate when Callaghan agreed Celeste might move to Hobart and complete the new nursing course offered at the General Hospital. Celeste had ground her stepfather down with her honeyed ways. Catherine voiced her longing to get away as they lay side by side in their big double bed.

'I'm envious you're escaping this prison. I wish I could go too.'

'I pray you will at the right time, Catherine. Seek the Lord, and he will guide you. Anger and bitterness are not becoming of you. You used to be the one to support me through sad times.'

'I pine for Adele and Miss Lucille, and now you're going too, I'll grieve for you more than you could ever know.' Catherine's eyes glistened, her emotions threatening to spill over.

♫♪ ♫♪

Callaghan instructed Thomas to drive Celeste in the covered wagon, as far as Campbell Town to catch the train to Hobart Town. Callaghan permitted Catherine and Stuart to accompany her. Catherine did not for a moment think Callaghan was generous, but guessed, he wanted them out of the way. The young people spent the night at their cousin's home, while Thomas found lodging at The Fox Hunters Return.

They met up with him at the station early in the morning, the train due to depart at eight o'clock sharp. A fine drizzle sprinkled the platform crowded with travellers jostling to position themselves first in line at the carriage doors. A tearful Celeste hung back against the wall.

'I'll miss you, Catherine, and as much as I'm pleased to be out of stepfather's clutches, I'm scared about living in Hobart.'

'Mother wrote to Aunt Elizabeth to tell her you were coming. I'm certain she will welcome a visit on your days off.'

Celeste flung her arms about Catherine's neck and released her reluctantly, only when the porter called, 'Last call, all aboard.'

Catherine waved until she could no longer see Celeste's arm dangling from her window.

'Come, Miss Catherine, we've only an hour.' Thomas waggled the list of items he had to collect at the general store. 'We ought to buy these things and be getting on home. It poured rain all night, and now it's starting again.'

Stuart went into the produce section with Thomas, and Catherine to the haberdashery display to browse. She was there but a few minutes when there was a tap on the window. Surprised to see Edwin beckoning her outside, she spun around so fast she bumped into something.

'I'm so sorry, please excuse me,' she said, looking into the face of a mannequin.

When she realized the absurdity of apologizing to a dummy, she laughed with several customers who had witnessed her blunder.

Stepping onto the pavement, she squealed, 'Edwin.'

He swiped his cap from his head, revealing his mop of black curls—how she loved his hair.

'Just met Thomas, said you was here. What a bit of luck this is.'

'Hello, am I surprised to see you,' she said.

'Been here visiting me cousin. I lived with her family for about a year when I was a kid. She asked how your mother was getting on.'

Catherine gasped, covered her mouth. 'Mother?'

Edwin screwed up his face. 'I'm sorry. I thought you knew she was from Campbell Town.'

'You must take me to visit the lady. I want to ask.'

'Whoa. My cousin lives out of town. Your mother was a young woman at the time. It was Aunt who mixed with your mother's folks, and she's passed on.'

Catherine frowned. 'Bother. There's so much I ...'

She caught the cautionary glance Edwin gave her. He took her arm folded it into the crook of his elbow and walked her along the street.

Catherine turned toward him. 'Where are you going now?'

'To meet your brother and Thomas.'

She laughed. 'You know what I mean.'

He snickered. 'You, Miss Nicolson, are as inquisitive as an ant at a picnic ... I'm heading to Fingal to try my hand at mining.'

'That's miles away. When do you plan to return?'

'No telling, but if I make it rich, I'll be back to court you, Catherine. Would you agree to that?'

Catherine's cheeks burned and looking into his eyes, she nodded her head and smiled. 'I'd be pleased to enjoy your attention, Mister Edwin Nelson. Indeed, I would.'

Edwin dipped his cap, pushed the door ajar and offered her a chair at the table where Thomas and Stuart had found a seat. A gust of wind caught the door, and it slammed shut. The tree branches, in the park across the road, waving erratically.

Thomas looked out. 'Getting nasty. Hope it doesn't set in.'

All four ordered meat pies, mashed potato and peas, and Catherine, a large pot of tea.

'Your sister will be pleased to have you closer.'

'So, she said ... she's been looking after the young ones as well as her own, since mother passed, and they've been a real handful for her, especially with Tom away all week ... but it's easier now the older ones attend the local school.'

The entire time they conversed, Stuart kept a wary eye on Edwin. Catherine was furious. She glared at him and shuffled her chair closer to Edwin. Thomas must have sensed her frustration because he began to chat with Stuart about his plans. Edwin moved his face closer to Catherine and whispered in her ear. He was the type of man she wanted to marry. Talking with him was such a pleasant encounter. She almost forgot her misery in saying goodbye to Celeste and having to return to face Callaghan's control.

A clap of thunder ushered in the storm. Thomas grimaced. The rain pelted against the store window and the proprietor rushed to close the doors. Thomas interrupted the chatter and explained he was keen to set out on the return journey before worse weather blew in.

'It's starting to rain mighty heavy.'

He lowered his voice and spoke to Edwin. 'The wet of the last few days doesn't seem to be letting up. The river was high on the pylons of the bridge yesterday, and it won't take too long for it to go under. Best be on our way.'

Catherine wrapped her scarf about her head. 'Edwin, get word to us somehow, to let us know how you get on.'

'Thomas will be sure to hear. I'll stop in at Avoca to see Edward and Betsy from time to time.'

'Just watch out Callaghan isn't around when you do,' Stuart chipped.

'I'll be sure to be careful, Master Stuart,' Edwin said and turned to leave.

Catherine waved her handkerchief, but he did not glance back. She drew a sharp breath—she would miss him. Thomas gripped her arm and guided her to the dray.

♫♪ ♫♪

Thomas steered the wagon along High Street, dodging the puddles—great chunks of the surface gouged from the road. Water lapped at the underside of the solid red brick-bridge as they traversed the river. Passing the stately Grange and St. Luke's church they headed north toward the Corners junction, the rain torrential.

The carriage barrelled by improved pastures, the grazing cattle huddling underneath the trees. The mountains on either side of the valley shrouded in dense cloud, and the cold breeze whipping under the canvas epitomized Catherine's mood. Normally the scenery would captivate her, but heartsick, having endured two painful goodbyes in one morning, she closed her eyes and sighed. Another deluge teemed upon the wagon, the incessant rain hindering their progress. The horses' breath curled up around their ears. Thomas gently slapped them, and seeming to sense they were homeward bound they increased their pace.

The crunch-crunch of the wagon wheels as they rolled rhythmically along the road and the pitter-patter of the rain on the canvas lulled her to a daydream state. She imagined travelling with Edwin to Fingal and smiled. The rain gave way to a fine mist. Thomas slowed the horses and turned left off the road onto a muddy track.

They crossed a small creek before Catherine questioned, 'Where are we, Thomas?'

'Calling into my friends, Robert and Alice Mc Donald's place, to give the horses a spell and a drink.'

Catherine admired Thomas, always careful with the horses—his father, Edward, having instilled in his son the need for excellence in his role as groomsman.

The track led to a grove of Cyprus trees. An axe-hewn slab-hut, with an ironbark roof partially hidden amongst the pines visible. A thin column of black smoke rose from the bluestone chimney.

'Ordinary folk,' Stuart scoffed.

'True, he's a squatter, Master Stuart, but a hard-working timber cutter. You'll notice his carvings, of the best quality and sought after all over the plains.'

As the wagon pulled up, Robert and Alice stepped onto the veranda. 'Good day, Tom, nice to see you again.'

'Hello, Rob, Ally, meet Miss Catherine and Master Stuart Nicolson, we're headed back to Willowbank, need to rest the horses for a bit.'

'Hello, Ally, hello Rob,' Catherine greeted them warmly, but Stuart merely grumped.

'Seems to be the week for drop-ins … Edwin called by here a couple of days ago.'

Catherine met Alice's gaze. Alice, a pretty girl, with dark curly hair that softened her face. Was she also a relative? Alice smiled, revealing a not so attractive mouth—missing her front teeth.

'How'd you do? Come on in and dry off a bit. The kettle's boiling, just in time for a hot cuppa.' Alice wiped her hands on her apron. 'I'll get the tea. Please have a seat.'

Catherine lowered herself onto the bench beside the fire burning in the hearth, glad of the warmth. Thomas had not overstated Rob's expertise with the chisel. The main room boasted a magnificently carved dining suite and sideboard.

'This is impressive, Mister McDonald.'

'I enjoy carving. It's relaxing.'

Catherine glanced about, the dining furniture the one luxury. Would such a situation be so bad if she were to wed Edwin? Rarely having seen the inside of ordinary folk's houses, she considered the simplicity of the lifestyle they enjoyed, noting the clay plastered over the interior walls and oiled calico nailed above two small windows. The calico served a double purpose, for privacy, though they hardly needed curtains deep in the isolated scrub, but vital, to keep the cold out. She chewed her bottom lip—her own window boasted heavy brocade curtaining. In the small room off to the side, two straw-filled mattresses covered by grey woollen blankets lay upon crude beds. Perhaps a couple of colourful knitted covers would be welcome—she would send a pair to Alice.

'Let's water the horses while we wait. We can't stay long, don't want to get cut off,' Thomas said.

Thomas, Robert, and Stuart led the horses to the creek, Catherine following them out. She laughed at the alacrity of a mother duck pushing her ducklings up the bank on the other side of the creek to safety. Returning to the house, she found Alice in the kitchen where a huge pot of water bubbled on the wood-fire stove. Alice sliced a block of cheese, wrapped the remainder in gauze and placed it into an old kerosene tin.

'To keep the rats out,' she said.

Catherine shivered, vermin—heinous. The ordinary folk lived in such austere conditions, so different from her own experience, even with Callaghan as a stepfather—how did she suppose she could improve their lot?

Alice cut five large slices of bread and placed them with the cheese on a tin plate. Reaching for a canister, she scooped two tablespoons of tea into a pot and poured in hot water.

'Mind grabbing them tin cups off the bench?' She motioned to Catherine, and they joined the others in the main room.

Robert and Alice proved to be an affable couple, and Catherine took an immediate liking to Thomas' friends.

Shortly after the meal, the travellers waved goodbye. 'Thank you, Ally,' Catherine's voice echoed along the gully, now filled so full with water it had begun to flow into the paddock. The rain had not let up.

They reached home well into the night, thankful to have received some protection from the roadside bush since the howl of the wind in the treetops indicated the storm continued to lash the countryside. Though Catherine sheltered under the canvas cover, her clothes clung to her. On reaching the house, Thomas steered the wagon to the rear of the house so they could enter through the kitchen. She twisted the hem of her dress to extract the water.

Catherine did not expect to eat tonight—Callaghan's edict—if a person missed the call to dinner, they went hungry. However, Sarah, aware of his ruling, set aside something for them, and they wolfed down corned beef and potatoes covered in cheese sauce.

'It is good of you to wait late, Sarah. I was starving,' Catherine said, scraping the last of her meal into her mouth.

Stuart, not so familiar with the servants, grunted his approval too as they slipped into the hallway and made their way to their rooms. Catherine tossed her hat onto her dresser, knocking something onto the floor. She scooped up a bunch of dried deep, blush roses and was still wondering about the posy when Mother came in to check on her. She whispered, 'Goodnight.'

'I'm awake, Mother.'

'I'm glad you're back with me. I've sad news. While you were gone, Mister Fraser had an accident on his new machine, and he died as a result.'

'That's dreadful, so sad for Andrew, he'll fret for his father awfully, they were very close.'

'Yes … my heart is breaking.' Mother's voice cracked.

The darkness enveloping them did not allow Catherine to see her mother's face, but her sorrow overflowed—her body trembling—poor Mother, she loved that old man. Catherine hugged her mother, and she allowed herself to slump in Catherine's embrace. Minutes passed. Mother loosened Catherine's grip, stroked her daughter's hair and tiptoed from the room.

Reflecting on all the happenings in the past two days, Catherine ached to share it. It was strange to be alone in the bed—she missed Celeste, and almost wished Louisa had moved in with her, but Louisa enjoyed the luxury of her new room, Adele's old chamber. Catherine snuggled into her warm quilt and slept soundly, very thankful for a place to lay her head.

Chapter Twenty

The rain continued unabated for days. Catherine went in search of Ebony and found Thomas in the yard.

'River has risen to levels unseen,' he said. 'The tracks and even the stone-metal roads have become impassable. Stuart helped me lift the pump, and we moved the sheep and cattle to higher ground, and the horses to the shearing shed, the stable swamped.'

Catherine looked over to the pump-house. Foliage hid all but a small section of the roof. The water must be lapping the shelf holding her notebook and the old chest. Could she ask Thomas to fetch them? No, Mother would be in a precarious position if Callaghan saw either one.

'It'd be best not to wander too far. You might get into difficulty,' Thomas said.

Catherine shrugged and retreated to the parlour for the day.

The following morning, she looked from her window shocked to see water lapping at the barn. Stuart led the horses out, taking them to higher ground. Slipping her dressing gown over her shoulders, she raced into the hallway.

'Catherine, slow down, it's not safe,' Sarah grasped her arm.

'What's happening?'

'The wheat crop in the lower reaches … completely ruined and the storehouse engulfed.'

She groaned. If the storehouse had gone under, then the pump-house flooded with all its treasures ruined.

'The water is lapping at Thomas' windows,' Sarah said. 'Thomas and Marjorie lifted their belongings into the hayloft, just in time for the surging floodwaters to wash about one foot of brown sludge through the cottage.'

Catherine's eyes widened her body tense. 'No wonder Thomas suggested I remain close to the house. I hope we're out of harm's way here,' she said, backing up and into her room.

She had not bothered to check the pump-house from her window earlier, but now as she stood looking across the paddocks, she saw just how far the silt-laden water had risen. Her secret place was gone, washed away. Tears slipped down her cheeks. She rested her head on the sill, pleased she had at least committed her writing to memory. Perhaps it was best Mother's drawing was gone. Slipping into her blue and white gingham day-dress, she went downstairs.

At breakfast, Callaghan said, 'More inconvenience, we'll have to shift everything out of the cellar.'

'But it won't reach the house.' Catherine sensed the strain in her mother's tone. 'Part of the reason Francis built the house on the rise.'

Callaghan huffed.

Simon was quiet, his lip trembling. He fiddled with the tablecloth, his eyes darting in his sisters' direction as he listened.

'I have to go to the lavatory,' Louisa grabbed at her skirt clearly in urgent need.

Callaghan pushed his chair back, crashing it to the floor, and cursed. Mother groaned and cradled her head in her hands.

♫♪ ♫♪

Catherine passed through the hallway. Thomas and Marjorie were speaking with Sarah.

'Not sure I want to sleep up there in the hay with the mice and the snakes flushed out of their holes. They'll undoubtedly be looking for dinner,' Marjorie said.

'Think of it as an adventure, me dear, our secret country house.' Thomas tried to sound reassuring, but Marjorie rolled her eyes.

'Perhaps there's something to be said for being cramped in the servants' quarters,' Sarah chuckled.

♫♪ ♫♪

'Catherine, have you seen Stuart?'

'Not since early this morning, Mother. I thought he was taking the horses further up the hill.'

Mother's face blanched. She raced to the kitchen. 'Where's Thomas?'

'In the hayloft, ma'am,' Sarah said, and a few minutes later, Thomas shot by on Callaghan's horse.

Mother paced, moved ornaments from shelf to shelf, and paced some more. She picked up her knitting and sat with it untouched on her lap.

Every few minutes she pulled the curtain back and peeped out the window. 'Where are they?'

'Mother, he wouldn't be here yet. To get to the top paddock he would have to wade through the creek flooding the gully,' Catherine said, picking up a magazine, thumbing through the pages, though barely absorbed the content.

Thomas whistled, and Mother leapt to her feet and tore out. Catherine followed down the steps. Stuart was lying across the horse's back, his torso unseen, his left leg twisted at an awkward angle.

'Get Mister Callaghan, Catherine.' Mother tapped her on the rear to hurry her.

Callaghan ambled to the pavement and grimaced when he saw Stuart's leg.

'All right, Thomas, let's get this over with. Catherine clear the way.'

The men lifted him from the horse, Stuart screaming and turning the colour of death. They lay him on his bed, and all the while Callaghan barked orders at Thomas and Sarah. Thomas ran to the barn, returning with the handle from some implement, and Sarah brought strips of cloth and a bottle of potion from the cellar. Stuart clenched his teeth.

♪♪ ♪♪

For days Mother stayed by Stuart's bed, damping his forehead and feeding him broth. There was no way to get him to the doctor or to have the doctor come to the house. Catherine carried some of Sarah's chicken broth to the pair.

'Stuart's rambling … something about sheep and an unknown brand in the top paddock,' Mother said.

'Did you say anything to Mister Callaghan?'

'He said to take no notice, reckons delirium causes a person to imagine things.'

It was too dangerous to verify his story, and besides, Callaghan had confined the family to the homestead, all buildings other than the house and the hay shed inundated.

The jersey cow's milk dried up, and Sarah made use of the tins of powdered milk Mother had ordered from the store the previous month. Mother realized the value of the new product on the market and purchased several tins in case of such an emergency. At the time, Callaghan strongly reprimanded her, calling her a stupid woman for wasting money on such an unnecessary item. Other basic stocks had run low too, but Sarah managed to create delicious meals with scarce ingredients. Catherine, surprised at her ingenuity, continued to worry. If the rain did not stop soon, even Sarah would run out of ideas.

Catherine knocked on the girl's door and signalled to her to follow. 'Sarah, Thomas and Stuart removed the pump before the water rose. Did they move anything else?'

'No, there was little else kept there,' Sarah said.

'But there was something else, wasn't there?'

Sarah clasped Catherine's arm, pulled her back into her room and closed the door.

'I've hidden the chest somewhere else, was your mother's wish. She sent me to fetch it. I knew you'd found it, things moved. You must forget you ever saw it.'

Catherine cocked her eye. Sarah, stone-faced gave nothing away.

The contents of the tin were clearly of vital significance to her mother, and Catherine was sure they pertained to Mister Fraser.

'Did you find a notebook in a bag?'

'Yes, jammed behind a post,' Sarah said.

'Did you read it?'

'No, I can only write my name, not much else. Besides, I don't reckon she'd want me snooping into her private matters.'

Catherine figured, if Sarah was unaware the writings belonged to her, she would not confess to owning the book. However, was her mother now privy to her thoughts?

♫♪ ♫♪

As soon as the water receded, Thomas transported Stuart to Grandma's where the doctor would set his leg. Meanwhile, Catherine and Marjorie shovelled the thick brown mud from the worker's cottage floor, the foul stench like the pigpen at Myrtleford. Catherine slipped, landing in a heap of the offensive waste, mud splattering her clothes. Try as she might, she could not get the smell out and burned the dress. The next task—whitewashing the walls, was a more palatable exercise. Catherine took her broom and swirled a circle pattern across the wall.

'You've a real knack for painting, Miss Catherine.'

'It's fun, and now it's your turn.'

Marjorie dipped hers in the paint and dabbed the next wall, the shape of the bristles forming blobs. Refilling their brushes, they covered the walls, giggling like children. Catherine smiled, her heart happy to help her disadvantaged friend. Mother popped her head into the cottage to deliver fresh linen and check on their progress.

'You've got the place looking almost new. I think I know the very thing to add a colourful touch.'

She returned with essential items to refurbish the couple's room, and handed Marjorie a pair of rose-coloured floral curtains.

Marjorie shook them out. 'They're pretty, Missus Nicolson.'

Thomas arrived, his wife's shining eyes causing him to colour. He pointed across the paddocks, 'The rain has been a godsend for the Midlands.' The friends laughed together—he sounded so like his father.

Catherine asked, 'Would you find out how everyone else fared? What about your parents, Edwin's family, and Grandma's home?'

'I'll let you know. I've got to pick up more clobber in Perth when I collect Stuart.'

'Thomas, would you pick up a newspaper or two at the store please?' Mother asked.

'Perhaps one from the south, too. The Hobart Mercury covers news all the way out to the east coast,' Catherine said, glancing at Thomas, who smirked undoubtedly aware of the reason for her request.

Slipping up to her room, she jotted a few lines to Edwin—oh, how she wanted to see him—to give the envelope to Thomas before he left for town, but on reaching the foot of the stairs, she paused.

'You will sign the paper, Evelyn or I'll—' Callaghan's thunderous voice badgered.

Catherine tiptoed back upstairs.

Chapter Twenty-One

There was a record grain harvest on the plains following the rain, most estates faring well. While Willowbank's oats were severely damaged, the estate had a bumper wool yield. Callaghan's spirits were high when the tally came in, Mother choosing the perfect moment to seek permission to visit Celeste.

'Patrick, I do believe it's time for me to visit Hobart Town to check on Celeste. I can stay with Elizabeth.'

Catherine shivered, astounded at her mother's boldness in confronting Callaghan with such a request during the family dinner, and even more so at Callaghan's response.

'I agree. It's a capital idea.'

Callaghan directed Catherine to accompany her mother, with the not so secret ambition she would find a suitor within their privileged classes. Lucille had good prospects, and Catherine regarded as the next to initiate an advantageous attachment.

Catherine sorted through her frocks, careful to choose her finest wardrobe. Looking at her nails, she grimaced a good deal of work on her manicure imperative. She soaked her hands in a solution of borax to loosen the grime from under her nails, black from weeding. It would not be wise to embarrass her toffy aunt. She smirked. How convenient that her outfits comprised gloves and were required on every occasion in fashionable society. Besides, she must look her best, because though still hankering after her Ordinary friend, no word came from him. Who was foolish enough to think she was the only girl who found him attractive and might entice him? A trip to a bustling centre of commerce was a welcome diversion and perhaps might present an agreeable suitor. If Celeste's communication was an indication, ample wealthy young merchants pursued suitable companions.

Thomas drove mother and daughter to Clarendon station in the barouche, and they caught the southbound train. The Corners Station their first refreshment stop—the passengers bustled their way to the tearoom. Catherine and her mother stood in line at the counter to order lunch.

'A plate of freshly made smoked-ham sandwiches and a pot of tea, please.'

The storekeeper wrote the order down, jingled the cash box and counted out the change.

'Let's make our way to the spare table, near the row of windows.' Mother pointed. 'Perhaps we can get warm by sitting in the sunshine.' Catherine agreed sitting so she could peer out the window.

'Well, hello, if it isn't, Miss Catherine Nicolson. Fancy meeting you here at The Corners,' the greeting originating from the table behind.

Catherine noted the cultured English accent and turned. 'Harriet! It's lovely to see you. You've met my mother, now Missus Patrick Callaghan, haven't you?'

'Yes, we've met. Hello, Missus Callaghan. It was at the church bazaar a few years ago when we girls won prizes for our floral displays, and your brother made his awkward announcement.'

'Stuart has a habit of being inept.'

'I recognised him as the lad caught up in the hilarious incident at the Morven Show. Remember his father lifting him over the fence by his britches when the bull got loose and charged at him. Graziers ran all over the paddock chasing their escaped charges. I couldn't stop laughing.'

'How could I ever forget? Poor Stuart.' Mother laughed.

Harriet's travelling companion joined her at her table.

'And you've met my stepmother, Missus Chapman, Elena, my former governess.'

'How do you do?' Mother smiled.

'Would you join us on our table?' Elena shuffled her chair to make room.

A waitress approached with a tray of sandwiches and a teapot. Mother motioned the girl to place the food on Chapman's table.

'When did you return from Cambridge?' Catherine asked.

'I arrived on the Odessa about two months ago. We disembarked in Georgetown.'

'Did you complete your studies?'

'Yes, and passed all my exams with top marks.'

'What are your plans?'

'I am travelling to Hobart Town to take up a position, English and History Mistress at the Macquarie Street School. I'll be boarding with Mister and Missus Chester at Overton Cottage. Their daughter also teaches at the school.'

'How splendid.'

Harriet continued. 'I met a wonderful gentleman on my voyage from England, a doctor, Jonathan, employed at the hospital, and I am to be married next year.'

'Congratulations.'

'And what brings you to Hobart Town, dear Catherine?'

'Mother and I are on our way to visit my sister, Celeste. She is completing her nursing certificate at the hospital. We're staying with my Aunt Elizabeth.'

A shrill whistle interrupted their conversation and the station-hand called, 'All aboard for the continuation of your journey to Hobart, ladies and gentlemen.'

'I have extra tickets to an orchestral performance, on Saturday evening at City Hall if you are interested. I'll meet you on the platform when we arrive and give them to you. We can exchange ...'

Harriet's voice lost in the noise of the hustle, Catherine mouthed, 'Thank you.'

The conductor directed the passengers to their assigned cars, Harriet and Elena stepping into the first-class carriage. Catherine and her mother entered the second-class car. Callaghan had demanded Mother buy the most inexpensive tickets.

'Mister Callaghan is such a scrooge,' Catherine grumbled through gritted teeth.

Why had mother married Callaghan and continued to put up with his offensive manner? Father would have ensured they had first class seats. Oh, she did grieve for him.

The train chugged forward, and Catherine toppled sidewards. Regaining her balance, she quickly resumed her seat and settled beside her mother, placing a woollen rug over their laps. Catherine brought a book to read, but she chose to rest back in the cushioned seat, stare out the window for a while entertaining her own thoughts.

Lifting her head to the sound of youthful chatter, she noticed several children in the forward section of her compartment—ordinary folk, their outfits resembling Edwin's sister, Mary's. A well-dressed woman ensured the youngsters remained well-behaved.

♫♪ ♫♪

The train stopped at Campbell Town to pick up more goods and passengers. Catherine watched from the platform as the rail workers hitched wagons, filled with large bales of wool, and huge logs, to the rear of the train. The smell of cattle dung and soot itched her nostrils. Memories flooded as she recalled Celeste's tearful farewell on the station and the surprise meeting with Edwin. A sudden wave of yearning overcame her—he would return for her.

Mother strolled along, staring over at the town—returned and regained her seat.

'Goods, off to the wharves in Hobart Town no doubt,' Mother's comment roused Catherine.

'Didn't you say Aunt Elizabeth's home is close to the wharf?'

'Her home is right beside the Derwent River. She says she has an excellent view of the harbour.'

'I can hardly wait,' Catherine said and settled again as they resumed their journey.

One of the young tykes whimpered, and an older girl placed her arm about the little one's shoulders.

Catherine's mouth gaped on hearing the girl say, 'It's all right darling, we'll all be together. Miss Emery says the orphanage won't be scary.'

Mother lifted her head, 'How sad, undoubtedly off to Queen's Orphan School.'

Mother turned to look through the window, a tear slipping down her nose. She dug her handkerchief from her handbag and blew, Catherine surprised at her mother's reaction. Edwin said the lady her mother lived with, in Campbell Town, was his aunt's neighbour. Maybe Mother was an orphan too. Perhaps her father died when she was young. She would ask her at a more suitable time.

Catherine scanned the scenery, the rail-line cutting a path through the thick shrub, and then across cultivated land. From time to time she caught glimpses of small cypress-pine huts, built strategically on creek banks, or of grand mansions on vast estates, where sheep and cattle grazed and yellow heads of barley waved in the breeze.

Staring out the east-side window, she mused. How was life for Edwin in the mines up at Fingal? Clickety-clack, clickety-clack, clickety- clack, the carriage wheels drummed on the line. The repetitive sound caused Catherine to yawn and finally drift off into an intermittent sleep.

'Arrival in five minutes, at the Hobart Railway Station,' the conductor announced.

Catherine jumped up, banging her head on the overhead rack.

The children laughed.

'Shush!' The woman slapped her hand over the biggest one's mouth.

'Ouch! He startled me.'

'You've been asleep. You missed the tunnel on the descent from Rekuna.'

'Train station terminal, ladies and gentlemen! Please take your tickets to the western end of the platform to collect your luggage.'

Catherine gathered her belongings and repositioned her hat.

A biting wind greeted them as they stepped from the train. Catherine buttoned her coat to the neck and put on her gloves. Patches of snow clung to the summit of what she believed to be Mount Wellington. She shivered as they walked along the platform.

Harriet approached. 'Missus Callaghan, Catherine, I'd like to introduce you to Doctor Lyndon-Swathe,' her affected accent intimidating.

'Pleased to make your acquaintance, Doctor.'

Should she have curtseyed, his demeanour bold?

'Catherine, here are the tickets to the performance I mentioned. It would be lovely if you and your party could attend the performance with Jonathan, Elena and myself.'

'This is very generous, Harriet,' Catherine said and crammed the tickets in her handbag. 'Aunt Elizabeth's home address is six Morrison Street.'

'Ours is fifteen Glebe. Send me a message, if you would like to have our carriage stop by to collect your party.'

'Mother, Catherine!' Celeste rushed toward them, arms and legs flailing in the most undignified manner, so out of character for a Miss Nicolson, and flung her arms around Mother's neck, Aunt Elizabeth trotting behind, tutting. 'I'm so pleased to see you. I've missed you all so much,' Celeste drew breath. 'I have permission to sleep over at Aunt Elizabeth's tonight.'

The ladies greeted Aunt Elizabeth, and Catherine proceeded to introduce the newcomers to Harriet's party.

When the Harriet's presented her fiancé, he said in his upper-class voice, 'I have met Nurse Nicolson. She has assisted on my ward several times,' he touched his hat, 'miss.'

'Good afternoon, Doctor Lyndon-Swathe,' Celeste nodded her head.

Catherine immediately realized why she felt so inferior in the doctor's presence. He exuded such confidence, considered himself most important. A pleasant gentleman indeed, she frowned.

On reaching the curb, Catherine checked Aunt Elizabeth's driver had placed their luggage trunk onto the rear section of the carriage.

'Harold will drive us to our home a half a dozen blocks from here. My cook has prepared a roast dinner to warm you up on this chilly day.'

From Park Street, the horses turned right into Davey Street. Catherine pointed to the tenement housing closest to the wharf—the quarters pocked as though a wrecking ball had pummelled them.

'The dwellings in Wapping belong to wealthy merchants. The ordinary folks pay them exorbitant rent. Molly, my maid's family live there.'

'Do you ever take alms packages, Aunt Elizabeth?'

'Never, Catherine! Unlike your grandmother, I believe they are happy just as they are. We need to leave them alone. Though, I believe our rector's wife takes the blankets we make and hands them out now and again.'

Catherine shook her head at her aunt's stance. She would rather hold to Grandma Kate's way of thinking—she cared about the ordinary folk.

The carriage took a left turn into Argyle Street. Catherine sat tall, her eyes agog. Huge traders, docked at the wharves, rolled up and down. Labourers, like ants, scurried between the warehouses and the vessels, carrying their loads up the gangplanks, disappearing into the bowels of the ships.

'I'm on duty tomorrow, but on Saturday, Aunt and I will take you and Mother on tour to see the entire town. The gardens are beautiful, and there have been some grand sandstone buildings constructed in recent days.'

'Will you have to work with that pompous Doctor Lyndon-Swathe?'

'Catherine, please refrain from such character assassinations.'

Aunt Elizabeth's scolding withering—Catherine had forgotten how class-conscious her Aunt was. Catherine's shoulders tensed, it would be a difficult few weeks if required to exhibit the ladylike manners Elizabeth expected.

'I'm sorry, Aunt Elizabeth.'

'Doctor Lyndon-Swathe is not too bad,' Celeste said. 'Some of the other doctors speak quite harshly, but at least, he has a caring bedside manner.'

Would the doctor also provide care to the people who lived in the shanties they had passed? Catherine hoped their tour of the town might include the Wapping district. She intended to ask the rector's wife about her charity efforts for the residents.

Chapter Twenty-Two

Aunt Elizabeth guided her guests through the French doors leading from the drawing room to a wide veranda. There, they viewed the expansive waterway Catherine knew to be the Derwent River.

'Magnificent, I've never seen anything like it,' Catherine said.

Elizabeth pointed out the various landmarks across the river, and after a few minutes, invited them to the dining room.

'The fishy smell is rather strong.' Catherine's nose wrinkled.

'One becomes used to it living so close to the salt water.'

Elizabeth gave instructions to her maid, 'Molly, time to close the shutters.'

Aunt Elizabeth's husband joined them for the evening meal. Ralph, an army lieutenant, deployed to the conflict in the New Zealand land wars, a quiet, reflective man happily allowed his wife to dominate the conversation.

♫♪ ♫♪

A large log burned in the small fireplace, and while it conveyed a sense of warmth, failed to produce much heat. Catherine examined the highly polished maple cabinet on the south wall showing off several exotic pieces of memorabilia. One unusual piece, the horn of a rhinoceros, sat prominently on the top shelf. She screwed up her nose. Strange why anyone found such an item worthy of display. However, she remembered Edwin telling her his uncle had mounted a wild duck on a wall.

Edwin—she was not supposed to be thinking of him. The short trip from the railway station to her aunt's home gave her fresh hope of meeting someone engaging. The town was full of luxurious residences, and undoubtedly housed noble young gentlemen from wealthy families, and Celeste would introduce her.

Bending, she inspected the piece again, and Aunt Elizabeth noticed Catherine's interest, 'Uncle Ralph procured the souvenirs on his assignments to Europe and South Africa.'

Elizabeth directed her guests to a maroon brocade-covered chaise with matching padded-chairs. The setting, placed around a large beige woollen rug, a comfortable conversation area. A few excellent watercolours hung on the walls, Elizabeth's name prominent on the plaques attached to the frames.

'Lovely work, my dear,' Mother said.

'I find it a most relaxing past time, Arianna.'

While the sisters-in-law chatted, Catherine examined the books on the bookshelf.

'May I peruse your library tomorrow, Aunt?'

'Of course, Catherine, it's pleasing to know you are interested in reading.

'I recommend Austen's, *Pride and Prejudice*. Its relevance will not escape you.' Celeste winked.

Catherine must engage her sister in private conversation as soon as the opportunity presented itself. Celeste was different since she had left home, was surer of herself and did not appear as stuffy as Catherine recalled from their discussions back at Willowbank.

'Let's play the memory game.' Elizabeth indicated a tray on a low table in the seating area, its contents hidden under an embroidered cloth.

Elizabeth lifted the covering. Knowing the object of the game was to remember and record as many items as possible within a given time, Catherine made a mental note of the scissors, a comb, various coloured buttons, a thimble, a piece of paper and pencils.

Aunt replaced the cloth. Catherine visualized the positions of the items, scribbled until she named eighteen pieces, looked over at Celeste and scratched her scalp with the pencil.

'Done,' Mother said and put her pencil down.

'You win. You are clever, Mother. I didn't remember all the colours of the buttons. So how did you do it?'

'I counted five, Catherine and then noted the colours were the same as our dresses.'

'But there are only four of us.'

'Ah, Elizabeth, but you forget about your maid.'

Without acknowledging Mother's candour, Elizabeth pronounced coolly, 'Well! I am sure you must be very tired after your long journey. I'll have my maid show you to your rooms, oh, and breakfast is at eight o'clock in the morning, on the veranda. I will turn in now. Goodnight.'

Snapping instructions to her maid, she swept out of the room. Her maid directed Catherine, Mother, and Celeste to their rooms, providing the necessary comforts but with minimal decoration. Turning the crisp white sheets down and fluffing up the shop-bought counterpanes, the maid retreated.

'Thank you, miss.'

'Call me Molly, ma'am. It's nice to know some of you cares about us ordinary folk and treats us with a little bit o' respect.'

'God has no favourites, Molly. He loves us all.'

'Yes, ma'am.' Molly bowed and left the room.

Catherine could hear her mother's soft whiffle, eased toward the edge of the bed and tiptoed to Celeste's room.

Celeste rolled over and tittered, 'I've been waiting. Hop under the counterpane, or you'll catch your death of cold.'

'Thank goodness for flannelette nightgowns and woollen socks,' Catherine said, pulling the covers up to her chin and turning toward her sister. 'Celeste … what's happened to you?'

'If you mean I seem to be having too much fun here in Hobart Town, let me enlighten. The nurses invited me to the Saturday night dances held in Glebe Hall, and I've met some handsome gentlemen. One, John Clarkson, a banker, and I plan to introduce him to Mother while she's here.'

'Dances? Do you think it is wise, Celeste?'

'Listen to you, smitten by the likes of Edwin Nelson.'

'I don't go out dancing, parading myself in questionable moves. Besides, Edwin is a Methodist, and I doubt he would approve.'

'But, Catherine, you enjoy the balls, Aunt Amelia and Missus Douglas hold at their mansions.'

Celeste's defence pierced. 'They're under complete supervision, and the dances are graceful, not unbecoming at all.'

'Really, Catherine, do you think I would be careless with my affections? You know me better than that.'

'I hope it's the case, dear sister.' Catherine sighed. 'I want you to be successful in finding a suitable husband who adores you.'

'I appreciate your concern, Catherine. You'll see, John holds me in the highest regard. His parents are wealthy trading merchants here in the city.'

Catherine kissed Celeste on the cheek. 'Sweet dreams, I'm off to bed.'

She was not at all convinced Celeste could protect herself in Hobart society. After tossing about, she finally drifted off to sleep.

♫♪ ♫♪

The jangle of the milkman's bell echoed. Mother already up, Catherine splashed water on her face, dressed, and arrived in the front hallway just as Molly passed through from the kitchen carrying the breakfast tray.

'Morning, miss.'

'Hello, Molly.'

Catherine followed the maid to the veranda. Her mother and Aunt Elizabeth were discussing the scenery. Catherine looked across the Derwent to Sullivan's Cove, the expanse of grey-blue water appearing icy.

'Good morning, Daughter. Come, we've got a warm spot out of the breeze from which to view the harbour.'

Catherine wrapped her arms about her mother's neck and kissed the top of her head. She shook out her serviette, noting the green and white checked gingham-cloth just like the one at home. The table set with plain ivory, porcelain-china, and highly polished silverware spoke of elegance. In contrast, a teapot covered with an oversized knitted tea cozy, placed in the centre of the table, looked gauche.

'Uncle Ralph left early for Anglesea Barracks, and Celeste for the hospital,' Mother said.

'Shame, they're missing this delightful morning.'

Two ships docked at the quay swung back and forth with the lapping of the wave. On the wharf adjacent all manner of farm carts and rail wagons in a line staggered under the weight of crates of apples, bales of wool, and stacks of timber. Several large traders anchored in the port nearby, waiting their turn to dock.

Across the cove, a gleam bounced from a high point, drawing Catherine's attention to a magnificent home set in endless gardens. 'Is that Governor Weld's residence?'

Aunt Elizabeth confirmed and reached for the bell pull, Molly dashing to her side.

'Please bring the porridge, Molly.'

Catherine grinned, Elizabeth's improved manner was almost contrite.

'Yes, ma'am, I'll get it right away.' Molly glanced at the Mother, smiled and skipped toward the kitchen, returning with a large bowl of porridge.

'Excuse me.' Catherine's stomach growled. 'Please pass the honey, Mother?'

Scooping polite sized portions of the mix into her mouth, she savoured the flavour. Reaching for a piece of hot buttered toast, she lathered it with raspberry jam. The Willowbank ladies had not enjoyed such a leisurely morning in years.

Elizabeth related her experiences of various social events recently attended, and was particularly excited about an afternoon tea at Government House.

She pointed across the bay. 'Only the upper echelons are invited to the governor's residence. The fine structure is considered the best in the British Colonies, the sandstone quarried on the property and hand-carved. The clock, in the main tower, came from the old St. John's church building.'

Catherine, keen to hear more, asked, 'You did say you've been inside?'

'Certainly, it's truly magnificent with its Huon pine flooring, carved cedar doors, and colourful plastered ceiling. Mena has the most beautiful gardens.' Elizabeth gave the distinct impression she was on first name terms with Governor Weld's wife.

'Do you suppose we might visit Missus Weld?'

'I'm afraid it is not possible—invitation only. Nevertheless, you may see the governor's carriage. He and his lady will likely attend the Theatre Royale next week.'

'We have three tickets to next Saturday week's orchestral performance. Do you suppose you could purchase extra for you and Uncle Ralph?'

'I believe I could arrange to acquire more tickets through our bank manager. He's on the committee.'

Molly approached waving an envelope, 'Addressed to Miss Catherine.'

Opening the seal, Catherine said, 'It's from Harriet. We're all invited to Missus Chester's home for morning tea on Wednesday.'

'I can arrange a curricle for you, Arianna, but I'm afraid I'll have to decline. It's my charity meeting at St. George's on Wednesdays. I will be attending to some business in town today though. It's within walking distance if you would care to join me.'

'Oh, yes,' Catherine said, however, her mother appeared to be quite content to remain on the veranda for the entire morning.

Chapter Twenty-Three

Catherine inspected her outfit in the duchess mirror and grimaced. Her dark tweed coat hid her womanly shape, and her walking boots did nothing to add glamour to her ensemble. Once out the door, she shivered, pleased practicality won over fashion—a chilly southeast wind blew across the water. She pulled her hat down over her ears and put on her woollen gloves. Aunt walked at a lively pace given her fifty-seven years and was several yards ahead by the time the ladies entered Franklin Square.

'John Franklin, former governor, loved by some,' Elizabeth said. 'He and his wife did much to beautify Hobart Town.'

Delicate snowdrops outlined their path, and pink Daphne bushes pulsated their fragrance, taking Catherine back to Grandma's garden. She plucked a flower from the bush, tucked it into the buttonhole of her coat and caught up to her aunt and mother. They were chatting to two well-dressed women with baby carriages—the young mothers sitting on a wooden bench overlooking the pond.

Elizabeth said, 'It's rather cold to have the children out, don't you think?' Not waiting for a reply, she bent over and poked her head inside the hood of one of the carriages. 'Looks like his father for sure, the pug nose is a dead giveaway.'

Catherine raised a brow, Aunt Elizabeth always blunt.

The mother bristled but replied, 'Yes, Arch is extremely proud of his new son.'

'Don't keep the children out in the cold too long. They might get pneumonia.'

Elizabeth resumed walking at her original pace. 'They are wives of men in Ralph's regiment. They need mothering some,' Elizabeth's voice too loud not to be heard.

She exited the park opposite the Commercial Bank, Catherine and her mother trotting behind. 'I'll be about half an hour, Arianna, if you and Catherine want to take a walk.'

♫♪ ♫♪

'The city is very modern with its paved footpaths and gas lanterns,' Mother said. 'I've something in mind.'

Catherine and her mother paused before crossing the street while a large mail coach, pulled by four sturdy horses, rolled by.

'We'd best not be too long. Aunt would be none too happy if we're late returning.'

Several gentlemen in dark suits and top hats acknowledged them—the charming sophistication of the city types winsome. Even Mother blushed.

'Catherine, Joyce's the watchmakers … let's take a quick look at their jewellery collection. I'm sure Elizabeth will be well occupied for a while yet.'

Mother led Catherine by the arm, off the pavement, and into the shop.

'Over here,' Mother said, and crouched to look through the window of a highly polished display counter. One shelf displayed various styles of pocket watches and one, silk-lined boxes of ladies' jewellery, including pearls, diamond pendants, and brooches.

'Oh, isn't that exquisite.' Catherine admired a brooch of gold in an oak-leaf design inlaid with rose cut diamonds.

'May I have a closer look please, sir?' Mother asked the gentleman behind the counter.

'Certainly, madam, it's a Hallmark. Our new Victorian-style

pieces are quite delicate, don't you think?'

'Indeed, they are, sir. I want to purchase this one for my daughter. Wrap it and place it in the box for us, please.'

Catherine gulped. 'Oh! Mother, you shouldn't. It's expensive,' Catherine protested further, knowing Callaghan would be furious.

'You know it's traditional for me to give a piece of jewellery to my daughters.'

'Not until they turn twenty-one though, and I'm not twenty yet.'

'I want you to have this piece in advance. It's rare when we get to the city, and a piece such as this is exceptional.'

'How do you intend to pay for this fine piece, madam?'

'I have a promissory note in my name.'

Mother pulled a yellowing scrap of paper from her handbag and laid it on the counter. Catherine's eyes opened wide. Her mother's sideways glance warned—the promissory note bore a coat of arms, a great buck with the words, Je Suis Prest, inscribed above it. Catherine looked at her mother and raised her brow. Mother ignored her, Catherine not daring to ask the knotty question. The gentleman cleared his throat, and a second shop assistant came alongside, studied the writ, looked intently at Mother and nodded.

The parcel in hand, they left the store just in time to see Elizabeth step from the bank foyer onto the pavement. She tapped her timepiece, 'I see you wasted no time in parting with your money, Arianna,' and dipped her head toward the brown paper package Mother carried. 'I need to call into Harcourt's store to see if they've mended my sewing machine. I broke my spindle, and they expected it to be in the workshop for about a week.'

Catherine browsed while Elizabeth completed her transaction, Aunt's voice reverberating throughout the store. Harcourt's showroom exhibited fine furniture, all manner of iron products, and general bric-a-brac. Admiring an oak, dining setting, Catherine checked the price of a matching leather lounge suite. Her eyes rolled heavenward at the ticketed price of four hundred pounds but considered it would look very handsome in a grand drawing room. A carved walnut sideboard with brass handles caught her attention. If ever, she had the opportunity to decorate her home, that would be her feature piece. Such a grand purchase would be unlikely, however, if she married Edwin Nelson.

♫♪ ♫♪

Aunt's house was as quiet as an abbey on Sunday morning; it was the servants' day off. Catherine donned her woollen coat and scarf and ran to catch the others as they hurried to the church across the way. Her eyes strayed toward the flock while the vicar thundered his threatening sermon, insisting they pay their dues, and should they failed to do so, be at risk of eternal punishment. Afterwards, on the church green, she overheard a couple of parishioners discussing the sermon.

'Goodness, gracious me, we certainly got a scolding today. I wonder if the Bishop chastened him this week?'

'I think he must be a little overwrought. He's been spending a great deal of time visiting the unfortunates down at the tenement housing of late. I hear reported there's been quite a deal of unrest, or so his wife confided at the guild meeting.'

Catherine spied the rector's wife, but as she turned to greet her, Elizabeth seized her arm and said, 'We need to be on our way.'

On returning to the street, the sting of salt whipping their faces on the stiff breeze, caught Catherine by surprise. She wiped her eyes with her handkerchief.

Elizabeth's brow furrowed. 'This wind is a little stronger than usual. We ought to be getting home.'

A strong gust picked up dead leaves and dust, sending a bowler hat tumbling toward them with the owner in hot pursuit. Catherine stuck her foot out to stop its progress and held it firm by the rim.

'Thank you, miss.' A middle-aged man nodded as he dusted off the hat. 'It's a strong southerly today. I believe the barometer is falling. We might be in for a bit of a gale.'

The ladies nodded in agreement. Huge trees swayed in the swirling wind. A snap above their heads caused Catherine to jump; a branch crashing to the ground missing her by inches.

♫♪ ♫♪

All afternoon, the sky overcast and air bitterly cold, Catherine and Celeste happily reclined in the drawing-room near the fireplace reading the books Elizabeth had recommended. Besides, their aunt had reminded them, it was unspiritual to engage in active pursuits on the Sabbath.

'I'm sure it wouldn't have hurt to at least walk to the park,' Celeste complained.

Catherine agreed, but she would rather have called on the rector's wife to ask when she might visit the Wapping crowd.

'It's freezing outside, Celeste, besides it's getting late. You ought to get back to your quarters. Harold might have taken you, but he drove Uncle out earlier.'

Ominous black clouds rolled about the southern sky as the girls stepped onto the pavement. Catherine, glancing at the choppy Derwent, pulled a face. Celeste waved and scampered away.

The front door slammed shut behind Catherine. She made her way to the drawing room, poked at the coals in the grate and threw on another log. The reignited flames licked the wood and spiralled up the chimney. Mesmerized by the quavering tongues, Catherine mused. It was as well she did not speak with Missus Birch—she may be adequate to minister to the poor folks in her small locality, but helping the rough characters in Wapping district would be a daunting prospect. Agitation ran through her soul, her sympathies fluctuating. With what personal fortune could she help the poor? Certainly, none if she married a man of no means.

♫♪ ♫♪

Catherine looked up when Uncle Ralph entered. He scanned the parlour and retreated.

'There you are, Elizabeth. We'd better batten down the hatches. It seems we are expecting some rough weather,' he said, his voice echoing in the hallway. 'Molly, you'd best be getting right on home.'

'On your way out, tell cook I want dinner served at half-past five,' Elizabeth's voice trailed off.

Uncle's military mode came to the fore, 'Harold, if you've finished seeing to the horse, close the upstairs shutters. Make up the bed in the room beside the kitchen for yourself.'

Catherine tensed as Uncle Ralph gave orders. He re-entered the parlour, followed by a worried Elizabeth, her brows locked in a frown.

'I can hear the sea spray pelting on the windowpane, I hope the water doesn't reach us here in Morrison Street,' Elizabeth said, lifting the drapes to look out.

'That's unlikely. Water hasn't ever reached here before.'

Uncle Ralph tried to sound reassuring but Catherine, unconvinced, lent over Elizabeth's shoulder to see.

By five o'clock, the wind howled like a banshee, loose items crashing against the eastern wall. The roar of waves rushing into the cove and slamming against the rocks was frightening—Catherine shuddered.

Catherine was pleased dinner was a quick affair, with Uncle Ralph excusing himself to attend to important matters. No one looked keen to stay up late. Aunt's eyes drooped, and she stifled a yawn. Catherine and her mother turned-in early.

Uncle Ralph, unaware his voice carried up the stairwell, said to Harold, 'To save the ships getting crushed, the director ordered them to lift anchor and move away from the wharves. The strong winds pushed another ship off course around the south coast. Poor beggars are likely to smash on the rocks. Who would be foolish enough to venture out on a night like this?'

♫♪ ♫♪

Catherine's teeth chattered. She had moved into the room across the hall from her mother, but sleep refused to come—the loud thumping of tree branches against the house wall alarming. She could not imagine anyone sleeping through the racket. Just after the mantel clock struck midnight, her mother tapped her shoulder.

'Mother, you frightened me.'

'Sorry, I'm not sleeping. Come to my room, and join me in the double bed.'

Catherine exhaled the moment she moved, but the wind continued to rattle the windows. 'The blow is getting stronger. I'm petrified.'

A rush of wind followed by a loud bang and the sound of splintering glass caused her mother to leap from the bed.

Catherine flung the blankets off. 'What happened?'

Uncle Ralph's voice bellowed above the howling. 'A branch of a tree fell, and one of the windows on the western wall smashed.'

Catherine ran into the hallway, Mother at her heels. Aunt Elizabeth leaned over the balcony, and the cook appeared on the landing wrapped in a cotton blanket.

'It'll be all right. Harold is boarding up the window. Go back to bed,' Uncle Ralph commanded, his superior military tone intimidating.

Heavy rain persisted, and it seemed ages until the morning light peeped through the edge of the shutters. The breeze had eased somewhat, noises from below reaching Catherine's consciousness. She reached across Mother's side of the bed, vacated. It had to be around six in the morning. At the sound of the doorbell, she grabbed her house dress, slipped it on and hurried downstairs.

Elizabeth held the door ajar, 'I didn't think you'd come, Celeste.'

'I came via Liverpool Street, but there are trees down,' she said, pegging her coat on the stand. 'There's water lapping at your neighbour's gate, Aunt. You're fortunate to be on a slight rise.'

Uncle Ralph rapped on the door, shed his leather-skin and launched into a description of his tour. He had walked up as far as Bathurst Street and down to the wharf to assess the damage in their immediate locality.

'There's a great deal of mayhem throughout town. There are outhouses, chimneys, and verandas shattered, debris across lawns and roads. Fences are down, and at the top of the street, I saw a sheet of iron twisted around the gas lamp. The few ships at the dock fared relatively well, being in the shelter of the bay. However, one rolled violently throughout the gale, and I saw several of its mooring ropes had snapped.'

'Anyone hurt in town?'

'No, a few lucky escapes though, I believe. The fellow at the newsstand said, a vessel was seen sailing at high speed up the river to New Norfolk, due to the strength of the wind, but they are all accounted for.'

Aunt handed Ralph a towel, and he rubbed his wet whiskers.

'I checked on the Rector and his wife. Found him hammering a board to a broken window at the manse. He said a telegram he'd received from Launceston confirmed the bad weather was widespread.'

The blood drained from Mother's face. 'I hope Louisa and the boys are all right at home.'

'They'll be well cared for by Evelyn and Sarah, Mother.' Celeste's confidence met with disdain, though Celeste could not see Elizabeth pursing her lips and waggling her head.

Catherine stepped behind her mother and put her finger to her lips. Celeste nodded, took her mother by the hand and guided her into the dining room.

'Harold heard from the milkman. The supplies were late because he couldn't get through with his cart due to several uprooted trees blocking the road. He reckoned a piece of sheeting iron sliced one farmer's cow in two.'

Elizabeth inhaled. 'Ralph, that information is hardly meal-time fare. Speaking of breakfast, I need to start the porridge. Cook's at home and Molly hasn't arrived.' Elizabeth bustled to the kitchen and began clanging pots and pans.

'Someone ought to find out what's happened, Molly could be hurt,' Catherine said.

Elizabeth huffed. 'Some of the squad headed down to check on the folks in the lower reaches, undoubtedly there will be muck everywhere. We'd be in the way.'

'I suppose our tour is off,' Mother's tone hopeful as Elizabeth served her porridge.

'The paper said, the wind will be blustery at times, and to anticipate periods of rain,' Ralph said.

'We'll not venture far,' Celeste put her hands together in a prayer-like fashion.

♫♪ ♫♪

Elizabeth instructed Harold to drive the carriage to the front of the house. 'Take the route via Macquarie to Wapping so we can see the damage, and sweep around to the Alexandra Battery.'

'Yes, ma'am.'

Catherine chewed her bottom lip, the evidence of the virulence of the gale clear to see: trees stripped bare of their leaves, windows shattered, chimney tops and slate tiles displaced, and fence palings strewn throughout the streets.

Aunt Elizabeth shook her head, shocked by the scene. 'The whole place is ruined.'

Harold navigated the scattered debris, but when they rounded the corner into Campbell Street, he tugged on the reigns, and the carriage slewed sideways before stopping. A torrent of water writhed across the street blocking the sightseers' path. The foul-smelling, syrup-like slush clung to the whitewashed walls of the tenement housing to a depth just below the window frames. The rivulet had receded but undoubtedly seeped under the doors. A woman dressed in men's overalls, screeching profanities, wielded a broom sluicing the dregs from her dwelling. Another, slouched on a wooden crate her head in her hands, her shoulders convulsing. She glanced in the direction of the carriage, wiped her nose on the hem of her dress and retreated inside. Further-up the row of houses, a stack of sodden and broken furniture blocked the footpath.

'Oh, Mother, we must do something to help them,' Catherine said.

Her mother turned toward Elizabeth, 'Surely your church guild could lend a hand. Serving in such a way would show these poor folks some of Christ's love.'

Without warning, a bottle flew through a door and smashed into a dozen pieces on the pavement.

'And that,' Elizabeth pointed in the direction of the pile of broken glass, 'is why to venture into this neighbourhood of debauchery is extremely unwise,' and leaning toward her driver said, 'Harold turn around. We'll go toward Alexandra Barracks.'

Catherine had no wish to continue touring, her heart torn. She ached to help the poor in the slum area, her eyes tearing as she glanced at Elizabeth's detached countenance. How could she be unsympathetic? Celeste squeezed Catherine's hand.

'Notice the attention to detail,' Elizabeth prattled on. 'It was a high priority of the architects of the Houses of Parliament, and the stately homes along the waterfront are to marvel at.'

Leaving Battery Point, they passed the Barracks. 'Uncle Ralph's office is the third window on the left.'

Celeste pointed. 'Look, to the right. See St. John's Park, the construction site of our new church.'

Catherine nodded, but her mind continually returned to the scene she had witnessed in the slum district. She would speak with Celeste the minute they were out of Elizabeth's company. The horses cantered along to Argyle Street and into Macquarie Street, passing by buildings even more impressive than the church: the Post Office, the Hobart Town Hospital and City Hall.

'A little different than the Wapping District.' A groan escaped Catherine's throat.

'For goodness sake, forget those vagabonds, at least they weren't hurt,' Elizabeth's tone scolded.

♫♪ ♫♪

The carriage drew alongside the gate at the Botanical Gardens.

Celeste jumped out, 'Come on, Catherine, let's go before it starts to rain again.'

The ladies walked along the promenade, Celeste tugging at Catherine's sleeve. 'This is the best section.'

'It's not so pretty now. The storm has wreaked havoc,' Catherine said, looking about at the remnants of the garden.

'I prayed long and hard hiding under the blankets, Catherine. I can't tell you the relief I felt early this morning when the gale died down.'

'I was pleased to see you come, Celeste. Mother and I worried so all night,' Catherine said, and sighed, 'is it any wonder after seeing the mess in Wapping.'

Celeste, paces ahead, called over her shoulder, 'Catherine, look, this is my favourite part. This enclosed garden is the most romantic place one could wish to find?'

'What do you mean romantic?'

'A special place for courting.' Celeste had lowered her voice to ensure only Catherine heard her last comment.

Catherine stole a sideways glance at her sister—Celeste wore a mischievous smirk.

They reached the pond and raced for the wooden bench, the clouds and the surrounding vegetation reflecting on the still water, Catherine amazed at the corner protected from the storm.

'Beautiful, isn't it?'

'So, you visit here often, Celeste?'

'Oh, yes.'

Catherine's temples pulsed. She could hardly believe her sister's boldness. She wanted to ask more questions, but what if Mother or Aunt Elizabeth heard something of which they might not approve? She would ask later.

The damage from the previous night was more evident in the next section; one Norfolk pine stripped bare. Catherine stepped around the branches strewn across the path. Society gardeners directed men in uniform to gather the debris into piles for collection. Inmates from the Hobart Town Gaol, Celeste informed her. Some of them could be fathers of the children living in the flooded tenement houses.

Elizabeth stopped. 'Look, Arianna, the native trees have been completely uprooted.'

'The imported oaks have fared better, deeper roots, I suspect.'

'We would do well to import more from the Motherland, and I don't mean flora,' Elizabeth said, cocking a brow in the direction of her nieces.

Catherine bumped Celeste's shoulder and increased her pace, forging a gap between them and the older women. 'Pretend to be interested in the exotic plants growing along the stone wall.'

Celeste curled her fingers, bent and looked intently at the plaque bearing the name of a plant. 'Tree-fern will suffice.' Celeste giggled.

'Oh, Celeste, you're such a clown.'

'What do you want to say that Aunt can't hear, Catherine?'

'Celeste, do you know much about the ordinary folk, those who live in the Wapping shanties?'

'What a curious question. Why would you ask about the down-

and-out?'

'I want to go help the ordinary folk clean up. I want to know if Molly's all right.'

'Might be a bit tricky, I'll give it some thought, perhaps the rector's wife—'

Elizabeth summoned the girls. 'Catherine, Celeste, we ought to be getting back now.'

Celeste quipped, 'She's quite the sergeant major, isn't she?'

Harold took the reins and steered the horses along Davey Street, the most direct way to Elizabeth's home, but the route required them to pass by Wapping once more.

After lunch, Mother said, 'Catherine, perhaps Celeste can help you decide which dress to wear when we visit Harriet and Missus Chapman tomorrow.'

Catherine immediately recognized her mother's suggestion as an opportunity to retreat. 'Yes, Mother.'

In the upstairs bedroom, the sisters chatted until it was time for Celeste to return to the nurse's quarters, her John Clarkson the subject of conversation.

Chapter Twenty-Four

Celeste wagged her head, adamant Catherine not attempt to go to Wapping on her own, and given Celeste's strong negative reaction to the idea, Catherine hunkered into the rattan lounge chair on the veranda and stared across the bay. She dared not broach the subject with Mother—she must find Molly, the servant girl, and offer help with the clean-up without her mother and especially Aunt Elizabeth knowing. She would find Harold and ask him to take her to the wharf area. He would know where to locate Molly. As soon as Elizabeth and her mother retired upstairs to take their afternoon repose, Catherine tiptoed past the parlour—Uncle Ralph's whiffling loud, as he snoozed in his large armchair.

Cleaning equipment necessary, she crept along the darkened hallway accessed by the servants, to what she believed to be the storeroom. She had seen the house-help entering via the heavy wooden door at the end of the passage. Only two days ago, Molly stepped through the entry lugging a bucket and mop.

The highly polished boards gave way to bluestone steps. As she placed her foot on the top step, it scooted from under her. She grasped the doorknob to prevent herself from falling, but her full weight fell upon the door. It flew open, and she tumbled into the ill-lit anteroom, the door slamming shut behind her. A trickle of blood warmed the palm of her hand. She patted the injury with her petticoat, examined the graze, and plucked out several small pebbles. A minor mishap would not prevent her mission.

Leaning against the door, she watched as a million dust fragments danced along the sunbeam originating from the tiny window high on the far wall. When her eyes became accustomed to the muted light, she saw buckets neatly lined up on shelves, and mops and brooms hanging from the wall, all according to their size—unsurprising, Uncle Ralph would be fussy about the equipment, given his military expertise?

Having gathered the supplies, she turned the large ring-handle to re-enter the hallway, but as she did, a metal pin fell to the floor. Try as she might, she could not open the door, the catch broken.

She flopped on the floor. Should she scream? Would anyone hear? If she needed rescuing, that would put pay to her plans, unless perchance she could attract Harold's attention alone. She could hear him tinkering with the carriage out back.

Climbing onto the shelf below the small window, she stretched and was able to reach the narrow bars set in the frame. She held tight with one hand and poked the other through the bars.

'Harold, can you hear me?'

Receiving no reply, she called louder. Other than a shuffle, there was no answer. She raised her voice to a screech. Silence. She would have to wait and hope someone might come looking for her. Feeling for the shelf below, she placed her foot in a bucket, and it clattered to the floor. She checked herself, trying to anchor her foot on something solid. A tapping noise at the entry allayed her fears. Should it? What if it were Uncle Ralph? The hammering in the hallway grew loud.

The door swung back with a thump, Harold's large frame silhouetted on the wall. 'Miss Catherine, it's not ladylike to be hanging from them shelves. Here, I'll get you down.'

'Thank goodness you heard me. I thought I'd be in here for hours. Why didn't you answer me?'

'Figuring you wouldn't be in the lockup, lest you was up to something Missus Webster was not to know about. Them walls are a foot thick. No one inside could hear you.'

Catherine breathed a soft whistle. 'Harold, drive me to Wapping.

I want to find Molly. Something's happened to her. She hasn't turned up today.'

'Was wondering myself. I'll ask the Lieutenant if I can use the buggy.'

'Can't you just take it?'

'Don't be daft. The boss would send me packing. Wait, I'll check.'

Catherine stood by the lintel with her gear at her feet.

'Miss Catherine wants me to take her for a turn. I'd drive the—'

'You can use the buggy, but be back before five o'clock.'

♫♪ ♫♪

Harold swung the buggy from the main road into a market-garden driveway on instructions from Catherine. Groaning at the quality of the produce but aware she was fortunate to purchase anything at all, given the many crops damaged by hail and sleet, she filled her basket to the brim.

Harold slowed the horse to a walk as it picked its way through the narrow alley of Hunter Street in the housing precinct. A steamy stench rose from the piles of rubbish dumped along the footpath, the sound of hundreds of buzzing blowflies pulsating. Catherine's stomach somersaulted. Two boys poked at one heap with sticks, and as the buggy drew level, she saw a mass of black fur, the body of a dismembered animal shoved into the drain.

The wheels ceased to roll. A Council barricade blocked the buggy's path. To her left, an open drain ran between two dwellings, a film of scum lapping this way and that; raw sewerage floating on top. Her skin itched. Loose awnings flapped in the breeze, and boards, defaced by profanity scribbled in charcoal covered windows. Mud clung to the brick walls up to flood level, the whole neighbourhood ruined.

'I'll walk the rest of the way. Can you point out Molly's place?'

'That's Molly's house, six doorways down. Wait in your seat. I want to check something.'

Harold hustled to the first doorway, spoke to someone through the door and returned without explaining his reason for the diversion. Catherine slid across her seat to disembark.

'Stop. I'm turning the buggy around.'

'We're not staying?'

'We are, but Lieutenant Webster says, always park the carriage in the direction you want to drive.'

'Strange man.'

'We're right to go,' Harold said, and assisted Catherine from the buggy.

Her shoes sunk into the slop, pleased she had donned the well-worn pair found at the bottom of the guest-room robe. With a bucket in one hand, the basket in the other, and Harold carrying the brooms, Catherine strode to Molly's door.

A petite girl of about twelve, answered Harold's rap, and opened the door a crack. Catherine's brows knitted—eyes lacking expression stared back.

'What do you want?' The girl eased the door wider. Catherine's shoulders sagged, mirroring the girl's stance.

Harold addressed the child, 'Is Molly in?'

'Mother is—'

'Who is it, Betty?'

'Tell her, it's Harold, with Miss Catherine.'

The girl withdrew and pushed the door shut.

Catherine raised her brows at Harold, but he held his hand up cautioning her. Catherine tapped her foot. After several thumps and bangs, the lass returned, hesitated and looked to the left and right. Was the girl going to send them away? Instead, she beckoned the visitors.

A row of brightly coloured cans neatly placed in order of size caught Catherine's attention. She thought of the Webster's storeroom. Perhaps it was Molly, not Uncle Ralph, who had arranged the equipment so neatly.

Molly lay on top of the cover on a bed of wooden slats, her head propped up by several pillows. At least the cot was off the floor. Molly's left leg rested over a stuffed hessian bag, swathed in a bandage strapped to a length of wood. Catherine wriggled her nose. The house stank of mould and faeces, the residue of the filthy slush that washed across the floor, thick clumps of the semi-dried mess stuck to the legs of the minimal furniture. Catherine handed the basket of fruit and vegetables to young Betty.

'Molly, I thought you were hurt when you didn't turn up. What happened?'

'The wind was mighty fierce when I left the other day. A big branch dropped from a tree when I cut through the paddock. I jumped away, fell over a rock and strained me leg. Lucky though, some soldier boy got a cart and took me here. He got a nurse, and now I'm trussed up like a Christmas turkey. Sorry not to get word to you. Me girl, it's not safe for her to roam about this here neighbourhood, and she's all I got.'

Betty sat on her mother's bed, rocking, Molly stroking the child's back.

'Harold and I'll get to the cleaning.'

Molly shook her head in protest. Ignoring the objection, Catherine put on her apron and tied a scarf about her knot hairdo. Harold disappeared with the bucket.

Catherine lifted the chairs and drums of chattels onto the table, and Harold returned with a three-quarter filled bucket of brown water. 'Water coming from the pump has a lot of muck in it.'

Molly leaned in to look. 'Same as always, all we got to drink down here in Wapping.'

Catherine grimaced. She always had fresh water to drink.

Harold moved to the doorway, rolled and lit a cigarette. After scouring the grime from the furniture with an old cloth, Catherine dipped the broom into the water and scrubbed the walls and floor. She sent Harold to fetch another load of water and sluiced the mess out the door.

'I need another one, Harold.'

'Miss Catherine, you is good for coming, not like them others. Me house was clean and tidy.'

'My Grandma once told me, Molly, God loves us and wants his disciples to show his love by being kind to others.'

Hearing a ruckus outside, Catherine popped her head out to investigate. A hefty fellow twisted Harold's arm behind his back and shoved his face against the brick wall of the tenement house.

Harold struggled, hollering, 'Let me go.'

Snatching the broom, she ran toward the men, a rush of adrenaline charging through her body.

'No, miss, out of here.'

The door whammed behind her, a bolt thrown. She had nothing to lose now. Hurtling at the pair, she slammed the broom across the attacker's shoulders. He fell to the ground, an oath colouring the air.

'Run, miss, run,' Harold yelled.

Catherine needed no encouragement. She lifted her skirt and tore toward the buggy. Leaping into the front, she picked up the reins. Harold threw himself into the back seat, and Catherine slapped the horse, the vehicle lurching forward. The buggy careered along the narrow street. Easing around the corner, she glanced back The attacker was still on the ground. A woman knelt beside him. Catherine pulled the reins, jolting to a stop. Had she killed him?

'What you doing, miss? Don't stop.'

'But, I might have killed him.'

'No, he near caught me. I only just made it. He tried to grab the back of the buggy, didn't see the pile of trash and fell right into the stinking mess.'

♫♪ ♫♪

Three heads popped around the sitting room doorway when Catherine made her entry. Though she removed her muddy shoes, her feet were black with slime. Her face and headscarf, which she had failed to remove, smeared, and her dress splattered with drops of the filthy water. She skittered along the hallway.

Elizabeth tutted, Ralph cleared his throat, and her mother exclaimed, 'You look like an urchin, Catherine. Where have you been?'

'A bath, all I want is a bath.'

Soaking in the warm water soothed her aching soul, her deliberations troubling. How wrong she had been to think slum dwellers did not appreciate order as much as the well-born. Molly's impeccable tidiness would put any of her family members to shame. What of Molly and Betty? She prayed for their protection and did not wish for her zealous desire to help to result in trouble for them. She would have someone look in on them, perhaps the rector's wife.

Chapter Twenty-Five

By Wednesday morning, the weather had cleared, the sky cloud free—a cool thirty-seven degrees Fahrenheit. Uncle Ralph collected the weekly edition of *The Mercury* on his morning walk to the wharf. He read the full description of Monday night's gale, lamenting, except for the possible loss of life, some of the old tenanted houses had survived. Catherine shook her head, recalling the shocking mess at Molly's home.

'That ghetto ought to be levelled and reconstructed. The squalor is no place to rear minors,' Aunt Elizabeth said.

'The paper also reported the narrow escape of the doctor at Harrington House, having just left his drawing room when bricks from a chimney smashed through the shingled roof and ceiling, breaking much of the furniture,' Uncle Ralph said.

'Poor Doctor Lyndon-Swathe, perhaps I should stop in on him.'

Catherine squealed. 'You know him, Aunt?'

'A wonderful physician, he sees to our men and their wives at the barracks,' Uncle Ralph looked over his spectacles.

'Uncle Ralph, he's engaged to my friend, Harriet.'

'Perhaps we ought to lend a hand, Ralph.'

'I'm sure there were plenty of hangers-on who will have done just that, my dear.' Uncle Ralph had a certain way with his wife.

'I imagine so, Ralph, but of course.'

He helped Aunt into her coat. 'Tongues will be wagging at the charity meeting at St. George's today,' he laughed.

♫♪ ♫♪

Missus Chester's carriage driver parked out front. Catherine had waited in the drawing room and, seeing him pacing on the footpath, stepped into the entryway. Glancing down she frowned. Would her home-sewn, sapphire-blue walking-dress be suitable?

Molly stuck her head around the door. 'Miss Catherine, thanks for helping yesterday. I'm sorry Betty locked you out. He who attacked Harold has the blackest heart.'

Catherine put her finger to her lips. 'Shush, Molly, no one is supposed to know I went to Wapping.'

Molly slunk along the hallway into the dimly lit pantry and covered her face with her apron.

Catherine rushed after her, 'Don't worry, Mother is none the wiser.'

Molly looked over Catherine's shoulder, her mouth dropping open.

'What was I not to know?'

Catherine spun to face her mother, who had followed her into the kitchen and swatted her mouth with her hand, Mother's scowl causing Catherine to shrink back.

The carriage driver's voice echoed along the hallway. 'I'd be begging your pardon, missus, if you don't mind, I has not got all day.'

'Come, Catherine,' Mother said, donning her warm coat, hat, and gloves.

The driver let down the step for easy access, Catherine's hot breath visible as she climbed into the vehicle after Mother. Though it was a clear day, there was no warmth derived from the sun. In the distance, patchy snow had settled on the mountain. Catherine's mother let the unexplained matter rest.

'It's an icy breeze.' Catherine pulled her scarf more tightly about her neck, pleased they did not have to travel very far in the open carriage.

They rounded the corner into Glebe Street, and she chuckled on seeing some children stamping with glee on iced-over puddles which had formed in potholes on the street, just as she had as a child. Within a few short minutes, they arrived at the gateway to Chester's cottage. Several workers straightening trellises supporting bean vines in the large market-garden looked up. Catherine caught the sweet scent of the Boronia bush, planted beside the cottage wall.

Missus Chester waited on the front porch. 'Welcome, Missus Callaghan and Miss Nicolson, it is an honour to have you visit.'

'We appreciate your invitation very much, Missus Chester.' Mother stepped forward, 'They're lovely violets you've displayed in the glass cabinet on the porch.'

'Fortunate, not to have broken.' Missus Chester indicated her entryway.

Harriet appeared at the foot of the staircase in the hallway, her cheeks flaming. She wound her hair into a knot and pinned it on top of her head and hurried to the door.

'Sorry, I'm late. I've been helping Doctor Lyndon clean up his house.'

'Oh, we thought there would be dozens to clean up his place, or we'd have helped,' Catherine said.

'Catherine, how could you have done more?' Mother said. 'It appears you worked like a galley slave all day yesterday, helping the shanty folks. Now I know why you came home exhausted and in need of a bath.'

'Surely, you haven't poked your nose in down at the public housing, Catherine. Best keep your distance. Scurrilous types occupy the slums,' Harriet said.

Missus Chester's head swivelled from one person to another, her eyebrows raised to her hairline. 'Beatrice, will you hang the ladies' coats and hats on the rack, please? Come in! Come in! I have arranged for my cook to provide a delicious morning tea in the dining room.'

Harriet led the way, a warm blast of air greeting them as they entered the blue-stone cottage, a two-storey building with pit-sawn, timber flooring. She guided them into the parlour, a heavily furnished room with polished, Huon pine pieces. A crackling fire enhanced the cosy atmosphere.

'Our cottage is quite small. No drawing room here, but we are having plans drawn for our new house. We'll build it closer to the front of the street.'

Catherine plumped one of the vividly coloured cushions, placing it behind her back.

'You have decorated this cottage exquisitely, Missus Chester,' her mother's approval rather animated.

Catherine caught a momentary look of amusement in Harriet's expression, interrupted when the maid appeared. She placed a tray of freshly baked pound cake and shortbread biscuits on the sideboard. Pouring the tea into translucent-china cups, she passed them to the women.

'The garden sustained damage, but the house remained intact,' Missus Chester said.

'We heard Government House suffered damage to the ballroom's slate roof and chimney pots. We also passed debris from Lyndon's conservatory in upper Elizabeth Street. It was scattered all over his neighbour's garden.'

Unable to hide the anxious twisting of her fingers, Mother said, 'The paper reported damage as far north as our estate. I'm worried about the children and don't know how they've fared. The line is damaged, and we can't return early.'

Harriet tutted. 'Then you'll still be able to attend the orchestral performance on Saturday evening, won't you?'

'Yes, of course, wouldn't want to miss it. We seldom have the privilege of hearing highly accomplished musicians. We're grateful for the tickets provided,' Catherine said.

'I am especially pleased because Mister John Clarkson is escorting my daughter, Kathleen, along with Harriet and Doctor Lyndon-Swathe. I'm hoping for an announcement soon. Our families would be delighted to be associated,' Missus Chester said.

Catherine frowned and pressed her lips together.

Harriet interrupted her uneasy train of thought. 'Come and see my room?'

Catherine followed her young hostess upstairs, trailing her hand along the carved banister.

Harriet patted the settee for her friend to sit beside her. 'I'm happy to be back, Catherine. England was fine, but I want to be part of forging a gentility in our burgeoning city.'

'I kept the letters you wrote me while you were at Cambridge. It's been good of you to keep in touch. You certainly had many wonderful experiences. It was refreshing to hear something of English society from your perspective, somewhat different from cousin Florence's, I must admit.'

'It was your letters that convinced me I should return to Tasmania, and I did miss the more temperate climate. The long and dark winters in England are depressing. It is advantageous to have found such a good friend as yourself.'

'I don't expect we'll see each other often. This singular pleasure is unlikely to be repeated,' Catherine said.

'A lamentable affair indeed, so perhaps you could do me the honour of accompanying my cousin, George Hampton, to the orchestral performance. While he's the son of a wealthy merchant of Sullivan's Cove, he requires assistance to find his place in Hobart society. His mother despairs of him ever finding a suitable wife.'

'I'd be pleased to accompany him, but there is something I've not told you. I'm enamoured with a young man considered unsuitable to my family. He's a friend of our estate workers.'

'The servants?'

'Yes, their fathers belonged to the same chain gang, and their mothers' are sisters.'

'Catherine, do not imagine for a moment I would give my approval for such a liaison. It is out of the question. You must not think of marrying someone from the ordinary folk. You would regret it for the rest of your life, cutting off your access to the gentility. Now, put it right out of your mind. I will have George send you an official request to Morrison Street, and I shall speak with his younger brother about accompanying Celeste.'

♫♪ ♫♪

As the women returned to Aunt Elizabeth's, Catherine was downcast, unable to recall the rest of her visit. Would her attachment to Edwin mean the loss of her family and friends? Perhaps she would need to reconsider her position. She would use the remainder of her time in Hobart to weigh her options—to think on such a grim prospect as isolation from civility, distressing.

Their vehicle lurched.

'Get out of the way!' Chester's driver swerved to miss a young lad. 'Stupid kids, playing chase in the alley, should be working in the factory with their hags, keeping out of mischief. No hopers, lucky I missed him.'

Catherine glanced back wide-eyed. The driver had struck the lad, the child screaming and holding his leg. A mate pulled him into the gutter by the shirt just before the carriage swayed around the corner.

'You didn't miss him, mister. Stop!' Catherine called out.

'Mind your own business, young lady. I didn't hit him.'

Catherine's mother touched her lips.

♫♪ ♫♪

Celeste stopped by Aunt Elizabeth's after her shift, and the girls took tea on the veranda.

'I think Chester's carriage wheel knocked into a small lad near Hunter Street when we rode home from our visit,' Catherine said.

'Did the driver stop?'

'No, reckoned he'd missed him, but I'm not convinced he didn't break his foot. I want to check if he's injured.'

'As you discovered, it's not advisable to go there alone. Those shady characters living in that part of town will be watching for you,' Celeste said.

'I thought you might come with me.'

'You heard Aunt Elizabeth say it was unsafe.'

Shortly after Celeste had gone, Catherine was surprised to see her sister return. She brought an invitation. Missus Birch offered to take her to Wapping.

'What do you think?'

Catherine bounded from the chair. Now, she could find the young lad and check on his injuries.

'Was a sensible idea of yours, Celeste, to ask Vicar's Birch's wife to accompany me to Hunter Street.'

'She was most keen to assist. She said, she and her guild members often take food parcels to the families of widows or those whose fathers are in the penitentiary. She already had boxes stacked ready to go. Here she is now. I'll come too,' Celeste said.

Missus Birch's driver helped Catherine and Celeste onto the seat in the wagonette, the tray filled with all manner of groceries.

'We'll not go empty-handed,' Missus Birch said.

♫♪ ♫♪

The overcrowded terraced housing in Hunter Street gave way to the few shanties along the shoreline. 'Missus Birch's 'ere,' an older lad called far louder than necessary.

'The Sentinel warns. There's plenty of dubious activity around here.' Missus Birch conveyed she was under no illusion concerning the seedy behaviour she might stumble upon should she knock on a Hunter Street door unannounced.

As she spoke, Catherine saw the lad hit. 'That's him. The one with the bandaged foot, see he's limping.'

'Come here, lad.' Missus Birch stepped onto the cobblestones. 'How did you injure yourself?'

'Got me foot stuck in them boards along the wharf.' He winced, apparently in pain.

'Come back 'ere you brat. Your mother don't want you talking to no strangers.' A scraggly dressed woman appeared at the doorway of a shanty. 'You'll cop a hiding when she knows you is talking to the likes o' them.'

'I got to go, ma'am.'

'Who's out there asking questions then?' A man lunged into the street, obviously extremely drunk.

Catherine drew a deep breath and ducked behind the wagonette. 'It's him, Chester's driver.' Catherine's mouth was dry.

Missus Birch took control. 'We brought some goods over for the widows and children. Here, all of you help us get them off the cart.'

She directed the bystanders to unload the wagonette. All but Chester's driver complied. He merely leaned on the doorpost and glared.

He held his fist in the air when the supplies were on the pavement. 'Now git.'

Catherine leapt onto the seat ahead of Celeste and Missus Birch. Without hesitation, Missus Birch's driver swung the wagonette around and whipped the horse into a trot.

'That was him. He's Chester's driver.' Catherine wiped her clammy skin with her skirt.

'Had he stopped, he would be identified. He must have known the lad,' Missus Birch huffed.

'He is an insensitive beast. The lad's situation seems hopeless. It looks like he has broken his foot. If it's not fixed, he'll always walk with a limp, not be able to earn a decent living, and they don't even care. This circumstance is so unfair,' Catherine said, tears forming.

'The misery of the ordinary folk is an unfortunate reality. At times, we can do little to help. There's no point upsetting the tenants further. I'll come another day with Vicar Birch and bring some goods from the guild.'

For the remainder of the day, Catherine considered how she might make a difference. She remembered Grandma Kate's motto— Contentment is found in a mission that inspires you. How could she help those more unfortunate than herself?

'You're very quiet, dear.' Mother crinkled her brow at her daughter.

'It's a complete disservice to oneself, and does no good to attempt to reach out to the poor in the shanty district, Arianna. The child is suffering the consequences of interfering. Catherine, I suggest you take your miserable countenance to bed and sleep off your feelings of charity. You'll feel so much better in the morning and wonder why you worried your head about them. It's entirely their own fault they end up in such dire circumstances,' Aunt Elizabeth said.

Catherine turned her face from her aunt. She wanted to scream.

'Perhaps Aunt is right, pop into bed, and I'll come up in a few minutes.'

Catherine mumbled, 'Goodnight.'

'Goodnight, whom?'

'Goodnight, Aunt Elizabeth,' Catherine said, and dashed to the door.

Her aunt wheezed an exasperated huff.

Mother stepped in as soon as Catherine pulled the cover under her chin, and keeping her voice low said, 'Oh, Catherine, I thought she would explode.'

'Her, explode, what about me? If she says one more thing about how ordinary folk are culpable for their predicament, I'll bite her head off. She's unrecognizable as the daughter of one as kind as Grandma Nicolson.'

'I know you have a tenderness for the impoverished, and by all means, do what you will to make their lives more agreeable, but I want to protect you from being entrapped in privation yourself.'

'Why, Mother? You've so often told me to follow my heart.'

'With the proviso, you choose well.'

'Is it true you were once merely a maid, come from the working class, if so, you know what it's like? Is that why you treat Edward's family with respect.'

'So many questions, but I don't deny it, though I don't know how you could know.'

'A long time ago, Stuart said you were, though I didn't believe him. There were further details suggesting an entanglement connected to you. I have an inkling.'

'You mean the drawing in the treasure box. I saw your eyes open the other day in the jewellery store when you recognized the insignia. Sarah let me know you'd discovered it.'

'The coat of arms is the same as the one on Fraser's coach, isn't it?'

'Definitely, but then Fraser is not an uncommon name.'

'Edwin said his aunt in Campbell Town knew of you.'

'Ah, so we're on first name terms with that scoundrel, are we?'

'He's no scoundrel, Mother. He's an honest, working man.'

'With no means to support a wife.' Mother shivered.

'I think you're trying to steer me away from the subject, but you're cold, hop in here, it's cosy under the bedspread.'

Her mother climbed into the bed fully clothed. 'There is more to my story, Catherine, but it would be extremely dangerous for you to know of it. Only Betsy and Sarah have any knowledge of my past, and that's the way it must remain.'

Mother trembled. The evening chilly, but Catherine convinced her mother's tremor was not a result of the cold night air, instead due to her disquietude.

Mother rolled over, and Catherine snuggled into her back and whispered, 'Don't worry, Mother, your secret is safe with me.'

Catherine wanted to ask if her mother had opened the canvas bag and read the contents of her notebook, but she resisted the urge. A more opportune time would present itself.

Chapter Twenty-Six

Catherine and Celeste dressed for their evening at the orchestral performance, while Elizabeth and Mother attended the hairdressers in Liverpool Street.

'You look pretty. The blue organza suits you, and your Hallmark brooch sets the outfit off superbly.'

'Thank you, Celeste, the dress is another hand-me-down from Florence. Here, let me help you to curl and pin your hair. I saw the latest styles in Aunt Elizabeth's English journal.'

Catherine had warned Celeste her man of interest was to accompany Kathleen Chester to the performance, and Celeste agreed to attend with Richard Hampton, George's brother. She also accepted Catherine's suggestion to pay scant regard to Mister John Clarkson during the evening.

'Men enjoy the chase. Ignore him altogether, Celeste.'

Celeste hugged her sister. 'Dear sister, I'm indebted to you. So glad you're here with me. You display cunning beyond your years.'

The Hampton brothers called for the girls and their mother, their carriage accompanying Uncle Ralph and Aunt Elizabeth's along Campbell Street to the Theatre Royale. Catherine glanced at the young Hamptons sitting opposite, the boys solidly built with ruddy English complexions. They were congenial enough—Catherine would endeavour to be affable.

Harriet's party had already occupied their seats in the Dress Circle, when Catherine and her party arrived. Harriet beckoned them, insisting she sit beside Catherine. Catherine smiled—Celeste seated next to Kathleen Chester and almost giggled at her sister's nonchalant response on being introduced to John Clarkson. His face coloured, undoubtedly uncomfortable about getting caught out, but neither one indicated they knew the other. On cue, the master of ceremonies commenced the programme. Catherine sat straighter, riveted when the orchestra began. Never had she heard such harmonious sounds. Enraptured, she clapped enthusiastically after each number.

'Wasn't the violin solo magnificent?'

George Hampton smiled at her and nodded in agreement, but was less demonstrative in his response to the items. Without a doubt, he attended many performances. As the curtain lowered at the interval, dozens of patrons on the ground level hopped over their seats and headed in the direction of the ablution block.

'Drunken prostitutes,' said Jonathan Lyndon-Swathe, 'they ought not to have been allowed in. Have they no respect for public property?'

The two parties made their way to the foyer where drinks and lollies were on sale. In the crush of the stairwell, John Clarkson moved close to Celeste and whispered.

'My mother and Missus Chester arranged for me to escort Kathleen, but it's you I'd rather be with. I hope you still plan to meet me at the dance tomorrow evening.'

Catherine leaned closer to Mister Clarkson and said through gritted teeth, 'Indeed she will not, Mister Clarkson. If you were a gentleman, you would ask for her attendance in the proper manner.'

'Shush! I wasn't talking to you with the caustic tone. Keep your voice down.'

'Excuse me! You're incorrigible. Come, Celeste.'

Catherine grasped Celeste's arm and caught up to the Hampton brothers. Celeste looked back wistfully, and John Clarkson smirked— her sister enamoured with such a man, surely not. George handed Catherine a glass of cordial. She acknowledged his hospitality, engaging him in lively chatter. He could not have been more attentive.

♫♪ ♫♪

During the second half of the concert, their conversation felt easy. Her pleasant young escort would make a wonderful husband for someone like Celeste—an unsuitable match for her. Regardless, she had no desire to live in Hobart Town. George was not of the same mind. At the end of the evening, he asked her and her mother to do him the honour of accompanying his mother and him to the museum and art gallery the following day.

'There's an exhibition of colonial artists I am sure would be of interest to you. Mister and Missus James, patrons of the gallery, have requested the pleasure of our company for afternoon tea following the tour. They stressed I should invite people with an interest in the Arts. They would like some financial assistance to procure further paintings for the gallery and more artefacts for the museum. I am more than willing to do what I can to further the culture of the citizens of Hobart.'

'Such an outing sounds pleasurable. I'll ask Mother. I'm sure she would be delighted to come. We have a John Glover landscape gracing our dining room.'

'Now, that is impressive. Glover lived in your district, did he not?'

'Yes, at Deddington, in the foothills of Mt. Ben Lomond, country any landscape-artist would be delighted to paint in any medium.'

♫♪ ♫♪

Catherine stretched across the bed, reminiscing about her delightful evening, Beethoven's Symphony reverberating within her soul. Enthralling!

A footfall on the lower landing alerted her to Mother's approach. An animated conversation between her mother and Aunt Elizabeth reverberated, Catherine's romantic prospects the subject of discussion. No need to strain to hear, their high-pitched voices carried up the stairwell.

'I was delighted Catherine and Celeste accompanied the Hampton brothers. I am very well acquainted with Missus Hampton, and I like her. We regularly attend St. George's charity meetings together,'

Elizabeth said.

'You would not be surprised to hear, Patrick sent Catherine with me for these three weeks, with the intention of our daughter finding a suitable prospect, and George Hampton does seem to be a reasonable fellow.'

'If only Callaghan's intentions were honourable. He's made it clear he does not like the girl, does not care for her to be under his roof. He is concerned about his reputation and worried she might disgrace the family. Oh! I don't know how you could have married the brute of a man, Arianna, after being married to such a gentleman as my brother.'

Poor Mother—Aunt Elizabeth's exasperated tone left her stammering, 'I ... I ... It was difficult, Elizabeth, I felt I had no option.'

Aunt let out a wheeze.

'Patrick is most concerned because a road contractor from the ordinary folk has been hanging about, some friend of Thomas, and he thinks Catherine has become fond of him.'

'It would be utter foolishness to marry a man devoid of financial means. She is a strong-willed young woman, no doubt, but I cannot believe she would allow herself to get entangled in such a liaison.'

Perhaps they were right. How could Catherine assist the ordinary folk if she became one? Catherine pulled the thick counterpane over her ears to block out the sound of their voices. She prayed earnestly for the Lord to direct her steps and drifted into a deep sleep.

♫♪ ♫♪

Catherine's visit to the art gallery proved exhilarating, mentioning it enriched her view of the Lord's marvellous creation. She was not as keen about the specimens in the museum. Admiring the paintings by local artists in the gallery, particularly the one of Lake St. Clair she said, 'Does such a piece not convince you there is a Creator God, Missus Hampton?'

'Truly it does my dear.' Missus Hampton stepped back to take a second look.

George did not comment. He had not declared his position concerning spiritual matters, in fact, Catherine noticed he had not said very much at all during their tour. Missus Hampton took Catherine's hand and guided her to an adjacent gallery while Mother lingered with George.

The two women studied various paintings of Hobart Town and its harbour and discussed the portraits of citizens who had contributed to Tasmanian society. Missus Hampton chatted readily and invited Catherine and Celeste to dinner the following week.

'I've been spoiled by your most courteous son these past two days. I'm sure we can arrange to attend your dinner. I appreciate your invitation.'

During the next two weeks, George Hampton found every excuse to call upon Catherine. Along with her mother, they visited every venue of significance in the city. Catherine impressed by the sandstone architecture, admired the Town Hall with its Italian Renaissance influence, and the elegant homes of Kelly Street.

'Tell me about Willowbank, Catherine. What is your home like?'

'Our Georgian mansion was built from a mixture of local slate and sandstone and constructed by convicts under the tutelage of a renowned architect, a former prisoner. Our estate, acclaimed for its wool production, Father considered an expert in the field, and our trusted servant, Mister Edward, the chief farmhand, ably assisted him.'

'Your mother's name is Missus Callaghan.' George's inflection indicated empathy.

'Yes … she remarried.' Catherine raised her chin. 'My father was respected throughout the district. His gentleness toward his servants the subject of many a discussion.'

'But Callaghan doesn't, huh? Now he has control of Willowbank? He must be an astute man to have moved in on your mother.'

Catherine's lip curled. 'He's a villain, sent Mister Edward away. I'm sure he's up to no good.'

'That's rather unkind, don't you think?'

'I'm sorry, I shouldn't have spoken out of turn, forgive me.'

George shrugged, threaded Catherine's hand through his arm and led her along the street. 'Let me show you the best fashion-store in town.'

Her visit to Connor's Family Store with George was indeed a

highlight. As she tried on various hats, she looked in the mirror and either grimaced or held a pose. George did not hesitate to give his opinion, and Catherine giggled.

One over-embellished, flowered number brought the comment, 'They may put you on display in the botanical gardens in that one.'

A straw hat with a gold thread made him laugh. 'You'll have a jackdaw nesting in that one.'

She purchased an exquisite bonnet and some matching material. 'This is to sew a gown when I return home.'

'Now, royal blue, I like. It enhances the colour of your eyes, good choice.'

George's praise thrilled Catherine. 'Your compliments are accepted. I'll wear it to my next garden party.'

What was she saying? She was acting all uppity and had hardly given a thought to Molly or the poor ordinary folk in Hunter Street. She had indulged in the society of Hobart's elite as though she were born to it. Had she reneged on her promise to serve the poor?

The carriage bumped to a stop in front of Elizabeth's home. When George entered the house, Aunt said, 'I imagine you two will be sad to say goodbye.'

George stared at Catherine. She had omitted to tell George she and her mother were leaving at the end of the week.

Catherine smiled weakly. 'We're leaving Friday morning. The time has flown by so quickly, I've had such a fine time.'

'This was unforeseen. I hadn't realized today was to be our last outing, but as luck would have it, I can call upon you again soon. Your mother kindly invited me to Willowbank.'

Catherine squirmed. She liked George but certainly did not love him.

♪♪ ♪♪

The morning of their departure was bleak, the wind whistling along the platform, scattering papers about. Celeste clung to her mother until the loudspeaker bawled, implying the urgency for passengers to take their seats.

Catherine was wistful, touched by a tearful Celeste waving

goodbye as the train pulled away from the station. She watched her sister until the carriage rounded a bend.

Mother spoke first. 'George asked me if he could come to visit us.'

'Oh, Mother, I am not so sure that's a good idea, I'm so confused.'

Visions of the sad faces of the ordinary folk in Wapping flooded her mind. George's values were at odds with hers. The train swept around a long curve. She glanced once more in the direction from which they had come. Patches of snow reached as far down as the foothills of Mt. Wellington. Maybe she could weave some blankets for Missus Birch to distribute.

Chapter Twenty-Seven

Catherine, tired and disenchanted with high society following her return home, kept her promise to knit for the ordinary folk. She also began to fashion novelty items for the Nicolson's Christmas scheduled to take place at Willowbank. Callaghan, always reluctant to have extended family or visitors, became irritable and argumentative when he learned of her mother's plans. Up until Father's death, Mother enjoyed entertaining folks on the estate. Since Callaghan's arrival, she had complied with his wishes to avoid his displays of foul temper.

Mother persevered, 'Patrick, it is my turn to host the season's festivities, and you may join in or spend Christmas in Avoca. I assure you, even you will enjoy the way we celebrate Christmas when I'm the hostess. Besides, your daughter's families are invited.'

Catherine could hardly believe her mother's arguing the point with Callaghan. It might have been enough to push him into a rotten mood, but her mother's jovial temperament won him over.

He relented and even offered his assistance. 'I'll catch the turkey and chop off its head.'

Callaghan caught Reginald the turkey—Louisa had named the pesky fowl. He held its legs tight and placed it on the chopping block. With one fall of the axe its head rolled. Catherine gasped. She had always hated the gruesome sight. Callaghan let it go, and the headless creature ran around the yard until it finally dropped dead.

He handed it to Sarah, who plunged it into hot water, 'To make the plucking easier.'

Callaghan also harvested a small pine from the forest for the children to trim. Stuart placed it in a tin bucket, adding gravel to hold it firm. Evelyn drew angel and star patterns on wrapping paper for the children to cut out and they tied them to the tree with strands of coloured wool. Once decorated, Stuart positioned the tree in the corner of the drawing room. Mother and Sarah made fruit-mince pies and plum puddings, adding the traditional silver three-pence. Sarah scrubbed floors and made up additional beds for the guests. Catherine and Louisa dusted and polished furniture, everything gleaming as new. Mother travelled to Evandale with Callaghan to purchase extra provisions to supplement the Christmas festivities and to collect the gifts she had placed on order from the mother country some eleven months earlier.

Catherine snatched a few minutes while Callaghan was away to complete her handicraft gifts for the family. The sound of a horse whinny in the front courtyard put a stop to the activity, and looking out, she was surprised to find Grandma Kate and Rowena's carriage parked in the quadrangle—two days before the remainder of the guests. Everyone arrived by Christmas Eve.

As soon as Celeste came, Catherine took her by the hand, ushering her into the rotunda in the centre of the rose garden.

'Tell me, Celeste, is your special beau taking good care of you?'

Tears welled up in Celeste's eyes, and she leaned her head on Catherine's shoulder.

Catherine waited a few minutes until her sister's sobbing eased, and then asked, 'Do you want to tell me what happened?'

'John was courting Wilhelmina Nicholls at the same time as he professed his feelings for me.' The sobs began again. 'I found out from one of the other nurses, he'd proposed to her.' Celeste reached for her handkerchief and blew her nose. 'When I challenged him about it, he simply said, she is a woman of means and likely to inherit property in Devon. I want to leave this rat hole, so bye my sweet little lady.' Tears rolled down her face again.

'I'm sorry, you don't deserve to be treated so, Celeste.'

They sat for a few minutes more until Celeste gained enough composure to re-join the family and strolled back to the house. Celeste excused herself to wash her face before returning to the drawing room.

Sweet smells of the cooking infused the house causing the atmosphere of excitement to increase, the visiting children's noisy play irritating Callaghan.

He grumbled and yelled at them, 'Will you keep those spoiled brats quiet. I need silence. How can anyone think around here?' He threw the newspaper onto the table and stamped out.

When he rode out to the north paddock, supposedly to check on the flocks, Catherine exhaled a long breath. She struggled to keep her temper under control whenever he was around. Grandma Kate raised her brow at Catherine's sigh and patted the chaise next to her, the signal for her granddaughter to sit with her.

'Catherine, Scripture tells us our good deeds heap coals upon our enemy's head.'

'What does it mean, Grandma?'

'The passage tells us to show respect and grace. Doing so induces remorse and a change of attitude.'

'I'm sure that may be the case with most, but I wonder about him. He is incapable of pity.'

'Regardless, it is your Christian duty to treat him kindly.'

'Pray for me, Grandma, I can't do it without the Lord's help.'

♫♪ ♫♪

Right after dinner on Christmas Eve, Callaghan excused himself while the rest of the family and their guests gathered in the drawing room—the folding doors opened between the rooms to accommodate everyone, the crowd spilling over into the refectory.

Louisa, seated on the stool at the piano, beckoned. 'Let's sing some Christmas carols,' she said, struck a C chord, and everyone sang with great enthusiasm.

In between each song, the children read the story of Jesus' birth from the Gospels, and Grandma explained the readings. 'God sent

Jesus into the world to show us how much he loves us and to reconcile us to himself.'

'Reconcile, what does that mean?' Louisa asked.

'It means to bring us back because our sins cut us off from God.'

That night, Catherine considered the things Grandma Kate had talked about. 'So, Lord,' she prayed, 'You even took Callaghan's punishment? You would forgive him. Then help me to forgive him too. I'll try to treat him with courtesy, even when he hurts us, but you'll have to give me the strength, there's no way I can do it on my own.'

The following morning, the household woke to the drumming of rain on the windows. The wind howled bending tree branches to breaking-point. The family had intended to go to the church service held at St. Johns in Evandale, but due to the inclement weather, remained at home and conducted their service in their chapel. In the absence of a priest, Callaghan deferred to Kate, since he made no secret of his contempt of Christianity, saying it was more apt for the dim-witted. Even so, he sat in the pew next to Mother while the congregation joined in singing a verse of a carol, after which Catherine read a poem she had written.

'The Shepherd's Joy

''Twas the sound of rustling angel's wings
Startled shepherds at their watch
Good news of joy to you I bring
A Saviour's born and ordained King.

'T'ward dazzling light they fixed their gaze
While angelic choirs proclaimed His praise
Hark the majestic song, 'til the echoes clearly ring
A Saviour's born and ordained King.

'The star in the east it glimmered bright
Pointed t'ward David's city this solitary night
The shepherds hastened, their song within
A Saviour is born and ordained King.

'There a peasant girl her baby lay
Gently wrapped, and placed on stable hay
In awe, they fell and worshipped Him
A Saviour's born and ordained King.

'The shepherds returned, their story to tell
They spread the word that all was well
Glory to God and peace to our King
A Saviour's born and ordained King.'

The congregation sang again, and Mother quoted a portion from the Gospel of Matthew.

Grandma spoke about the wise men's search to find the child Jesus, and challenged her listeners by posing a rhetorical question, 'What gifts do you to bring to the Lord?'

Catherine nodded—she would help the disadvantaged.

'Remember this,' Grandma Kate concluded her sermon, 'Contentment is found in the mission that inspires you.'

The family, the workers, and the guests trouped back to the main house, the children running ahead. It was time to open the presents stacked under the tree. Sarah added a log to the waning embers to warm the refectory and the adjoining room.

Each of the Nicolson girls received a suitable book ordered from the Oxford Publishing House in London—Catherine's *Little Women*, by Louisa May Alcott. Delighted, she hugged her mother.

Catherine and Louisa gave each person a piece of their handicraft, the gifts greeted with 'Ooohs' and 'Aaahs'. Grandma Kate examined hers, voicing her approval.

The younger children played with the carved animals and the rag dolls they received, the boys yelping or growling appropriate noises representative of their gift. The bell signalled for dinner, a traditional English style meal befitting Willowbank. The children passed coloured-paper crowns to everyone, and while some fitted well, most did not, causing great merriment among the diners.

Mother passed a jug of rich gravy and a bowl of sweet sauce around the table. Catherine licked her lips, the meat with crispy baked potatoes, pumpkin, fresh garden peas, and carrots delicious. All was quiet except for the clink of cutlery.

'Thank you, Miss Sarah, the meat was very tender.'

'Arianna, there's no need to thank the cook? That's her job,' Callaghan said.

A unanimous wheeze escaped from the guests.

'Sarah has excelled herself. It is merely a courtesy to offer thanks,' Grandma said.

'Humph.' Callaghan glared after the girl as she disappeared through the kitchen door.

Steamed plum-pudding and custard served, Catherine scooped a spoonful of whipped cream onto her portion.

Shortly after they commenced eating, Callaghan found a threepence earning him a special prize from Mother, a box of English toffees. Catherine grimaced, Mother pandering to Callaghan having arranged with Sarah to add the coin to his piece of pudding. He did seem jollier than usual, and Catherine supposed he had fortified himself with the imported Scottish whiskey he kept in his cupboard.

'I'm off to the barn. I have work to do,' Callaghan said, pushing back from the table.

'Umm!' Catherine's interjection spontaneous but unwise—she ducked as his opened palm swiped passed her head—hardly surprised, Callaghan avoided participation in the afternoon activities to sleep off dinner. At least the mood would be pleasant in the house. Her grandmother frowned.

'Let's do mimes,' Louisa said.

There was much laughter and merriment while they played the game, and an impromptu concert brought cheers of approval before the first of the guests made a move to leave.

'Before you go, we have some gifts to distribute to our workers.'

Mother called the children to gather, and they presented Thomas, Marjorie and Sarah, boxed-gifts wrapped in brightly coloured paper. Catherine and Louisa had sewn the handkerchiefs cut from squares of white linen, crocheted around the edges, added an initial embroidered in the corner and placed in boxes along with English toffees.

Simon tugged on Thomas' sleeve and said, 'I painted your wrapping.'

Thomas ruffled Simon's hair, 'Thank you.'

'Please accept these small gifts as a token of our appreciation for your service,' Mother said.

'Much obliged for your kindness, ma'am.'

Mother smiled. 'We're all part of God's family.'

Thomas bowed, the girls nodded, and they took their leave.

♫♪ ♫♪

Thomas wheeled the carriages into the courtyard.

'We've had an enjoyable stay and are glad you included us,' Callaghan's daughter, Meg, said.

'We were happy you were all able to come.' Mother had taken great pleasure in hosting the Nicolson relatives and Patrick's daughter's families.

They appeared reluctant to leave, but it was sensible for the Avoca residents to make their first stop before dark. The carriages departed the driveway to the calls of 'Goodbye' and 'God's speed.' Mother had given Meg a parcel to deliver to Edward and Betsy. Catherine had slipped in a brief note in an envelope to Betsy, asking her to pass an enclosed letter to Edwin, pleased with her clever little scheme.

'I'll give Betsy the parcel as soon as we arrive in Avoca,' Meg had promised.

Catherine settled in the drawing room intending to read the first chapter of her new book. Instead, she closed her eyes and dreamed of a handsome man with the bluest of eyes.

Chapter Twenty-Eight

The weather improved somewhat as summer progressed, the month of February particularly hot. Catherine, her sister, and brothers spent a deal of time outdoors picnicking on the riverbank and swimming in the waterhole. Callaghan demanded they all make themselves scarce after they completed their morning's work. It was as well, for Catherine itched to speak her mind, his constant berating of Mother insufferable. She cupped her hands and scooped water from the horses' trough, splashing it on her face.

Catherine watched her brothers take it in turns to swing from a rope tied to a willow branch. Dropping into the deep waterhole in the centre of the river, they swam back to the bank. It reminded her of Edwin and his gang enjoying the same pastime at the Narrows near Grandma Nicolson's home. Edwin would have received her letter weeks ago, and she hoped to get a reply soon.

The boys had brought their lines to catch a trout and moved to their favourite place to fish, the slow-moving section of the river where the current converged. They threaded earthworms onto hooks and cast their lines upstream, allowing the bait to drift until they felt a tug. As soon as they pulled their fish in, Catherine scooped them into a net. Meanwhile, Louisa, basket in hand, collected watercress along the bank and picked blackberries thriving along the paths.

'Here you go, I caught dinner.' Stuart dumped the catch in a tub outside the kitchen door.

'Perhaps you can scale them for Sarah, Stuart.'

'No Catherine, Mister Callaghan reckons that's woman's work,' Stuart said, his lip curling.

Catherine threw her hands in the air, 'What? Since when did you side with that?' She smacked her cheek.

Stuart lifted his chin and grinned. Sarah rolled her eyes at Catherine.

Wiping and sharpening a paring knife, Sarah cleaned the fish and covered the pieces in flour. 'I'll serve the fish with the fresh watercress, tomatoes, and mayonnaise.'

Catherine took a bowl from the shelf, washed the blackberries and took off their stems.

'Thank you, Miss Catherine, I'll make the pastry later.'

'Blackberry pie with fresh cream, how spoiled we are.'

♫♪ ♫♪

One particularly hot day, Catherine plunged into the river, fully clothed. She had joined her brothers as they swung on the rope and dropped into the middle of the river. Louisa screeched, her face contorted. Catherine did not care. If Mother could see her now, she would despair saying, "Whatever became of the lady I've tried so hard to raise."

Too late, Catherine discovered she was drifting downstream. She struggled to swim to the bank, her dress floating up around her head. The current crashed her against a log wedged by a rock, her shoulder slamming against it.

She let out a yelp. 'I can't get to the side. Help!'

Louisa yelled to Stuart and Simon, 'Quick! Come! Catherine needs your help.'

Louisa snapped a branch and stretched it out to Catherine, but she could not reach it. She sank, surfaced, sank and bobbed up choking.

'Help me,' Louisa screamed.

Simon ran along the river's edge. He grabbed at Catherine's dress—

the lace ripped away. He snatched again and dragged her up, onto the bank. She lay panting in the dirt, coughed, vomited, and curled in a ball, clutching at her shoulder—the pain excruciating. Simon squatted by her.

'You saved my life, thank you.' Catherine gasped for air. 'Where's Stuart?'

Catherine hoisted herself onto her elbow. Stuart was down the river and had resumed fishing, or had he even stopped? Catherine sobbed. He had not even attempted to rescue her? Did he care she nearly drowned?

♫♪ ♫♪

Catherine looked at her filthy dress. Not only was it dirty, but it was also torn from the waist down to the hem. 'We'd better be getting on home.'

Simon led them along the track toward the house. As the group drew level with the garden, Stuart dashed past Catherine and ran to the stables. Approaching the house, she considered what route to take to avoid detection. Callaghan would thrash her if he caught her in such a state.

Callaghan came into the courtyard, his fist raised. 'Girl! What're you doing swimming in the river? You're a complete and utter idiot! You were supposed to take care of those brats, not involve them in horseplay.'

'Stuart ratted on me?' She clenched her teeth, closed her eyes and waited for the blow. It did not come.

'Meet our guest.' Callaghan's tone changed, was almost civil.

Catherine swung around, her eyes opened wide. George Hampton was standing in the doorway to the stable.

'Oh, no!' Catherine picked up her sodden dress and ran to the rear entrance of the house through the back door, wincing at Callaghan's devil-like cackle.

Sarah's mouth dropped open.

Catherine gave no explanation for her condition but simply pleaded, 'Sarah, please pour a bath for me,' and she bounded up the staircase into her room.

♫♪ ♫♪

Catherine soaked in the tub trying to figure out how George Hampton happened to be visiting Willowbank. What was he doing here? At least he saved her from the beast.

The dinner bell clanged. Callaghan and George Hampton were already seated at the table when Catherine entered the room.

George stood. 'How are you, Catherine? It is good to set eyes on you again.'

Heat rose up her neck and into her face. 'Hello, George, nice to see you, too.'

The family found their places, Callaghan directing George to the seat next to him and clipped Stuart under the ear to move along for Catherine. Louisa sat opposite. Callaghan clapped his hands, the signal to Sarah he was ready for the meal to be served.

George shuffled his feet from side to side, bumping Catherine with his knee at intervals. She glanced down and saw Louisa's bare toes rubbing against George's shoes. The flirt was playing with George's feet under the table. Catherine looked across at her sister and frowned. Louisa ignored her, smiling, and signalling George with her eyes. He looked at his food and pushed his fork about his plate—beads of perspiration shining on his cheeks. Callaghan either did not notice or could care less and chomped noisily at his chop bone. Mother coughed a gentle warning to Louisa, who tossed her head and sat up straight.

'Catherine, come to the drawing room following dinner, and you too, Arianna. The rest of you up to your rooms, and that includes you, Evelyn. I don't want to see any of you before breakfast,' Callaghan said.

'I'm not a baby. I don't want to go to bed this early.'

'Stop your whining, Son. Do you want a thrashing?'

Simon chased Evelyn up the stairs without further argument, Catherine pleased he did not kick up more fuss—it would not do for George Hampton to witness Callaghan's temper in full flight. Callaghan took George to the drawing room, and he beckoned Catherine.

'Your mother and I have decided, it would be advantageous for you to begin seeing Mister Hampton. He made it known he is interested in courting you.'

Callaghan had hardly waited for Catherine and her mother to be seated before he launched into his speech, George Hampton looking decidedly uncomfortable. He sat opposite with his chin almost touching his chest. His ruddy complexion had taken on a distinctly crimson glow. Catherine looked away—her fingernails digging into the leather upholstery of her chair. She wanted to punch her stepfather for his lack of manners.

'I think we ought to leave Mister Hampton and Catherine alone for a short while, Patrick.' Her mother stood to leave.

'You amaze me, woman. For once you have a brilliant idea,' Callaghan said, and followed Mother into the hallway.

Catherine waited for them to move out of earshot. 'He has a difficult character, George. I'm sorry he embarrassed you so … he's never considered others' feelings.'

'Well, I guess at least he's saved me the awkwardness of broaching the subject with you. Moreover, he's made me an offer too good to refuse. Reckons he can sew up a deal for me here with the estate owners in the Evandale district. I'm a merchant broker you know, and I'd make a fortune if I can arrange the transport. Mister Callaghan wants lambs and cattle sent by rail to Launceston or Hobart, the meat salted and shipped to Europe.'

'Yes, I know, but how does it concern me?'

'I had a letter from your mother to say you missed me and wished I'd be able to visit Willowbank.'

Catherine grimaced. What a monster. He must have forced Evelyn to write that letter on Mother's behalf. 'Oh, I didn't know … Now, I'm the one embarrassed.'

How could she tell him, she didn't have feelings for him? Callaghan had placed her in an untenable position.

'Mister Callaghan plans to introduce me to the owners of the district's largest estates tomorrow. Missus Fraser has invited us, along with the other estate owners to a luncheon at Braeside. Mister Callaghan insists you and your mother accompany us.'

'Oh, my goodness, Mother.' Catherine grasped the rear of the nearest chair and said, 'Well then, I guess I'll see you in the morning. Oh, by the way, have you been shown the guest quarters?'

'I have. Goodnight, Catherine.' George bowed and took his leave and went to Louisa's room. Louisa had moved in with Catherine, her room confiscated.

♫♪ ♫♪

Catherine sat on the sofa and buried her face in her hands. What could she do?

'Ah, you're still here, Catherine.' Her mother tiptoed into the drawing room.

'Mother, how dare Callaghan demand George courts me? Hampton is a perfect gentleman, but I'm not interested. When I tell him I cannot accept his proposal, he will be deeply hurt.'

'He hasn't proposed yet, and perhaps you might change your mind. Tomorrow we will enjoy calling in on our good friends. Visiting the grand estates will remind you of what it is like to be the wife of a wealthy gentleman.'

'But Mother, we're supposed to be dining with the district lords at Braeside, the Fraser family estate.'

Mother's brows knitted. 'Oh, Patrick didn't mention Braeside.'

'He doesn't know about the promissory notes, does he?'

Mother turned, her furtive glance toward the door warned Catherine to keep her voice low. 'He mustn't.'

'How have you avoided detection? You are so like—'

'Arianna, what's going on?' Callaghan strode across to Mother and pulled her up, out of her chair.

She shook her head and mouthed, 'I'm speaking with Catherine about our outing tomorrow.'

'All right, I'll go with you,' Catherine said, 'But, I'll not be pressured to make a quick decision.'

'I'm thankful at least you have agreed to come. Now let's get some sleep. It will be a long day tomorrow,' Mother said, and she brushed past Callaghan and climbed the stairs with Catherine, leaving Callaghan leaning on the mantel.

'Goodnight, Mother.'
'Night, sleep well.'

♫♪ ♫♪

Catherine did not sleep well at all. Louisa had moaned all night, but now her side of the bed was empty. The morning light made Catherine blink, her eyes hurt and her head ached. She dressed and made her way to the kitchen. On the way, she saw Louisa entertaining George in the parlour. They had their heads over a book. He threw his head back and chuckled.

'Sarah, do you have anything for a headache? My head hurts so badly I feel ill.'

Sarah sighed. 'I expect so, Catherine, I'll make you some ginger tea and bring it up to your room. You go, close the drapes and lie down on your bed. Place a drop of lavender oil on your temples and a damp cloth on your forehead, and draw in deep breaths.'

Catherine was grateful for Sarah's advice because, in a short while, she was well enough to prepare for her day out. She chose to wear a silk frock, a hand-me-down from Florence, and pinning her gold oak-leaf brooch to the bodice, examined herself in the mirror.

Her mother greeted her in the hallway. 'You do look lovely, my dear.'

Catherine snatched her hat off the stand on her way to the door, the one she had purchased while with George in Hobart.

'Good choice, Catherine.' George had come in to escort her and her mother to the carriage. Callaghan had waited outside.

'Right, Thomas, off to Fraser's then.'

Catherine appraised her mother's ensemble. Mother had chosen a simple floral dress with a pretty, matching bonnet, not a style she wore often. She had twisted her hair into a tight bun and pinned it securely, not a strand of auburn visible.

Chapter Twenty-Nine

'Doesn't Braeside Estate look a picture?' Catherine indicated the rose-garden in the centre of the circular driveway as the carriage came to a standstill.

'It is beautiful, indeed. Missus Fraser is waiting to greet us.'

George assisted the women to alight, and they walked toward the entrance, Callaghan remaining in the carriage.

'Welcome, dear, it's Adrianna, isn't it?'

'Arianna actually, Missus Fraser.'

Felicity Fraser raised an eyebrow. 'You may call me Sylvie ... my friends do. You've met my son, Andrew, haven't you?'

'Yes. Hello, Andrew.'

'Good-day,' Andrew said and nodded toward Catherine and George Hampton.

Catherine introduced George to the Frasers, and Missus Fraser grabbed his arm and escorted the party to the foyer where the maid took their shawls and hats. Catherine smothered a giggle when she saw her mother had tied a wide band about her head. She resembled the ladies pictured in Evelyn's history book.

The maid seated Catherine and George alongside the John Carrick family of Relbia Park Properties and her mother on the opposite side of the table—Catherine's nose twitched. Missus Fraser introduced the remainder of the guests. Catherine nodded. She had met most of them. Callaghan arrived some ten minutes late, and without so much as, a how do you do, flopped onto the chair next to Mother. He looked completely spent. Perspiration ran down his temples, and his hair was dripping wet.

A waitress brought in several large silver dishes filled with vegetables, and a second waitress followed carrying platters laden with a variety of meats and served the guests. Catherine savoured her meal, the lamb, flavoured with rosemary; succulent. Around her, the conversation animated and interspersed with much laughter, everyone in the room involving George. He and Andrew talked on and on, undoubtedly had plenty in common. Catherine wished she felt as warm toward him.

George turned to chat to Mister and Missus Carrick, omitting Catherine. She cared less and perused the family pictures covering the walls. One family portrait, taken some years ago, showed Mister and Missus Fraser with a young Andrew seated upon Missus' lap. Catherine scanned another older painting assuming those seated were Andrew's grandparents and his father as a younger man, given the style of clothing worn. A fourth person in the picture, a young woman, was—Oh! She gulped. The woman's features were so like—Mother. Who was the woman?

Catherine's mouth opened and closed. She turned and lowered her gaze, and did not dare draw attention to the canvas. She shot a glance toward her mother. Her mother's face was taut. Callaghan, locked in conversation with his neighbour, had not noticed.

One of Braeside's maids approached the dining table, her face as white as a frosty lawn. She leaned over between Catherine and Missus Carrick, and spoke quietly but urgently.

'Come quickly, Missus Carrick, to the stable. Something terrible has happened.'

The maid led the guest through the rear hallway of the house. A few minutes later Catherine excused herself and followed, sickened when she came upon Missus Carrick. The woman was holding a small bloodied white dog and moaning.

'My precious little Snowball is dead.'

'Strangled is my guess, ma'am. I found her over by the hawthorn hedge. I am very sorry, she is a beautiful puppy,' Thomas said, his face pale.

'Who would have done such a wicked thing?' Missus Carrick began to wail and shake uncontrollably.

Catherine met Thomas' gaze. Thomas picked up the dog from Missus Carrick's arms, and Catherine steadied her, guiding her back into the house. Mister Carrick met them in the hallway. After speaking briefly with the maid, he called for their carriage and left without another word. Missus Fraser, unaware of the circumstances of the noise and Carrick's departure, called for dessert.

'Tell her we're leaving,' Callaghan muttered through clenched teeth into Mother's ear but not quietly enough.

'Patrick, that would be very rude.'

'Do it, woman.'

'Missus Fraser, I thank you for the delicious dinner. Please excuse our party. We'll not stay for dessert and need to leave immediately.'

'What on earth have I done so wrong? Everyone is leaving. What of my luncheon. The men haven't even signed off on the proposal.'

'George and I will meet with your son tomorrow.'

Once back on the main road Callaghan said, 'Thomas take me to the Blenheim in Longford, I need a b… drink. That blasted dog bit me on the ankle.'

Not one of the Willowbank passengers uttered a sound. Catherine looked from one to the other. Neither her mother nor George asked why they needed to depart urgently. Of course, Callaghan knew.

She stared across the post and rail fence toward the Western Tiers. Gibbet Hill rose in the foreground, the place, where following a lashing from the cat-o-nine tails, the convict hangings had taken place. Callaghan deserved a lashing, he was cruel. O Lord, help, she cried deep within her soul.

'Find a table and order pudding. I'm getting a drink.' Callaghan pushed Mother into the Blenheim Hotel dining room.

'That ridiculous fuss back at Braeside meant we missed out on dessert. Come on, George, let's get a beer.'

George hesitated. 'Would you like a drink, ladies?'

'They can wait. Bring them a lemonade afterwards.'

Catherine and Mother sat silently for a few minutes.

'What happened back there?' Mother kept her voice low.

'Missus Carrick's dog was killed.'

'You don't suppose Mister Callaghan had anything to do with the little dog's death?'

'I think you know the answer, Mother.'

'Here we are, one for you, Catherine, and one for you, Missus Callaghan.'

'Kind of you, George, thank you.'

'Well, son, it seems you made quite an impression today. We're in business. They bought the idea, box and dice, especially young Andrew Fraser. We'll sign him up tomorrow.'

'I'm very pleased. The deal will be beneficial to all.'

'More importantly, you and I have set in motion a plan to propel ourselves into the upper stratum. We'll soon be very rich.'

'I'll move to Evandale next month then,' George said.

'I'll speak to the rector, and we can arrange a wedding as soon as possible,' Callaghan said.

'Sir, don't you think I ought to propose first?'

'She's yours, Hampton. There's no need for that. Catherine, you'll move into Ferngrove as Missus George Hampton. I'll even provide a wedding feast.'

Catherine was dumbstruck. How could she ever forgive her stepfather?

'Please, Patrick, allow the girl a day or so to consider this offer.' Mother said.

'All right, two days, that will give you time to help her get the trousseau organised.'

♫♪ ♫♪

Catherine spent hours tossing the covers off and dragging them back over her head.

Could she learn to like George? She liked Ferngrove House, with its cottage garden and curved cedar staircase. She recalled the polished marble mantelpieces at the house. They were quite remarkable, and the conservatory a wonderful place for afternoon teas. If they were well-to-do, she could engage in charity work in the same way her Grandma Kate did in Perth.

She sweated one minute, froze the next and heaved the covers up again. George did not react as she might have expected when he discovered the reason Missus Carrick was upset at Braeside. He said, after all, it's only a dog. Perhaps George did not care for pets. He was not as sensitive as Edwin, but she had not seen Edwin in ages. He might never return. Catherine decided what she must do. She drifted off to sleep just as dawn peeked through the curtain.

♫♪ ♫♪

'Good gracious, Catherine, what on earth's the matter with you? You were moaning and talking in your sleep all night.' Louisa tossed the cushions onto the bed.

'Not all night, I hardly slept.'

'What's bothering you so? Is it something to do with your intended?'

'Why does everyone assume George is my intended?'

'Well if he's not, let me know. I'd have him in a second. He's good looking, well-mannered, and plenty rich.'

'You're welcome.'

'What, Catherine? You'd be foolish to pass him up.'

Catherine backed out of the room leaving Louisa with her mouth gaping.

On reaching the foot of the stairs, Catherine beckoned George to follow her, 'George, may I have a word with you in the drawing room, please?'

'Yes, Catherine, what is it?' George sat on Callaghan's chair behind the desk.

'I have considered Mister Callaghan's suggestion we become husband and wife.'

'I do hope you're in agreement … I'm pinning all my hopes on you assisting me with the business.'

'George, it is a very wonderful offer. I like you, and I like the house in Evandale.'

'You sound somewhat hesitant.'

'I am, George. I'm afraid, I'm in love with someone else, and I really can't marry you.'

'Catherine, how can you be so heartless? I had no idea. I was given to believe you cared for me, and now I'm entrapped into this scheme Callaghan has dreamed up, and with no wife to support me.'

'I am sure you will find a suitable wife, but it's just not going to be me.'

George Hampton turned on his heel and left the room. Catherine escaped to the pond and sat on the bench under the elm tree until she was sure George had left Willowbank.

♫♪ ♫♪

Catherine froze at the top of the stairs.

'What's she thinking?' Callaghan screeched.

'She told him she doesn't love him. He's gone back to Hobart. He said he'd still move into the Evandale house and begin trading as arranged.'

'It's your fault. I've heard you tell the girl often enough to follow her heart. What stupid advice is that?'

Catherine slipped along the hallway and climbed into a closet. Her mother pounded upstairs and into her room. Callaghan followed.

'No, don't, please, Patrick.'

Thump! The door opposite slammed against the wall. Heavy footsteps retreated along the hallway.

Callaghan let go a string of profanities. 'Where is the girl? I'll kill her if I find her. If she won't marry him, then her sister shall.'

He flung a door against a jam, most likely Catherine's. She was thankful, Louisa and the others left earlier to collect mushrooms.

He stomped down the stairs. Catherine did not move for several minutes. Wriggling, trying to free her cramped leg, her foot caught in something at the rear of the closet.

'Catherine, you can come out now. He's ridden off.' Mother opened the cupboard door.

The bright sunlight illuminated the space. Catherine reached over and dragged at a strap.

Mother's eyes opened wide. 'A holster.'

'And a handgun in it.'

'Put it back quickly.'

'Wait, let me see if it's loaded. No bullets.'

'He's gone to Evandale, no doubt to drink himself into oblivion. Keep out of his way for a day or so.'

'I will, don't worry. I'm sorry that thug struck you on my account. Let me see to your graze.'

'I'll be in my room.' Mother closed the door.

Sarah was not in the kitchen. Catherine discovered the lantern high on a shelf. She poked a thin stick into the coals of the woodstove and transferred the flame to the wick. It flared. Descending the cellar stairs, she gripped the rough wall. She held the light high and searched for Marjorie's concoction of mutton tallow and herbs. She shifted several bottles of preserves and discovered the jar marked, "salve".

The lantern flickered and died.

'Oh, dear me.'

Reaching for ointment, she knocked a bottle. It crashed to the stone floor and shattered. She moved her hand to the side and scraped a cold metal surface.

'A canister?'

Tracing her finger over the lid—it was her mother's jewellery box. She poked around behind the tin and discovered her canvas bag, her notebook undamaged inside.

She kicked a piece of broken glass in the darkness and hoped the jar she held was the salve. Seeing a shaft of light from the open door, she made her way to the kitchen and placed the lantern back on the shelf.

She scribbled a note for Sarah about the broken utensil, and shook her head. Of course, Sarah could barely read. She scrubbed the words out, drew a large cross on the paper and stuck it to the cellar door with a tiny ball of bread-dough mix she found under a cloth.

♫♪ ♫♪

With gentle strokes, she rubbed the ointment into the bruise forming on her mother's cheek.

'Mother, I found your box.'

'You went into the cellar?'

'Yes, I knew where Sarah kept the potions.'

'Sarah told me she'd hidden the tin there. Only the girls go down those stairs, they are so steep.' Mother lay back on the pillow. 'Sit with me a while.'

Catherine dragged her mother's brocade stool from in front of the duchess and placed it beside the bed.

'I followed your eyes at Braeside. I am like her, am I not?'

'Who is she?'

'Mister Fraser's sister, but long gone, I'm afraid.'

'He came here often before he died. How are you related?'

'He was my father.'

'Ooh! Mother.' Catherine covered her ears.

Catherine moved around the bed and closed the door even though no one could have heard her mother's revelation. Everyone was out.

'My mother, his mistress, was his first wife's maid. She died of consumption on the voyage to Tasmania, and his wife soon after they arrived.'

'Is the drawing in the jewellery case a picture of her with you? How old were you?'

'It is. I was just three years old.'

'Did Mister Nicolson know of your lineage?'

'Your father, of course, but he wanted to protect Mister Fraser's reputation. He liked him. It was Mister Fraser who asked your father to hire me.'

'How is it Sarah conceals your box?'

'When Mister Callaghan sent Betsy away, Sarah became my confidant. My promissory notes and keepsakes must remain safeguarded. The items are the only evidence of my background.'

'I think my Edwin knows you were related to Mister Fraser.'

'Your Edwin, Catherine, please tell me you're not still in love with him?'

'I've not seen him in so long. I don't know.'

'Edwin's aunt was a neighbour to Missus Beatty, the woman who cared for me in Campbell Town. He learned of it during a visit and verified it with Sarah, she told me,' her mother said.

'Why does it matter if people know? Mister Fraser has died.'

'If Andrew and his mother knew of my existence, they would cut off my allowance. I especially need it now. Mister Callaghan refuses me sufficient funds on which to live. An amount placed in the Hobart Bank in the Fraser name is available. I can draw on it with the promissory notes. Mister Fraser also stipulated that each of his grandchildren was to be given a personal memento at their coming of age.'

'Thus, my charming, oak-leaf brooch, his guilt offering.'

'No, Catherine, that's unfair. He was always generous toward us.'

'We're back!' Simon's singsong voice floated up the stairwell.

'Let's not mention this morning's events.'

'I won't.'

Catherine escaped to the pond. The shadows clambered over the mountains and meandered across the plains, and she shivered in the cool breeze. Yellow leaves twirled at the bottom of the giant elm—Autumn spent.

Entering the rear door, Catherine leaned on the kitchen bench and watched while Marjorie sliced peaches. Sarah stirred the first of the cooked fruit and spooned it into preserving bottles. The warmth of the stove and the friendly chatter of the servants soothed her soul. She almost envied the girls' simple existence. Her stepfather had certainly caused her life to become difficult.

He calmed down in a few days, and conditions returned to normal at Willowbank, but Catherine avoided being alone in his presence in case he beat her or worse, forced her to marry George. George Hampton was not prepared to accept Louisa as the second choice.

Stuart sought Catherine out. 'Seems I had you figured all wrong, Catherine. I thought you were Callaghan's underling, but Celeste put me in the picture. Callaghan has duped us, especially me, and you were on to him. I'll let bygones be bygones.' Stuart slapped her shoulder.

♫♪ ♫♪

Catherine shivered. The long winter evenings ushered in with a blast of freezing air across the plains from the Tiers. She huddled by the open fire and knitted blankets for the ordinary folk in the slums of Hobart, recalling her visit. How was her sister faring in the city as a newly married woman? She smiled as she relived the events of Celeste's recent wedding on the estate. Celeste had met Thomas Schofield soon after returning to work in Hobart following her last visit. Catherine worried, Celeste had recovered rather too quickly from the jilting by her former man, but on meeting Thomas, Catherine's doubts dispelled.

She enjoyed the privilege of sewing Celeste's violet, satin and Chantilly lace gown. Celeste chose her as her maid of honour, and the whole family were involved in decorating the chapel and preparing the garden for the reception to follow. Many relatives and friends attended the happy occasion, and Catherine was pleased to belong to such a close-knit family. Even Patrick Callaghan had been in a jolly mood.

♫♪ ♫♪

Catherine contemplated Celeste's letter. Celeste had joined Missus Birch's guild not long after she had returned to town. Catherine persuaded her mother, Evelyn, and Louisa, to give her a hand with the knitting. Adele sent a supply of wool skeins. They were all keen to contribute.

A thank you note arrived from Missus Birch:

> *How pleased I was when you said your group would knit blankets for the ordinary folk in Wapping. I'm so excited about the charity work you're doing. You should have seen the people rush toward Celeste when she lifted the package you despatched from the carriage.*

Catherine hoped to weave more blankets to send to the Wapping Folk, but Callaghan refused to supply any more wool for Mother to spin, and this was the last of Adele's skeins.

She overheard her mother's comment to Evelyn. 'She seems rather too preoccupied with helping the poor and hardly speaks of anything else. Mister Callaghan insists it's a waste of time and money, and I'm afraid he's going to forbid us to continue supplying any goods at all.'

'People often keep themselves busy to cover up some disquiet.'

'It's so unlike her. Catherine's usually moderate, but these days she is utterly consumed.'

Evelyn was right. Catherine did miss Edwin more than she could bear, and working herself to the bone was not helping. She wished he would come back to her.

Chapter Thirty

Catherine hummed—chilly days gave way to warm summer breezes. She settled in her armchair near the window, picked up her craft and lay it down again. It was too good a day to be stuck inside.

'I'm going for a ride.'

Catherine hoisted the saddle across Ebony's rump.

Marjorie, standing nearby, rested on the broom and shook her head. 'I wouldn't do that if I were you. Thomas said Mister Callaghan had confiscated Ebony for himself.'

'What, how dare he, father bought him for me.'

'Besides, he told Thomas, he don't want you wandering off, sticking your nose in his affairs.'

An abrupt shout sounded across the quadrangle.

'Quick, pull it off,' Marjorie said.

Catherine yanked the saddle off and placed it on the hook, Callaghan's silhouette appearing in the door frame. He glowered in the girls' direction, snatched a shovel and retreated.

Catherine wandered down to the river with her basket. She hated injustice—he had seized all that mattered to her.

'Lord, I know vengeance is yours, but oh, what I wouldn't like to do to that man.' She huffed, and when far enough away from the house, screamed until her throat rasped.

Looking out across the plains toward Mt. Ben Lomond, she sat quietly for a long, long time until relief washed over her. Late pockets of snow gripped crags near the peak, and low cloud lay trapped in the valleys. She surveyed the foothills to the south. Edwin would be deep underground at the mining enterprise out at Fingal. While she longed to see him, she questioned whether they would ever meet each other again. From time to time, they relayed messages via Thomas, but it had been many months since Thomas had visited Edward and Betsy in Avoca, or they Willowbank.

'Lord, I do love him so much. Why hasn't he come back?'

She had stayed too long, her arms pink from the sun. She shrugged. Setting out along the path, she picked daffodils for her mother's vase. Spying mushrooms in the paddock adjacent, she collected them for the family's breakfast. A movement in the reeds distracted her—a platypus slid from the bank into the river.

'How odd you are … Lord, you've made some comical creatures.' She giggled.

As Catherine strolled toward the garden, she noticed a pair of yellow wattlebirds darting in and out of the Banksia foliage calling, "Look out, miss, look out, miss!" 'Oh, Edwin, I miss you.'

She entered the house via the kitchen door to deposit her load. 'Hey Sarah, I found some mushrooms.'

'Ah, they'll be delicious cooked in butter, and I'll serve them on toasted whole-wheat, with eggs and tomatoes.'

Breakfast was almost over when a rider galloped into the driveway, all eyes turned toward the door to see who had arrived in such a hurry.

'Come through, sir.' Sarah led a gentleman, still in his riding habit, into the hallway and approached Callaghan.

'Mister Callaghan, the gentleman is asking to speak with you and Missus Callaghan.'

'Let's go into the drawing-room?' Mother said, rubbing her hands through her hair.

The rest of the family remained in the dining room, not privy to the conversation.

Callaghan returned to the parlour. 'The messenger came from your Aunt Rowena's house. Your grandmother is dead.'

♫♪ ♫♪

Catherine and Mother rode in Callaghan's new, sleek black hansom. Catherine might normally take pleasure in such a ride, but they were on their way to Christ Church, Longford, for Grandma's funeral. Tears slipped down her cheeks, and she fiddled with the thin ribbon of tulle around the neck of her black dress of heavy serge, her bonnet tied so tight it almost covered her face. She stared at the blinking sunlight as the horses rushed through the brush, Callaghan perched high on the driver's seat. Thomas had not returned from his work in Avoca.

A surprising number of vehicles had parked in the adjoining grounds.

'We welcome you to this celebration service in honour of Grandma Kate Nicolson,' the bishop's voice echoed throughout the sanctuary. 'We thank you, God, for the grace extended to us by our dear departed.'

Mister Jessop, the church choirmaster, led *Amazing Grace*, the congregation singing as robustly as they might at an evangelistic meeting—Grandma would be delighted. The minister read a Psalm, Grandma's favourite Scripture passage. He spoke of the many charitable acts of kindness Grandma Kate had performed within the community.

Weeping families lined the street as the funeral cortege passed along the main road on its way to the Cypress Street Cemetery in Launceston, where Kate was to be buried next to her beloved Philip.

'You know,' commented one middle-aged woman, 'she taught me to sew.'

A neighbour added, 'And me to cook.'

The daughter of the middle-aged woman sniffled. 'I first learned, *Jesus Loves Me*, in her sunroom.'

'Oh my, my, we'll miss her so much,' another burst into tears.

Aunt Rowena approached. 'Arianna, bring Patrick and Catherine, and come along with the other relatives to the William Street house for afternoon tea.'

At Rowena's the extended family shared stories, as they reflected upon Grandma's years, yet no one would miss Grandma Kate more than Catherine.

'Grandma taught me so much, but it was not only the lessons, rather the way she lived. I'll never forget her adage, "Contentment is found in a mission that inspires you".'

'She would be happy to hear you speak of it, Catherine.' Aunt Rowena patted her on the cheek.

Callaghan interrupted, 'I need to collect something at Evandale, Arianna.'

As they neared town, they came across a road gang. Catherine recognized some of the young men. They had worked with Edwin.

'Hello, Missy Nicolson,' shouted one. 'Edwin's back in town you know. He's working on the other side o' town.'

'Quiet there, scum,' bellowed Callaghan. 'Catherine, look away now.'

She snapped her head around and focused on her mother's hat, though the muscles around her mouth twitched and her face burned. Mother's eyes met hers.

♫♪ ♫♪

Callaghan and Mother stocked up on provisions from the general store, while Catherine moved to the newsstand and flipped through a magazine.

'Girl, carry these out to the carriage.'

Catherine almost lost her balance when Callaghan dumped a heavy package into her arms.

Her stepfather hitched the horses to the mounting rail near the Clarendon Arms. 'I'll be an hour or so, Arianna … you and the girl find something to occupy yourselves while I'm gone.' He stepped into the hotel.

'We could have arranged to visit Missus Turner, the new minister's wife, had we known we were stopping for a while,' Mother huffed. 'She could have come back with us this afternoon.'

'Can we take a walk along High Street? I like looking at the gardens in Evandale,' Catherine said, not waiting for her mother to object.

Catherine walked alongside her mother, passed the Royal Oak, the Saddler's Shop, and then rounded the corner into Russell Street to Solomon House. The town oozed grandeur. The scenery soothed her senses after the draining events of the day, and she breathed in the perfumes emanating from the gardens as they strolled.

'Grandma Kate aided me to find my peace with God.'

'But, Mother, you've always been an upright lady.'

'Not so, I'm afraid. I was enamoured with your father before Margaret Nicolson died.'

'Oh! Mother.' Catherine's pulse quickened. 'Did you and father?'

'No, but it was hard. We shared an unspoken yearning, though your father remained honourable, and when Grandma Kate guessed, she kept me amenable.'

Catherine fell silent. Why would her mother reveal this detail to her? Was she fearful Catherine might fall prey to temptation? Her mother's Christmas gift was evidence she knew where her daughter's affections lay.

On returning to their meeting place, Callaghan leaned on the hotel rail, his head drooping. He staggered to the carriage, drunk. He reached in and handed a moneybag to a skinny young chap. The fellow snatched it. He had a ghastly burn scar on his left hand.

He asked, 'When will I get the rest?'

'When I'm ready, now be off, Slim,' Callaghan's speech slurred.

The Slim character sneered and said, 'Don't think of crossing me, Pat Callaghan. You're in as deep as me.'

Catherine pulled a face—an illegal arrangement, for sure.

'You girl, take the reins. Drive us home,' Callaghan said.

No sooner had they left the outskirts of the town than Callaghan called, 'Stop.'

He slumped to the road, was violently ill, and lay moaning on the grass. Mother knelt beside him. He pushed her away and flopped backwards.

Catherine looked up and down the road. Some three hundred yards away, road workers were packing up equipment. Edwin must be with them. She saw him approaching and climbed down from the hansom.

'May I be of help, miss. I see you're in some trouble.'

He did not address her by name, and his formal manner surprised her. However, Catherine assumed, because Edwin had only been to

Willowbank at night, he thought he was safe from detection. Mother leant over Callaghan and loosened his neck ribbon.

'It's Mister Callaghan. He seems to have taken ill.' Catherine addressed Edwin with the same aloofness, though her knees knocked together.

'He'll be all right in a few minutes,' Mother butted in.

Edwin must have perceived Callaghan's condition and wanted to avoid embarrassing the family further, and he turned to leave. Catherine moved to the opposite side of the hansom and met him.

He lowered his voice to say, 'Bit under the weather, eh?'

He took her arm and moved her further away from the vehicle.

'I'm sorry to hear about Granny Nicolson. You'll miss her. Any chance you could slip over to Thomas' hut later tonight? I don't think Callaghan's likely to catch you this time, not by the looks of him.'

Catherine nodded, and Edwin jogged to his gang. It was several minutes before Callaghan climbed into the carriage. He slipped to the floor. Catherine took the reins and guided the vehicle home, driving to the rear entrance of the house.

Mother helped Callaghan to his room, while Catherine called for Thomas to attend to the horses. She mentioned Edwin's plan to visit.

'Be careful not to be noticed leaving, Miss Catherine. We don't want any more trouble.' Thomas tone was kind but firm.

Chapter Thirty-One

The household settled for the night, and all was quiet except for Louisa's soft breaths. Catherine slithered out of bed, pulled a pretty day-dress over her head and tiptoed down the stairs. The last step squeaked. She stopped dead, and then dashed out the kitchen door. Sitting on the step, she tied her boots.

She tapped lightly on the door of the worker's cottage, and when it opened, Marjorie grasped her sleeve, pulled her inside, and pushed the door closed. She clicked the lock. It took a few seconds for Catherine's eyes to adjust to the dim candlelight.

'Hello, Catherine.' Edwin greeted her warmly. 'Come sit with us.'

Marjorie waggled her finger. 'Now listen up you two, we're happy you get on, but we can't afford to be caught together otherwise we'll be chucked out. We've nowhere else to go, and I'm having a baby. The old grump, Callaghan, will make sure no one else puts us on.'

'I'm sorry, Marjorie. We won't cause you trouble. We'll leave right away,' Catherine turned the knob.

Edwin leapt from his seat, 'Sorry, Tom, I didn't mean to make it awkward for you, friend.'

He grabbed Catherine's hand, guided her out and closed the door behind them, the pitch-black yard swallowing them.

'I know where we can go, follow me,' Catherine said and led him to the hayloft. 'We'll be safe here for a few minutes. Everyone is well asleep. We really can't drag Thomas and Marjorie into our mess—it's too risky.'

They sat side by side among the hay bales, their intense conversation re-awakening Catherine's desire for her friend, and he left her in no doubt about his feelings toward her. His hand caressed her hair at the nape of her neck, and she turned her face toward him. His eyes danced. He held her face in his hands and pressed his lips to hers. A surge of passion ran through her being, and she moved toward him. He pressed her to himself, parted his lips and groaned.

'Achoo.'

'Shush.' Edwin jumped up.

'Hay … it always makes me sneeze.'

He smirked and pulled her to her feet.

Catherine sighed, 'Sorry.'

He stuck his thumbs in his braces, and she plucked a straw of hay from his hair.

'I'll come again soon, but I got to go now. I don't want to get caught by the brute.'

'Be careful of Slim too.'

'He's not been down this way lately. I think he's working up Breadalbane way. It seems he had a falling out with Mister Callaghan.'

The earlier exchange between Callaghan and Slim would indicate otherwise, Catherine puzzling over Slim's threat.

'This will be our secret place then. Let's devise a signal, so I know when you've come.'

Having agreed, he swiped his cap from his pocket and twisted it over his curls.

♫♪ ♫♪

The call of the wattlebird vibrated, "Look out, miss, look out, miss!" so distinct she almost laughed aloud. Edwin must realize, the bird does not usually sing late at night, but, if someone heard it they would not think of it either.

Their regular meeting in the hayloft, the feverish intimacy and the discussion of future-plans excited Catherine. Her conscience smarted—so untoward for a young woman to be in the company of a man alone—the rules of propriety emblazoned upon her heart. However, smitten with Edwin and indeed he with her, confirmed by his tender embrace, she yielded. Occupied with thoughts of Edwin, Catherine set aside her mission to help the poor, temporarily, she reasoned.

The shackles of gentility squeezed her vitality. Callaghan threatened her she would never be allowed to leave Willowbank unless she did his bidding and accepted George Hampton's hand. Knowing her family would never approve of a marriage between Edwin and her, she would have to find a way to escape. Gnawing irritation turned to cold anger, and Catherine snapped at Louisa and her brothers. Though her mother was sympathetic to her feelings, she argued such a marriage would jeopardize Catherine's standing in the family.

Each day, she ached for Edwin's touch. Every night she tiptoed out of the house and climbed into the hayloft. Following their trysts, she found it difficult to sleep, and tears drenched her pillow. Her heart was heavy, racked with guilt.

♫♪ ♫♪

Catherine rested her head against the barn wall, and Edwin snuggled close. He smelt so good. His curls were slicked back with violet oil, and his eyes shone in the moonlight. He had plucked a red rose from the garden and presented it to her. She kissed him, sniffed the petals and stuck the stem between the floorboards.

'Catherine, my love, I really oughtn't to ask you to come away with me, but I've grown to care for you. I want you to be mine. Will you marry me?'

He rolled toward her, took her in his arms and kissed her tenderly. She ought to have wriggled from his embrace, but the warmth of his body against hers was electric.

She pressed closer, 'Oh, yes, yes, I love you, Edwin.'

He spoke into her hair. 'It'll be hard, Catherine, and not the kind of life you're used to.'

'I've worked hard since my father died. I could manage as well as any of your ordinary folk.'

Edwin looked at her knowingly. His expression told her, he thought, she had no idea how her life would change.

'We'll have to keep it secret … elopement. It's the only way. There'll be no fancy wedding for me.'

'Could you be ready to leave by the end of the month?'

♫♪ ♫♪

Her sister's warm body brought guilt. They had shared the bed for the past months since Louisa's room was retained for guests. Catherine was glad her sister slept so soundly. She could not understand her agony quite like Celeste might. In the morning, Catherine turned the pillow to hide the evidence of her distress, the pillowcase badly stained. Washday was a long way off—she could not change it yet. Teetering on the edge of a dark precipice, and aching with remorse, she could bear the burden no longer.

She prayed, 'Father, I'm sorry. I was disobedient, forgive me for dishonouring Mother. Oh, but I love Edwin so.'

Her mouth moved, but she emitted no sound. Louisa stirred, and Catherine tensed—waited, lay still.

'Lord, Callaghan … I can hardly mention his name without feeling nauseous. I thought I could live to please you, but I can't. I can't love him, as I ought, I'm no better than he. A little sin, big sin, it makes no difference. I've broken your commands, but I know, you are my Redeemer. I trusted you as my Saviour when I was a child, and now again, I need to be forgiven, be reassured.'

Her head hurt. She could imagine no other way, she must leave. Her breathing slowed, the tension flowing from her body. Inching toward the edge of the bed, she swung her legs from under the counterpane. When her feet felt the floor, she crept toward the door. A sideways glance in the mirror stunned her. She looked closer, even in the dim light of dawn, she could see her eyes were red and puffy. She tiptoed along the hallway, down the stairs and into the drawing-room. She flipped through the big, black bible on the sideboard. It did not take long to discover the verse Evelyn had taught her.

She interpreted as she read, 'If I own up to my sinfulness, you are faithful and righteous, and you will pardon me. Thank you, Lord.'

Edwin's familiar shrill call shattered the black silence.

Catherine drew a sudden breath. 'Edwin, shush.'

She pushed the kitchen door. It squeaked. An arm reached out clamped a hand across her mouth and yanked her into the room. Her breath caught in her throat. She spun, lost her balance and staggered into the bench. A low light burned in the lantern above her head.

'Oh, Catherine, please don't ...'

'Ooh!' Catherine rubbed her arm. 'Mother ...'

Her mother closed the door, grasped her shoulders. Mother's eyes bore into her daughter's.

'Catherine, I know you yearn for him, but consider your future. If you choose this Ordinary man, you will never enjoy your entitlement. You won't be in a position to help the impoverished.'

'Mother, that barbarian Callaghan has made our lives miserable. As long as he controls Willowbank, we will never be free to enjoy cultured society as we did while Father was alive. He won't even allow us to help the poor.'

'Go back to bed before Mister Callaghan wakes.'

Catherine looked over her shoulder. Edwin was waiting in the barn, would he come back again if she failed to meet with him?

A shuffle in the hallway sent blood rushing to her head, her temples pulsed. Mother stepped away, crouched behind the bench, her eyes open wide. A footfall landed on the wooden floor outside the door. Catherine leaned against the door, sweat beads forming on her lip. Mother put her finger to her mouth, and Catherine held still, the footsteps retreating up the rear stairs.

♫♪ ♫♪

When Catherine met Edwin the next evening in the hayloft, she apologised to him, tears coursing down her cheeks. He dabbed her face with his handkerchief.

'Catherine, my poor darling, I'm sorry. I've caused you trouble.

Forgive me?'

Catherine felt Edwin's chest rise and fall. He remained quiet.

'Do you still think we ought to go ahead with our plan to elope?' Catherine looked intently into his blue eyes.

'I do.'

'I want to too, but ...'

'We love each other. Callaghan won't ever let us get hitched, nor the rest of your family either.'

'You're right, except perhaps for Celeste.'

'Let's leave soon. The longer we hang around here, the more chance of getting caught,' he said.

'Let's wait a while, and pray.'

♫♪ ♫♪

A scratching barely audible pattered on Catherine's bedroom door. She cocked her ear and listened. The latch clicked. She gulped air, scrambled from the bed and stood, her back against the wall. A muted glow infused the room as the door eased open. Catherine's temples thumped and her legs wobbled. She clenched her hands and raised them above her head ready to drop the intruder. An obscure figure stepped inside.

'Catherine, are you awake?'

'Evelyn, you scared me to death. Why are you creeping about so late at night?'

A squeak of a hinge along the hall caused Evelyn to scamper around the breach. She twisted the handle, closed the door and engaged the lock.

'Quick. Back into bed,' she said, and came around to the far side of the bed and crouched for a moment, silent.

She pushed herself up and sat on the edge of the bed. Catherine shifted over. Louisa rolled and groaned.

'Catherine, I didn't mean to alarm you. I must warn you. You must leave, get away, you're in danger.' Evelyn's breathless rasp and canine-like odour sent shivers over Catherine.

Her former governess, so contrary to her composed self, as tight as a coiled rope. Should she tell her of her intentions? Perhaps she was already aware. Was this a trap of Callaghan who may suspect her scheme to elope?

'When I was in at the Evandale bakery today, I bumped into Lucille and Missus Douglas.'

Evelyn took a moment to catch her breath, Catherine wishing the woman would hurry and divulge her message. Catherine curbed her tongue, did not want to blurt the details of her plans.

'Lucille called me aside, supposedly to show me a newspaper article. Out of the other's earshot, she said Missus Butler's new maid, Pat, informed her Callaghan means to harm you. Not to kill you, mind you, only to scare you off, enough to have you quit with the road worker fellow.'

Catherine puffed. 'Wretch, he'll stop at nothing.'

'It appears the maid is an associate of Slim. Slim learned of Callaghan's intent at the hotel. Missus Butler said when the maid applied for the job she gave a reference from an Edwin Nelson. He's supposedly a close relative.'

Catherine grinned, pleased the room was black as pitch—of course, one of Edwin's sisters.

'She also said Edwin asked her to get a message to you. He'll come for you tomorrow night.'

Tomorrow was sooner than Edwin had planned. Should she trust this information? Perhaps Callaghan would lie in wait in the barn and—the image made her shudder.

'I will help you, Catherine.'

Catherine had no reason to doubt Evelyn would aid her. The governess deplored her boss as much as she.

♫♪ ♫♪

Catherine packed a few clothes into her cloth bag, along with some special trinkets, including her expensive Hallmark brooch Mother had given her. The brooch would be her emblem of remembrance. She examined the gold, oak-leaf design, inlaid with rose-cut diamonds and placed it in a small pouch, before putting it into her carry bag, and shoved it under her bed.

'Well, Mother, you always said I should follow my heart. I'm ready to do so now.'

♫♪ ♫♪

The wattlebird called, "Look out, miss, look out, miss!" She wriggled to the edge of the bed, slid out, and dressed in her travelling garb. She heaved her bag over her shoulder and lingered at her bedroom door, taking in the scene. She had must hurry. Edwin would be waiting for her at the bottom of the ladder. She was taking longer than usual, leaving was harder than she imagined. She was deserting her mother and her brothers and sister, and Evelyn. Everyone.

She had looked longingly, at each of the family at dinner, met her mother's gaze across the table, and a wave of guilt had threatened to overwhelm her. Her mother would miss her. Deceit niggled at her. Had Mother guessed something was amiss? She had looked at her strangely tonight. Catherine was sure, however, when she returned as a married woman, her mother would embrace her, as she had always done. Evelyn had sat, shoulders squared and lips locked in a perpetual smile. Catherine could only imagine how her accomplice planned to ensure Callaghan slept well tonight but a bottle of brandy, laced with one of Sarah's concoctions, would be an asset.

She took one last glance around her bedroom, smiled at Louisa who slept soundly, opened her door and crept down the stairs.

Wretched step, it squeaked again.

She glanced through the drawing-room door. Memories of sewing bees and Adele reading her stories rushed into her mind. She hesitated, then stepped across the hallway into the kitchen. One more thing she must get.

The cellar smelled dank. With utmost care, Catherine eased the canvas satchel containing her precious compendium to the front of the shelf, opened it and lifted the journal out and checked her personal promissory note remained between its pages.

'Your secret remains with me, Mother.'

Returning to the top of the stairs, she puffed her cheeks and blew, dropped her notebook into her bag, stepped out, and re-latched the kitchen door. She would miss home, but she would be back.

The rear courtyard was bright as day. She looked up. A myriad of stars blinked. The moon high in the sky, glimmered like a giant lemon eye, watching. She peered about. If the wily Callaghan were waiting, he would have seen her every move. She would have to hurry.

She ran to the barn, weighed down by her bag and waited at the bottom of the ladder. She worried Edwin would be cross since he had advised her to bring very little for the journey. One of Ginger's kittens curled its body about her leg. She bent to stroke it.

'Hey! Over here.'

She spun around, Edwin's silhouette at the side doorway. He leant against the railing butting up against the east-side wall, the horses saddled and ready to go.

'Thought you'd changed your mind. I was getting pretty antsy.'

'Sorry I took so long, Edwin.'

He took her bag and smiled, the grin he gave, that said, I told you so.

They agreed to ride Ebony and his stablemate, as far as Epping Forest to Robert and Alice's place. They started along the southern track, by the river's edge, to avoid the main driveway. Catherine slowed her horse to a walk and looked back wistfully. Nymph's white arm stretched skyward, pointed. Catherine's eyes traced the imaginary line to the spot.

'Oh!' The filmy curtains of her mother's bedroom window billowed in the breeze.

She jerked the reins. Had Mother seen her leave? 'She will be distraught, and poor Louisa won't have my shoulder to cry on, but no, I'll not turn back,' her lament mumbled.

'Finding it tough to leave, eh?'

'Just a little … someday they'll agree it was for the best.'

Edwin steered his steed close, slapped Ebony on the rump and charged toward the river. The horses needed no further stimuli, they were off. A mile along, they slowed to a trot—they were safe. Callaghan could not follow, the estate horses turned out to the bottom pasture days ago.

The track led up a steep incline. Edwin took the reins of her horse and digressed toward a clump of myrtle trees. He slid from his saddle, lifted her down and took her in his arms, caressed her cheek, his lips soft against her skin. She lifted her face and smiled into his eyes.

'I love you, Catherine, me darling. You'll never have cause to regret your choice to come with me.'

She wrapped her arms about his neck and murmured. Beyond his shoulder, Willowbank Estate stood tranquil, bathed in silver moonlight.

Continued in Book 2 of *The Willowbank Series*

The Emblem of Remembrance
by Victoria Carnell

Acknowledgements

To my parents Victor and Norma, whose love of literature permeated our family home, I owe my gratitude. Loving thanks to my gregarious husband Graeme, who's comment, when asked if he has read my book, replied, 'I'm waiting for the movie to come out.' He ensured I stayed sane by insisting I take time-out from the project. To my children, Sharon and Darren, who enthusiastically supported my endeavour to write this story, and to my sisters, Barbara and Maribeth, and my brother, David, for the laughs and memories along the way, I owe my grateful thanks.

My warm appreciation goes to Sharon, Darren, Tina, Daphne, Barbara and Maribeth who read the initial manuscript and gave me valuable feedback. Thank you to Alan Fletcher for his delightful photo of the Yellow Wattlebirds of Tasmania. I sincerely thank Nola Passmore of *The Write Flourish* for appraising this manuscript and my friend, Jeanette O'Hagan, *By the Light Books*, who assisted me with the publishing of the first edition. Both, fellow Christian writers, encouraged me to persevere. I would also like the thank Julieann Wallace of *Lilly Pilly Publishing*, for editing and publishing the second edition. How grateful I am to the Great Author, the Sovereign God, for his Word reveals his multi-faceted character.

The little wattlebird, honeyeater, uses its long, brush-tipped tongue to extract food from nectar-laden shrubs like grevillea. Pairs are often seen foraging together, catching small insects and chuckling their melodious call. The cup-like feathered nests provide a comfortable home for their chicks.

Victoria Carnell

About the Author

Victoria Carnell comes late to the field of writing, though her mother's avid love for reading and her father's passion for the philosophy of language strongly influenced her formative years. Due to the many opportunities to interact with people from all walks of life, she has garnered an abundance of material to inform her writing.

Victoria serves in Christian ministry in Wesleyan Churches in Australia, alongside her husband. Being employed in the spheres of management and education in the wider community has afforded her many valuable experiences. Her children, their partners and her grandchildren delight her life.

She approaches life from the perspective of a Christian worldview and her aim is to encourage her readers to develop a relationship with the Redeemer, by identifying with her characters as they wrestle with the issues of life and faith.

Find more about Victoria and her writing at:
www.VictoriaCarnell.com

The Emblem of Remembrance
by Victoria Carnell
Book 2 in *The Willowbank Series*

Bibliography

Andersen, H.C. (1869). T*he Marsh Kings Daughter.* London: George Routledge and Sons, the Broadway, Ludgate. (Sighted: June 24th, 2017). http://onlinebooks.library.upenn.edu/webbin/book/lookupname (June 24, 2017)

Austen, J. (1813). *Pride and Prejudice.* London: Thomas Egerton. Military Library (Whitehall, London). https://austenprose.com/category/jane-austens-pride-prejudice (June 24, 2017)

Crane, W. and Evans, E. (1874). *Goody Two Shoes'* Picture Book. London: George Routledge and Sons. http://www.metmuseum.org/art/collection/search/337788 (June 24, 2017)

Davis, M.L. (1855). *Home Stories.* Collected by the Brothers Grimm. Translated by Matilda Louisa Davis. Illustrated by George Thompson. London: G. Routledge and Company. http://www.pitt.edu/~dash/grimm-engl.html (June 24, 2017)

Escott, J., Alcott, L., and Cottam, M. (2008). *Little Women.* Oxford: Oxford University. (Sighted: June 24th 2017). https://global.oup.com/ukhe/product/little-women-9780199538119 (June 24, 2017)

Penny Illustrated-Paper and Illustrated Times, v. XX1, no. 523, Saturday October 7, 1871. https://library.villanova.edu/Find/Record/vudl%3A300031 (June 24, 2017)

Wordsworth, W. (1807). *Daffodils.* http://www.textetc.com/workshop/wr-wordsworth-1.html (June 24, 2017)

Luther, M. (1852) *A Mighty Fortress is Our God.*
http://hymnary.org/text/a_mighty_fortress_is_our_god_a_bulwark
(June 24, 2017)

Rous, F. T*he Lord's My Shepherd.*
http://hymnary.org/text/the_lord_is_my_shepherd_i_shall_not%20want
(June 24, 2017)

Newton, J. (1779). *Amazing Grace.*
http://hymnary.org/text/amazing_grace_how_sweet_the_sound
(June 24, 2017)

Alan Fletcher (2012). *Tassie Birds.*
http://tassiebirds.blogspot.com.au/2006/07/yellow-wattlebird.html
(June 24, 2017)

www.ingramcontent.com/pod-product-compliance
Lightning Source LLC
Chambersburg PA
CBHW030636110726
47901CB00002B/470